"YOU'LL STOP THEM, WON'T YOU?" SHE PLEADED.

"I can give it a good try," Cimarron replied. "Of course, it's a dangerous, lonely mission." He watched as her eyes roamed down his hard torso and came to halt below his belt. "A good woman would be such a comfort. . . ."

"You're speaking of a Western woman," Victoria said. "We Eastern women are too tame for a man like you."

"You don't look tame to me." Cimarron smiled and wrapped his arms around her.

At first Victoria pulled away. Then she thrust against him and her hand began its journey downward to claim the prize her eyes had scouted. . . .

CIMARRON
IN THE CHEROKEE STRIP

Ø

SIGNET Westerns You'll Enjoy

(0451)

☐ **CIMARRON #1: CIMARRON AND THE HANGING JUDGE** by Leo P. Kelley. (120582—$2.50)*

☐ **CIMARRON #2: CIMARRON RIDES THE OUTLAW TRAIL** by Leo P. Kelley. (120590—$2.50)*

☐ **CIMARRON #3: CIMARRON AND THE BORDER BANDITS** by Leo P. Kelley. (122518—$2.50)*

☐ **CIMARRON #4: CIMARRON IN THE CHEROKEE STRIP** by Leo P. Kelley. (123441—$2.50)*

☐ **LUKE SUTTON: OUTLAW** by Leo P. Kelley. (115228—$1.95)*

☐ **LUKE SUTTON: GUNFIGHTER** by Leo P. Kelley.
(122836—$2.25)*

☐ **LUKE SUTTON: INDIAN FIGHTER** by Leo P. Kelley.
(124553—$2.25)*

☐ **COLD RIVER** by William Judson. (098439—$1.95)*

☐ **DEATHTRAP ON THE PLATTER** by Cliff Farrell.
(099060—$1.95)*

☐ **GUNS ALONG THE BRAZOS** by Day Keene. (096169—$1.75)*

☐ **LOBO GRAY** by L. L. Foreman. (096770—$1.75)*

☐ **THE HALF-BREED** by Mick Clumpner. (112814—$1.95)*

☐ **MASSACRE AT THE GORGE** by Mick Clumpner.
(117433—$1.95)*

*Prices slightly higher in Canada

Buy them at your local bookstore or use this convenient coupon for ordering.
THE NEW AMERICAN LIBRARY, INC.,
P.O. Box 999, Bergenfield, New Jersey 07621
Please send me the books I have checked above. I am enclosing $_____
(please add $1.00 to this order to cover postage and handling). Send check
or money order—no cash or C.O.D.'s. Prices and numbers are subject to change
without notice.
Name_____
Address_____
City _____ State _____ Zip Code _____
Allow 4-6 weeks for delivery.
This offer is subject to withdrawal without notice.

4
CIMARRON
IN THE CHEROKEE STRIP

by
LEO P. KELLEY

A SIGNET BOOK
NEW AMERICAN LIBRARY
TIMES MIRROR

PUBLISHER'S NOTE

This novel is a work of fiction. Names, characters, places, and incidents either are the products of the author's imagination or are used fictitiously, and any resemblance to actual events or persons, living or dead, is entirely coincidental.

Copyright © 1983 by Leo P. Kelley

The first chapter of this book appeared in *Cimarron and the Border Bandits*, the third volume in this series.

SIGNET TRADEMARK REG. U.S. PAT. OFF. AND FOREIGN COUNTRIES
REGISTERED TRADEMARK—MARCA REGISTRADA
HECHO EN CHICAGO, U.S.A.

SIGNET, SIGNET CLASSICS, MENTOR, PLUME, MERIDIAN AND NAL Books are published by The New American Library, Inc., 1633 Broadway, New York, New York 10019

First Printing, June, 1983

1 2 3 4 5 6 7 8 9

PRINTED IN THE UNITED STATES OF AMERICA

CIMARRON ...

... he was a man with a past he wanted to forget and a future uncertain at best and dangerous at worst. Men feared and secretly admired him. Women desired him. He roamed the Indian Territory with a Winchester '73 in his saddle scabbard, an Army Colt in his hip holster, and a bronc he had broken beneath him. He packed his guns loose, rode his horse hard, and no one dared throw gravel at his boots. Once he had an ordinary name like other men. But a tragic killing forced him to abandon it and he became known only as Cimarron. *Cimarron,* in Spanish, meant wild and unruly. It suited him. *Cimarron.*

1

"Oyez! Oyez! The Honorable Court of the United States for the Western District of Arkansas, having criminal jurisdiction of the Indian Territory, is now in session, the Honorable Isaac C. Parker presiding. God bless the United States and the Honorable Court!"

As the bailiff concluded his announcement, Cimarron, lounging in the rear of the courtroom in the area reserved for witnesses, folded his arms across his chest and crossed his booted ankles.

Judge Parker, seated at his cherrywood desk, which was covered with a piece of green felt and mounted on a raised platform, peered out at the spectators in the courtroom. Then he glanced at the two tables just inside the railing that was not far from his desk where the defense and prosecuting attorneys sat in readiness.

He looked down at the table that was placed between his desk and the attorneys' tables and nodded to the court clerk seated there.

Cimarron's eyes fell on the court reporter, who was seated at a small table directly in front of the empty jury box.

The man caught Cimarron's eye and smiled a greeting as a short man with a shiny bald head was led into the courtroom to take his place before the bar.

The man's defense attorney rose and stood beside the accused.

Judge Parker took off his spectacles, breathed on them, and polished them on the sleeve of his coat. He was a tall man, and his height was apparent even as he sat behind his desk. He wore a tawny mustache and goatee, but his cheeks were clean-shaven. Streaks of gray were faintly visible in his hair, mustache, and goatee. As he put his spectacles back on, his piercing blue eyes seemed to grow larger.

He said, in an evenly modulated tone, "The two cases the court will hear in this day's concluding session will not be jury trials, since both defendants have waived the right to such trials. The court will pronounce judgment and sentence, if warranted, in each case. Let the indictment in the first case be read."

The bailiff, who wore the badge of a deputy sheriff, read the grand jury indictment against Patrick Murphy, which accused him of having stolen a horse from a farmer near Okmulgee in Creek Nation.

As the bailiff resumed his seat, Judge Parker stared down at Murphy and said, "Well, Pat, here you are again. The last time you came before me, as I recall, it was on a charge of peddling the ardent to the Kickapoos, for which I fined you three hundred dollars. How do you plead this time?"

"Your honor, sir," Murphy responded, "sure and do I have to answer that now?"

"You do, Pat. Why would you not want to enter a plea before this court?"

"Well, your honor, I want most mightily to plead innocent but I don't want to get myself tripped up on a perjury charge."

Titters ran through the spectator section of the courtroom.

Cimarron smiled.

So did Judge Parker. "Pat, you are not making your plea under oath."

"Then in that case I'm as innocent as the newborn day, your honor, sir, and any misguided soul who says otherwise, well, I know the kick up the behind his mother would be giving him for saying such a sinful thing."

"Very well, Pat," Judge Parker said, lowering his head to try to hide his widening smile. "Now, you just go ahead and tell the court your version of what happened. You'll get justice in this court, of that I can assure you."

Murphy moaned. "Oh, your honor, now isn't that the very thing I'm most fearful of, sir?"

Cimarron guffawed, and the spectators' titters turned to loud laughter.

Judge Parker rapped his gavel for order, and the courtroom quickly quieted. "Proceed with your story, Pat."

"Well, your honor, sir, in the first place I didn't steal that horse. It just walked up behind me and as near as dammit put its head between my legs and the next thing I knew I was sitting in its saddle. Then that horse and me, didn't we travel now, the two of us, and then . . ."

Cimarron, as Murphy's trial proceeded, turned his attention to the blond woman seated near the front of the courtroom. Her hair was piled high on top of her head and pinned rather haphazardly in place. She wore no hat. Her shoulders were bared by the dress she was wearing.

As if she could feel his eyes on her, the woman shifted position and then glanced covertly over her shoulder. When she saw Cimarron, her lips parted in a broad smile.

She was a pretty woman, but her face was fleshy and in a year or two, Cimarron knew, it would be fat. Her gray eyes danced merrily between their folds of flesh. She had used grain-flour powder on her face, and the effect, Cimarron thought, was gaudily alluring. She brought her fingers to her lips and blew him a kiss.

He returned the gesture.

". . . sentence of this court is that the accused prisoner, Patrick Murphy, is guilty and will be remanded to the federal penitentiary at Leavenworth, where he will serve not less than two and not more than ten years at hard labor." Judge Parker rapped his gavel. "Next case."

The bailiff rose. "The people versus Lily Saunders."

"That's me, Judge!" said the woman who had blown the kiss to Cimarron as she got to her feet.

"Miss Saunders," Judge Parker said, "you are accused of having attacked one"—he glanced at a paper on his desk—"Mrs. Martha Heppelwhite."

The bailiff gestured and Lily sat down in the witness chair next to Judge Parker's desk, her gray eyes on Cimarron.

As Judge Parker began to question her, Lily finally admitted that, yes, she had chased Martha Heppelwhite, who was far from fully dressed, down Fort Smith's Second Street while brandishing the paddle of a milk churn.

"But I didn't intend to hit her with it," Lily insisted. "I just wanted to scare her a little bit."

Lily's defense attorney, as the questioning proceeded,

made several objections to remarks made by Mrs. Heppelwhite's counselor, none of which Judge Parker sustained.

Martha Heppelwhite took the stand, and Cimarron listened to her tell her side of the story. Martha claimed that Lily had tried to murder her. "Because she was jealous of me," Martha stated enthusiastically and emphatically.

Several minutes later, as the bailiff summoned him to the stand, Cimarron rose and headed for the front of the courtroom. After seating himself in the witness chair, he crossed his legs.

"You were in the plaintiff's—in Martha Heppelwhite's—home at the inception of this unfortunate incident?" Judge Parker asked him.

"I was there," Cimarron answered.

"Tell the court what happened."

"Nothing much. Martha—Mrs. Heppelwhite—well, we were busy at the time and unable to answer the door. Lily and Martha, you've got to understand, Judge, they're friends. They live right next door to each other. Anyway, Lily barged right in—Martha and me had both forgotten to lock the door, I'm now sorry to say—and when she found the two of us in the bedroom—well, she started carrying on like a starving screech owl."

The questioning continued.

Judge Parker elicited the information that Cimarron had, on several recent occasions, been as busy with Lily as he had been with Martha on the day in question.

The defense attorney, when his turn came, drew from Cimarron the information that Martha Heppelwhite had tried to attack Lily Saunders with a wooden potato masher and that, when Cimarron tried to break up the battle, both women had turned on him before, as he put it, "I hightailed it out of Martha's house in one real big hurry."

He was asked more questions by both Judge Parker and Lily's counselor. After answering them, he was dismissed.

The defense attorney then told Judge Parker that he believed it was "crystal-clear" that his client was guilty of nothing more than "a simple temper tantrum not unknown in the colorful history of the fair sex."

Cimarron, once again lounging in the rear of the courtroom, listened as Judge Parker announced that he was fining each of the two women twenty-five dollars for disturbing the peace of Fort Smith.

"And the court must observe," he continued, his eyes on Cimarron, "that it is a shame if not a sin that an officer of this court—in fact, a deputy marshal—should have conducted himself in such a fashion as to have aroused the jealous passions of two otherwise respectable citizens of the Fort Smith community."

As Judge Parker raised his gavel, he added, "The minions of the law, I respectfully submit, would do well to conduct themselves more circumspectly in affairs of the heart. Let me remind interested parties that although this court is principally concerned with criminal cases, it is not at all averse to listening to civil cases such as those involving the alienation of affections."

As Judge Parker's gavel banged down and the courtroom began to empty, Cimarron hurried outside and started down the steps, eager to be on his way, although he had no place in particular to go.

He didn't get far.

"Cimarron!"

He turned to find Martha Heppelwhite, her skirts raised and clutched in her left hand, running toward him. He groaned as he saw Lily Saunders leave the courthouse and stand, hands on hips and an angry expression on her face, staring at him.

"Cimarron," Martha cried breathlessly when she reached his side, "We can go home now, you and me." She took his arm and squeezed it playfully. "We can finish what we had hardly even started when that harridan"—she turned and jabbed a stiff finger in Lily's direction—"came barging in on us."

"Martha, honey, I think—"

Cimarron's voice died as Lily came running toward him. He freed himself from Martha and placed her behind him as Lily skidded to a halt in front of him. "Lily," he said, "now, don't you—"

"Shut up, you!" she snapped. "I won't listen to any more of your lies. You swore you wouldn't see that mantrap anymore!"

"Lily, I didn't say any such thing. I said it wasn't likely

I'd be seeing her on account of I had to head out after a couple of robbers."

"He doesn't want any more to do with you, Lily Saunders!" Martha cried from behind Cimarron.

"Martha Heppelwhite," Lily snarled, "your husband must be spinning in his grave because of the scandalous way you've been conducting yourself with this good friend of mine!"

"Don't you dare say another word about Mr. Heppelwhite!" Martha shouted. "I'll sue you for libel!"

"So sue me!" Lily countered at the top of her voice. She shoved Cimarron aside and lunged for Martha.

Martha screamed.

From the steps of the courthouse, Judge Parker shouted, *"Ladies!"*

Both women froze at the sound of his voice.

"Go home, ladies," he called out to them. "If you don't—"

Apprehensively, they turned to face him.

He pointed to the squat wooden building within the stone-walled compound.

It was enough.

Both women glanced nervously at the building Judge Parker had pointed to—the building in which female prisoners were housed—and then Martha turned to leave the compound.

She stopped, came back, and kissed Cimarron on the cheek.

Lily *harumphed* and, not to be outdone, stood on tiptoe and kissed him on the other cheek.

Then both women, keeping their distance from each other, marched out of the compound.

"Cimarron!" Judge Parker beckoned to him.

"Sorry about the ruckus," Cimarron said a moment later as he joined Judge Parker on the steps of the courthouse.

"Are you?" was the judge's skeptical rejoinder. "Walk along with me, Cimarron. Or have you pressing business elsewhere?"

"I haven't, Judge. Not pressing business. But Marshal Upham told me to go out on the scout in the Territory once I'd testified at that trial you just heard."

"No specific assignment this time?" Judge Parker in-

12

quired as the two men strolled toward the gate of the compound.

Cimarron shook his head as they passed the looming gallows, which he was keenly aware of but at which he forced himself not to look. "Upham just wants me to go out and see what I can turn up."

"And you will turn something up," Judge Parker commented sadly as they went through the gate and out into the surrounding town. "You could not fail to do so," he added mournfully. "Not with the way things are in those thousands of square miles in which infamy flourishes and every second person one meets is a scoundrel."

"There are a few good people out in the Territory, Judge," Cimarron said, remembering those he had met in his travels.

"Perhaps. But I daresay many of those good people you refer to have no permits to reside legally in the Territory."

"Hello, Judge."

"Well, hello there, Davey," Judge Parker said, greeting the small boy who blocked his path. "Shouldn't you be home now? It's suppertime, or very nearly so."

"I guess so," Davey agreed, but he did not move.

Judge Parker reached into the pocket of his coat and withdrew a brown paper bag. "Gumdrops in here," he said. "But some boys I know can't abide gumdrops. They prefer licorice."

"I hate licorice," Davey declared.

"Do you, now? What, in your considered opinion, is the best kind of candy being made these days?"

"Gumdrops," Davey replied without hesitation. "Red gumdrops," he added. "The cinnamon kind."

Judge Parker opened his paper bag and held it out to Davey. "I wouldn't be surprised if you could find a red gumdrop—very possibly several—in there."

Davey leaned over and peered into the bag. His grimy fingers disappeared inside it.

The paper bag crackled and then Davey's fingers emerged from it clutching two red gumdrops. His fingers flew to his mouth as his lips parted.

"Davey!" Judge Parker shook his head.

The fingers froze. Davey's lips closed.

"After supper, Davey. Put them in your pocket and en-

13

joy them for dessert. Will you do that? If you won't, your mother will chastise me, I fear."

Reluctantly, Davey pocketed the gumdrops. "Thanks, Judge." He was about to turn away when he seemed to notice Cimarron for the first time. He gave Cimarron a searching look and then turned back to Judge Parker. "He's the deputy who's a friend of Miz Heppelwhite, ain't he?"

Judge Parker nodded grimly.

"My mother says she wouldn't get closer to him than a country mile. I guess she's afraid he might arrest her for something."

"Run along home, Davey," Judge Parker said. "Give my regards to your mother. And remember, those gumdrops are for dessert."

"Yes, sir, Judge."

As Davey raced up A Street away from them, Judge Parker and Cimarron resumed their journey.

" 'Arrest her for something,' " Judge Parker murmured, shaking his head. "Cimarron, I have a request to make of you."

"Judge?"

"Try to confine your amorous adventures to the Territory, where they will, in all likelihood, neither be noticed nor cause any great harm."

"I'll try to do that, Judge."

"It's not a matter of morality. Well, perhaps it is in part. I'm a Christian and I— Never mind about all that. What I'm trying to say is that the law, if it is to be respected, must be supported and enforced by men who themselves are worthy of respect."

"You think that because I have an eye for the ladies I'm not worthy of respect?"

"No, that's not what I meant. I meant—you know damn well what I meant. It's a serious matter I mentioned. It's nothing to grin about, Deputy."

"You may know the law both back and front, Judge, but I guess you don't know much about a man like me."

"I know more about you than you think I do. Now, I expect you at least to consider my request."

"Judge, where might we be heading?"

"Evening, Mr. Chalmers," Judge Parker said, nodding

14

to a man who was standing in front of his shop. "The weather's been most pleasant lately, hasn't it?"

"Judge," Chalmers said, "have you got a minute?"

"What is it, Mr. Chalmers?"

"It's the school board, Judge. We've run out of money and the school term's not nearly finished and we're in dire need of some new books."

Judge Parker reached into his pocket and withdrew his purse. He snapped it open and took out several bills. "I'll set an example by making this small donation, Mr. Chalmers. I suggest that you talk with Reverend Kingsley and tell him that it might be a good idea if he were to urge his parishioners to make donations, however small they might of necessity be, to the school board to enable them to buy the books you say are so sorely needed."

"Good idea, Judge," Chalmers said. "I'll do that."

"Reverend Kingsley might also want to remind his flock that they have an obligation to aid in the education of their children to the very best of their ability. They will be making a sound investment in the future of this country as well as in that of their children themselves. Good evening, Mr. Chalmers."

"Thanks for the donation, Judge."

Judge Parker and Cimarron moved on as dusk descended on Fort Smith. "We're going to my house," Judge Parker declared.

Cimarron realized that he now had the answer to the question he had asked earlier. "Why?" he asked bluntly.

"You said you had no pressing business elsewhere. You said Marshal Upham had ordered you to go out on the scout. Well, I may have a more definitive task for you to perform."

"What might you have in mind, Judge?"

"Mrs. Parker and I are expecting guests for supper this evening. Mrs. Parker, I should mention in case you have any reluctance about joining us, has baked a chocolate cake."

Cimarron swallowed the saliva that suddenly filled his mouth.

"Roast beef," Judge Parker said. "Carrots fresh from Mrs. Parker's kitchen garden." He raised his hat as a woman nodded to him from her front porch. "Marcus

Doby is coming to supper. He visited Marshal Upham and told him that he wants to talk to me."

"Don't know the man."

"I know Mr. Doby only by reputation as a member of the Cherokee legislature from Tahlequah. A fine upstanding gentleman. I wish the Territory had many more men like him. I extended him, through Marshal Upham, an invitation to supper tonight."

"He's in some kind of trouble, is he?"

"Not personally, no. But he fears, I understand, that Cherokee Nation might be, and he thinks the court might be of some help in avoiding the trouble he apparently perceives."

"What kind of trouble exactly?"

"Ah, here we are." Judge Parker swung open the gate in the fence that surrounded his house and went through it.

"You said 'guests' before," Cimarron reminded him as he followed Judge Parker up onto the porch. "How many other guests are you expecting?"

"One other. A lady."

"A lady," Cimarron repeated and tried to ignore the stern glance Judge Parker gave him just before he opened his front door.

"A lady," Judge Parker said, "of impeccable breeding and reputation. Her name is Victoria Littleton. She was born in New York City but has resided for the past several months, according to Mr. Doby, in Tahlequah."

Cimarron followed Judge Parker into the house.

"I'm home, my dear." Judge Parker hung his hat on a wall peg just inside the door.

Cimarron did the same as Mrs. Parker came hurrying out of the rear of the house to greet her husband. "Isaac," she said, and kissed him on the cheek. "Did you have a difficult day, dear?"

Judge Parker shrugged off the question. "I've invited Cimarron to dine with us tonight, since we will be discussing a matter with Mr. Doby and Miss Littleton that may prove of interest to him."

"Good evening, Cimarron," the ample Mrs. Parker said. "You've been a stranger to this house and I consider that a personal insult."

"I apologize for insulting a fine lady like yourself, Mrs.

Parker. It's just that I'm in and out of town so much that I get to see a lot less of the people I like than suits me."

"Cimarron," Mrs. Parker said, beaming at him, "you have a way about you, you most certainly do. What a nice thing to say."

"Oh, he can be charming to ladies, there's not the slightest doubt about that," Judge Parker declared gruffly. "Not to mention hot-blooded where they're concerned," he added even more gruffly.

"Isaac, Cimarron's a young man and it will be a goodly number of years before his blood begins to cool. Don't you remember when we were—"

"I believe I know what you are about to say, my dear, and, yes, I do remember but I decidedly do not want the matter made a part of the public record."

Mrs. Parker, as her husband headed into the parlor that opened off the hall, winked at Cimarron.

He gave her a smile and then strode into the parlor.

"Cigar?" Judge Parker asked him, offering him a walnut humidor.

Cimarron shook his head.

As Judge Parker picked up a cut-glass decanter and offered Cimarron brandy, there was a cry from the rear of the house.

"My word!" Judge Parker exclaimed in consternation, nearly dropping the decanter. "What was that?"

But Cimarron didn't hear the question because he was already out of the parlor and dashing down the hall.

As he burst into the kitchen, he found Mrs. Parker on her knees near the stove, her large arms enfolding her younger son, James. The outside kitchen door was open and near it stood James's older brother, Charles, an expression of fury on his face.

"What's the matter?" asked Judge Parker as he hurried into the kitchen behind Cimarron.

"Just look at what they did to our boy!" Mrs. Parker wailed, displaying James's broken lip, which was bleeding freely. "They might have killed him!"

"They?" cried Judge Parker. "Who are 'they'?"

Charles answered him. "Some of the boys who live around here. They were beating James. I saw them and chased them away."

"Why did they attack James?" Judge Parker thundered.

17

"They didn't attack me, Father," James volunteered. "I attacked them."

"You—" Judge Parker began in dismay and then, "I have told you boys repeatedly not to engage in fisticuffs. Is that not so?"

"Yes, Father," James said sheepishly. "But they called you names."

"Aha!" Judge Parker glanced briefly at Cimarron, who nodded to indicate that he too had now guessed what had caused the fight, and then back at James. "You should have ignored them, James."

"But they called you Bloody Parker. Butcher Parker too. They said everybody calls you the Hanging Judge."

Mrs. Parker went to the sink and pumped cold water onto her handkerchief. "Let me wipe your lip, child."

Judge Parker said, "I don't want you fighting. Under any circumstances. Is that clearly understood?"

"Yes, Father," James mumbled and was promptly echoed by his brother.

Judge Parker turned and left the kitchen.

"Cimarron," James said, "I couldn't have just run away."

"I reckon you couldn't, boy. But your daddy's right. Fighting's no way to solve things. Men, if they have their differences, ought to sit down and talk them out."

"You boys," Mrs. Parker said, "go on into the parlor. Supper will be ready in no time. James, you hold that wet handkerchief against your lip until the bleeding stops, you hear?"

"Yes, Mother."

Cimarron followed the children from the kitchen. Charles walked briskly down the hall and disappeared into the parlor. But James hung back and looked up at Cimarron.

"Why do they call Father those bad names, Cimarron?"

Cimarron hesitated a moment and then hunkered down so that he was facing James. "Your daddy's a good man. He's a man who does his duty, and his duty is to uphold the law the way other men have written it. Folks get things mixed up sometimes. They call him those bad names because he sentences men to hang when the crimes those men committed call for your daddy to do just that. If a man kills somebody and gets caught, your daddy—if a jury finds the man guilty—he's got no other choice but to sentence the killer to hang.

"It seems to me that it takes courage for your daddy to do what he has to do. But it doesn't mean that he likes to see men hang. Fact is, he doesn't. But as long as he has to enforce the law some men who come before him are going to be found guilty and they're going to hang. Your daddy doesn't hang them. The law does."

"You like Father too, don't you, Cimarron?"

"Why, sure, I like him. What's more, I respect him."

"I guess I don't just like him. I mean I guess I—" James blushed and looked down at the floor.

Cimarron reached out and gripped James's shoulder. "Let me tell you something, boy. There's never a need to feel ashamed because you love somebody."

James looked up at Cimarron and smiled. "Would you give me a ride again like you did the last time you were here?"

"Climb on."

James climbed up over Cimarron's bent back until he was sitting on his shoulders.

"Hold tight now," Cimarron told him and rose, gripping James's ankles in both hands. He started down the hall, but before he reached the parlor the doorbell rang.

"We'll answer the door, Father!" James called out, his hands clasped against Cimarron's forehead.

Cimarron went to the door and, after releasing James's right ankle, opened it.

"Judge Parker?" The slender man with the sober face who was standing outside beside a young woman stared in obvious surprise at Cimarron.

James giggled at the man's mistake.

"No," Cimarron said. "The judge is in the parlor. Come on in, you and the lady."

Cimarron stepped aside and watched them enter the hall.

"Mr. Doby, I presume," Judge Parker said as he came out into the hall, his hand outstretched.

"Yes, I'm Marcus Doby."

As the two men shook hands, Cimarron closed the door and the woman beside Doby announced, "I'm Victoria Littleton, Judge Parker. I am most delighted to make your acquaintance."

"Miss Littleton." Judge Parker shook her outstretched hand.

"Time to get down, boy," Cimarron whispered to James. He hunkered down and James climbed down to the floor.

"Charles!" Judge Parker called, and when his son appeared from the parlor, he said, "You and James—both of you will get ready for supper now, if you please."

Cimarron was about to straighten up when James leaned over and, cupping Cimarron's ear in his hand, whispered, "When I grow up I'm going to be a lawyer and then a judge just like Father."

"You'll do it, boy, I know you will," Cimarron assured James, who then scampered up the stairs behind his brother.

As Cimarron entered the parlor, Judge Parker said, "May I present one of my deputy marshals. Mr. Doby—Cimarron. Cimarron—Miss Littleton."

"I'm pleased to know you both, I'm sure," Cimarron said amiably.

Moments later, when everyone was seated, Judge Parker turned to Doby. "I think there's time before supper is served for us to begin to discuss the problem that concerns you, sir."

"It's a major one, I believe," Doby began seriously. "We—I speak of the Cherokee people—are very much concerned, Judge, about the threatened invasion of the Outlet by would-be settlers."

"Invasion?" Judge Parker frowned.

"Perhaps you haven't heard," Doby said. "We have had reliable reports that there are a number of people gathering just north of the border near Hunnewell, Kansas. They are being organized and led by a man named Bill Lee Lomax, who believes that the Outlet and its six million acres of land should be made available to white settlement.

"But as I'm sure you know, Judge, the Outlet was given to the Cherokees by the federal government in 1828 and then patented to them in 1833 and—"

"One moment, Mr. Doby." Judge Parker cleared his throat and said, "I also know that the Cherokees have been forbidden to settle there by one of the provisions of the treaty your tribe made with the government in 1866,

20

since the land may, at some future date, be designated a homeland for other tribes. I know that no Cherokee is permitted to settle in the Outlet or make permanent improvements to any part of the land within its borders, since the government has stipulated that it has the right at any time to sell said land to some other tribe or tribes."

"That's true, Judge," Doby admitted. "But the point I want to make is simply this. Regardless of the restrictions placed on Cherokee use of the land in the Outlet—what some call the Cherokee Strip—if settlement does take place there, the Cherokees will lose that land."

"Ultimately they will lose more," Victoria Littleton stated. "Lomax is also talking about settling the Unassigned Lands west of Creek Nation. He claims that the Strip and the Unassigned Lands are public lands and are therefore open to settlement. If he is proved right, what is to stop him and others like him from eventually appropriating *all* of Cherokee Nation?"

"Perhaps, my dear," Judge Parker said, "you are unduly alarmed. After all, as the law now stands, no white man may trespass on the Outlet or the Unassigned Lands without a permit, and I would imagine that Mr. Lomax and his people know that."

"Of course they know it!" Victoria declared hotly. "That is why they are clouding the issue by insisting that the land is in the public domain."

"Excuse me," Cimarron said, and Victoria turned her luminous brown eyes on him. As he met her gaze and became fully aware of her beauty—the smooth skin of her face, her full moist lips, and soft auburn hair—he almost forgot what he had been about to say.

"Cimarron?" prompted Judge Parker.

"Mr. Doby," Cimarron said, "I'm wondering why you're so worried about this Mr. Lomax when you've already got white men ranching up in the Strip."

"It's true that there are ranchers there, and it is also true that some of them have not been licensed by Cherokee Nation to graze their cattle there. They are in the Strip illegally and are part of our growing problem there, along with the railroad interests who are lobbying fiercely in Washington for land allotments along their rights-of-way. And that is not to mention other forces that are at work to appropriate our land. I am referring to the small

21

towns along the Missouri, Kansas and Texas Railroad which are eager for settlement to take place so that they may grow."

"Marcus," Victoria interjected, "don't forget to mention that businessmen from as far away as St. Louis see the opening of the Cherokee Strip as a way of increasing sales of their wholesale goods."

"Miss Littleton is correct, Judge," Doby said soberly. "We see this pressure—this rapidly mounting pressure—as a serious threat to the integrity of Cherokee Nation."

Judge Parker turned his attention to Victoria. "Miss Littleton, what, may I ask, is your interest in this matter?"

"Certainly you may ask, Judge. I am president of an organization headquartered in New York City. Our little group calls itself Champions of Cherokee Rights. We intend to prevent Mr. Lomax, in any way we can, from crossing the Kansas border and entering the Strip. It is more than merely a matter of principle with us. It is a matter of honor, and we will not let our honor be besmirched."

Cimarron noted Victoria's flashing eyes and the firm set of her jaw. "How do you plan on stopping Lomax, Miss Littleton?" he inquired politely.

"Any way I can," she replied vehemently.

"Sounds like you might have a battle on your hands if Lomax is as bound and determined to settle in the Strip as Mr. Doby claims he is."

"I am not a coward," Victoria shot at Cimarron as if she were challenging him to deny her statement. "I will do battle with whomever I must wherever I must."

"I admire your spunk, Miss Littleton," he told her sincerely, thinking of how much he also admired her full breasts and bountiful body.

"Cimarron," Judge Parker said thoughtfully, "I believe it would be a good idea if you were to go up to the Strip and see just exactly what is going on there. You might have a talk with Mr. Lomax and explain to him the legal situation as it affects the plans he is apparently formulating. Make him understand that the federal court in Fort Smith has jurisdiction over the Strip just as it has over the entire Territory and the land in question is decidedly not public land."

"Is Lomax a man likely to listen to reason?" Cimarron asked Doby.

It was Victoria who answered his question. "He is not. He is a zealot, and such men are not to be reasoned with."

"Then it looks like I might have a battle on *my* hands," Cimarron said to her, "once I get up to the Strip and start standing toe to toe with Lomax."

"I'm sure, Cimarron," Judge Parker said, "that you can handle the situation."

"You're going to send just one deputy marshal out against all the forces arrayed against us, Judge?" Doby asked, sounding both incredulous and disappointed.

"I'll send more if such an action should prove to be necessary," Judge Parker responded. "But no others may be needed if Cimarron is successful in stopping Mr. Lomax from proceeding with his plans."

"I'm not at all certain that even an entire army could stop him," Victoria stated flatly and then added, with a glance in Cimarron's direction, "but I am quite certain that one deputy marshal won't be able to stop him."

"Well, Miss Littleton," Cimarron said, "you're looking at a deputy marshal who'll be happy as a heifer who's found a new fence post to at least try to stop Mr. Bill Lee Lomax from sneaking down into the Cherokee Strip."

2

Marshal Upham looked up as Cimarron entered his office the following morning.

"You're up before your breakfast," the marshal commented and began to shuffle through papers that were spread across the surface of his desk. "I have a job for you, Cimarron."

"Well, Marshal, you might best be assigning whatever job you're talking about to one of your other deputies."

Upham looked up, his hands poised above his desk, both of them clutching assorted papers. "What are you talking about?"

"Already got myself a job. Came to tell you about it. Judge Parker gave it to me last night."

"What sort of job did Isaac give you?"

Cimarron recounted the conversation that had taken place the night before in Parker's home and concluded, "Mr. Doby, he's pretty sure that there's trouble brewing up in the Strip."

"I'm not the least bit surprised," Upham commented. "Think of it. All that fertile land—all that relatively empty land up there just waiting for someone to come along and lay claim to it. Never mind that it belongs to Cheokee Nation. There are those who want it and some of them won't be easily dissuaded from taking it."

"My job's to do some dissuading, Marshal."

Upham nodded absently and put down the papers he had been holding. From the pile, he chose one and held it out.

Cimarron took it and looked at it. "You'd best get somebody else to bring in this lady who's wanted for attempted murder. It'll only slow me up. From what I heard last night the sooner I get to the Strip the better

24

chance I'll have of nipping in the bud any trouble that might be brewing up there."

"This won't take you long and it's not out of your way. Lucy Raleigh lives in Skullyville."

"I grant you that Skullyville's not far off, but Marshal, by the time I get there, arrest the lady, bring her on back here, and then start out again for the Strip—"

"You are one very argumentative man, Cimarron. Now, listen to me. Bud Billings is out in the Territory with a small posse. I had a letter from him yesterday and he's traveling back here along the California Road."

"Why not let Billings handle the matter?"

Upham scowled and banged a fist down on his desk. "By the time I could get word to Billings and— Never mind. Are you going to take orders from me or are you going to find yourself a job somewhere else?"

"Now Marshal, where would I ever find a job as good as this wonderful one I got? Why, I earn near to five hundred dollars a year. I get to travel through wind and rain and snow and haven't been shot more than twice so far. I hope you aren't figuring on firing me, Marshal. I truly hope you aren't going to turn me loose so that I'll be forced to find myself a job that won't make me risk my neck every day and my ass every night. I always figured you for a kindly and compassionate man, Marshal."

"Damn you, Cimarron, I—"

"I'll arrest Miss Raleigh, Marshal. I wouldn't want you to take away my deputy's badge that makes me a target for every desperado hiding out in the Nations."

Upham, scowling more fiercely now, said, "This is an important case, Cimarron. You can rendezvous with Billings and turn the lady over to him." Upham's scowl became a leer. "I think you're the man to arrest her. I've heard rumors that you have a way with you where the ladies are concerned."

"You oughtn't to listen to rumors, Marshal. They're usually a pinch of fact mixed in with a whole pint of fiction. Besides which, the ladies I've known—well, none of them ever tried to murder anybody, although I'll admit maybe one or two might have wanted to do me in. Now what can you tell me about this Raleigh woman?"

"Lucy Raleigh," Upham replied, ignoring Cimarron's grin, "stands accused by Roy Catlin, who lives here in town, of having tried to kill him. Roy says a friend of his gave him some powders and told him to take them because they were guaranteed to increase his—ah, potency. Well, Roy, being the suspicious sort that he is, badgered his friend until the friend admitted that Lucy Raleigh had given him the powders to pass on to Roy.

"Roy claims that Lucy was chasing him in a shameless fashion and had been doing so for some time. It appears he told her he had his eye on another woman and he asked her to stop bothering him. Well, what it all finally came down to is this. Roy took the powders to the Empire Drugstore here in Fort Smith and had them analyzed. They turned out to be pure strychnine."

"I take it that if Lucy Raleigh couldn't have Roy Catlin, she was bound and determined to make sure that no other woman would have him either."

"That's about the size of it. Now, you get a move on, Cimarron. Handle this matter as I've suggested."

Cimarron started for the door, pocketing the warrant as he went.

"And Cimarron."

He turned back to face Upham.

"Good luck up in the Strip."

"Thanks, Marshal. From what I heard last night, I'll no doubt be needing it."

Cimarron left the office and then the courthouse that was housed in the building that had once been an army garrison. He walked out into the courtyard of the stonewalled compound and, without a glance at the wooden gallows that stood so silently and so ominously not far away, he headed for the gate set in the stone wall.

He was a tall and slender man, and as he strode across the courtyard the early-morning sun sent his shadow snaking westward, a long lean line darkening the ground. He walked easily with the faintly rolling gait of a man who was more comfortable sitting a saddle than standing on his own two feet. His shoulders were the widest part of his body, his hips the narrowest. He moved with the natural grace of a stalking mountain lion and the confidence of a grizzly well aware of its power and its ability to use that power. His hands, strong and long-fingered, swung easily at his sides as he walked.

26

His face was composed of sharp angles and smooth planes. He had flat, slightly sunken cheeks bordering a narrow, wide-nostriled nose beneath which the thin line of his lips seemed to lurk. His forehead was broad, and there were wrinkles engraved upon it. Other wrinkles, deep and enduring, were to be found at the corners of his eyes, and they told their tale of days spent squinting into the sun and blinking to avoid trail dust. Once the skin of his face had been soft, but now it was as darkly burnished as any cured hide. Sun and wind had done their work and left their marks upon it. His deep-set emerald eyes were restless, roving here, there, missing nothing, finding little remarkable in the world. Keen eyes, quietly appraising.

His was a face people noticed, although had they been asked what it was they had noticed, their answers would have varied. "Tough hombre," a man had once said when he sighted Cimarron striding down a Tucson street. "Gunfighter," another man had once speculated and was not entirely wrong. "You're a man," a woman had said when he had been introduced to her, and her remark had amused him because he knew himself to be that—and all it implied—first and foremost. He wondered why she bothered to state the obvious with such apparent delight.

Black hair, straight as bullrushes, grew thick on his head. It buried both of his ears and the nape of his neck.

His face and lithely muscled body identified him as a man more at home under the sky regardless of the weather than beneath the roof of any shelter. He was a man who needed to be on the move, to feel himself alive and eagerly living.

He was handsome—or so some women had sworn—but now that handsomeness was marred because of the welted scar of flesh, livid and lifeless, which ran from just below his eye on the left side of his face to curve down over his cheekbone and end just above the corner of his mouth.

He wore jeans which were bleached by countless washings and threatening to give way at both knees. There was a slickly polished spot on them below the holster which rested against his right hip. In the holster was a single-action .44-40 Frontier Colt. His jeans were tucked into knee-high black boots. Their underslung high heels were worn and their pointed toes were scuffed.

He wore a gray flannel shirt beneath his buckskin jacket, and around his neck was tied a blue bandanna. On his head, tilted low on his broad forehead, was a battered black slouch hat which had a curled brim and indented crown.

The loops of the black leather cartridge belt which rode low on his hips were all filled.

After leaving the compound, he made his way west along Rogers Avenue until he came to the docks on the eastern bank of the Arkansas River. He stood waiting for the ferry which was making its way across the river toward him, idly gazing south toward Belle Point and the juncture of the Arkansas and Poteau Rivers. As the ferry pulled into the slip and its deckhands secured its lines, he climbed aboard and stood leaning against a railing, his eyes on the western bank of the river where the tents of the court's deputies could be seen standing like the last outposts of civilization beyond which stretched the thousands of acres known as Indian Territory.

He was still staring at the camp and the men moving through it when the ferry whistle sounded and the deck hands scurried about freeing the lines. As the ferry moved away from the limestone-and-sand embankment, the deckhands manned the sweeps and the boat moved slowly out into the current of the odorous river.

When it docked on the west bank of the river, Cimarron was among the first of the men on board to leave it. He headed south toward the camp, and when he reached it he weaved his way among the tents toward the tepee he had built to serve him as a home between his forays into the Territory.

Once inside the tepee, he gathered up his gear, then took it outside and over to the rope corral which contained his chestnut and several other mounts. He ducked under the rope and went in among the horses, shouldering them aside until he reached the chestnut.

He shook out his blanket, folded it, and placed it on the horse. Then, after saddling and bridling the animal, he tossed his saddlebags behind the saddle and shoved his '73 Winchester into the boot. He loosened one of the ropes of the corral which was tied to a sapling, led his chestnut out of the corral, and then retied the rope.

"Where you headed, Cimarron?" a man called out.

28

"Skullyville."

"Business or pleasure this trip?" the deputy, whose name was Peterson, asked.

Before Cimarron could reply, a deputy ducked out of a tent and said, "From all I've heard, Cimarron has a knack for turning business into pleasure and vice versa."

"Now what in the world's that supposed to mean, Wylie?" Cimarron asked.

"Just that you're a man who always seems to have a bit of fun and frolic with the fairer sex even when you're out gunning for somebody."

"I take my pleasures where I find them."

"Them," Wylie repeated. "Jane, Sarah, Mandy—"

"You got time for a hand or two of poker before you set out, Cimarron?" interrupted Peterson.

"Peterson, you know I wouldn't sit down with you and a deck of cards if my life depended on it. Not after the way you damn near cleaned me out the last two times."

"Peterson claims he doesn't cheat," Wylie commented, "but if that's true, he's the luckiest man ever drew breath since Adam saw what wonders the Lord performed with that spare rib of his."

Cimarron nodded, and a faint smile appeared on his face. "Peterson, I'll tell you something. When you ask me to play cards from now on, I intend to keep one hand on my watch—if I ever own one—and the other on my pocketbook. I'll trust to luck as to my hat."

Wylie guffawed and slapped his thigh. "He's pegged you for sure and certain, Peterson!"

"Well," Peterson drawled, "I hope the good people of Skullyville'll survive the visit you're about to pay them, Cimarron. Look at him, Wylie. He's slick as a knife blade, he is."

"What are you talking about, Peterson?" Wylie inquired.

"That buckskin jacket he's wearing. It's only a shade or so lighter than that chestnut he rides. Standing there like he is, he kind of fades right into the horse. From a distance, a man might miss seeing him altogether. He's not flashy nor even very noticeable. No silver doodads on his hat. No white shirt or bright-red bandanna. Those Texas spurs of his haven't the least little bit of a shine, so that were he to walk by an anthill the ants wouldn't be likely to notice that he's even wearing spurs."

"I don't like to call attention to myself with bright clothes or anything else fancy," Cimarron said. "A man—especially a man who works at the trade we do—does well, I reckon, to sort of let himself fade into the background of wherever he happens to find himself. There's no use skylining yourself when you don't know what might be at the bottom of the ridge you're riding."

"But what if it should turn out to be a loose-living woman riding all alone down there?" Peterson asked, grinning.

"I'll spot *her*," Cimarron answered and stepped into the saddle. "You can bet on that."

"And when she spots *him*," Wylie volunteered, "it won't be what he's wearing that'll make her sit up and take notice. She'll attend to matters straightaway once she gets an eyeful of those tight jeans an important part of him looks like it's fixing to bust right out of."

Peterson pulled a deck of cards from his pocket, fanned them, and held them up. "High card wins a dollar?"

Cimarron reached down and pulled a card from the deck.

Wylie, when Peterson turned to him, chose one.

"Well, gents?" Peterson prompted.

Wylie held up the nine of clubs.

Cimarron displayed his card—the queen of hearts.

Peterson selected a card, then flipped it over so both men could see it. King of diamonds. "Sorry, boys."

Wylie groaned and paid Peterson.

Cimarron rummaged about in the pockets of his jeans, came up with a silver dollar, and handed it to Peterson, who archly asked him if he wanted to try his luck one more time.

Cimarron shook his head and picked up the reins. "I'm going to consider that little bit of action we just had us a kind of fortune-telling game. Maybe I did lose a dollar on it. But I did draw the queen of hearts, and that just might turn out to be a good omen concerning what lies waiting up the trail for me."

He headed west, leaving Peterson and Wylie behind

him, their raucous laughter fading fast as he rode hard into Creek Nation.

Lucy Raleigh was a disappointment to Cimarron, and he thought wistfully of the queen of hearts he had drawn and decided the card hadn't been an omen at all. At least, not a good omen.

Because Lucy Raleigh, he thought with vague disappointment, was decidedly plain. To put it charitably.

He had easily found her small clapboard house once he arrived in Skullyville, because her address was written on the warrant he carried in his pocket.

Now, as she stood in the doorway facing him, one hefty hand still gripping the door she had opened only moments after he had knocked on it, he took in her face and body with one quick practiced glance.

Her eyes were as gray as laundry water. The skin of her face seemed never to have seen the sun. It was pale and wan, and there were puffy dark circles beneath her eyes. Her nose was slightly off center and her lips almost nonexistent. Her hair, the color of rotting hay, hung listlessly, looking, as did Lucy herself, bereft. She was tall and strongly built, reminding Cimarron of an oak tree that might never have been a sapling.

"Who are you?" she asked bluntly.

"Deputy marshal, ma'am, from Fort Smith."

"It's miss."

"Yes, ma'am—Miss Raleigh," He pulled the warrant from his pocket and showed it to her.

She glanced at it and then at him. Indignantly, "This is preposterous!"

"Maybe so. But whether it is or not, I have the sad duty of seeing to it that you get to Fort Smith to answer the charge of attempted murder Roy Catlin's gone and brought against you. I noticed you got a horse and wagon out back when I tied my chestnut to that apple tree on the side of the house. You'd best get that horse of yours ready to ride."

"I'm not going anywhere, not with a strange man, I'm not!"

"Oh, I'm not so strange once you get to know me."

"That's not what I meant." She started to close the door.

31

Cimarron thrust out one booted foot and blocked her effort. "You keep pushing on that there door, Miss Raleigh, and you're likely to bust my ankle. Now, why don't you just go pack yourself some things and come along with me peaceable. There's no need for you to make a fuss."

Lucy let go of the door and smiled.

"That's better," Cimarron said, relieved.

"Come in if you like," Lucy said. "I won't be long."

As she moved into the dim interior of the house, Cimarron stepped into the parlor and closed the door behind him. He looked around, and as his eyes became accustomed to the gloomy light in the room he made out an overstuffed sofa and several chairs. There was a dead plant in a pot on a wrought-iron table. A Sears Roebuck catalog lay open on the floor. An orange cat sat preening itself with its pink tongue on the sill of the only window in the room.

He went over to the sofa and sat down to wait.

He heard sounds from the rear of the house. Someone bustling about. The creak of a pump. The clang of metal.

He got up and made his way out of the parlor. He halted abruptly as he came into the kitchen. "Beg pardon, Miss Raleigh."

He turned quickly, but before he could leave the kitchen she said, "Please be good enough to hand me that bar of soap."

"Soap?"

"There. On the shelf above the sink."

He went to the shelf, found the soap, and handed it to Lucy, who stood naked beside the galvanized bathtub she had filled with water.

"Let me put my hand on your shoulder," she said, reaching out to him. "I don't want to slip stepping into my bath."

Cimarron obliged and she held tightly to his shoulder, so tightly that he winced, as she stepped into the tub and then sat down in it.

He stared down at her huge breasts that floated just above the waterline. He could dimly make out the dark patch of her pubic hair that was drowning in the tub.

"I couldn't go with you without bathing first," Lucy said, calmly soaping her arms and shoulders.

"I suppose not," he said, wanting to leave the room but remaining where he was.

"Just what exactly did Mr. Catlin accuse me of?" she asked, and Cimarron blinked and looked away from her spread legs.

"Murder. I mean, attempted murder." He told her about Catlin's charge.

"That's preposterous!" she declared heatedly when he had finished. "Why would anyone want to try to murder that—that *mouse*?"

"I'm sure I don't know, Miss—"

"My given name is Lucy."

"Lucy."

She smiled up at him.

He tried a grin which didn't work and then gave it up.

"Do you happen to know Mr. Catlin?"

"Never met the man, no."

"Skinny fellow. Shifty eyes. He fidgets all the time. Can't seem to stand still, and when he puts his hands in his pockets the way he seems so fond of doing—well, I can tell you it's scandalous. No woman would want to murder him. It would be like going out of your way to crush a bug you'd barely noticed. And dumb! Mr. Catlin is so dumb he couldn't teach a setting hen to cluck!"

Cimarron looked away as Lucy began to soap her left breast. He looked back.

Was she doing it purposefully? The nipple was growing hard as her fingers touched and seemed to tease it. It stood at attention. Cimarron thought it was watching him. He knew Lucy Raleigh was watching him. He felt himself stiffening and was about to put his hands in his pockets to adjust himself so that she wouldn't notice when he remembered what she had just said about Roy Catlin and his hands-in-his-pockets habit. He shifted position, angling his body. Could she still see?

"If Mr. Catlin was as equipped as you apparently are, Deputy," Lucy cooed, "I could understand why he would want to play with himself."

She was working on the other nipple now. It peeped out at Cimarron from a froth of suds. He suppressed the idiotic impulse to wink at it.

"I'd best wait in the parlor," he managed to mumble.

"My back," she said, bending forward in the tub. When

33

Cimarron stood staring stupidly at her, she held the bar of soap out to him. "My back," she repeated.

He reached out for the soap.

She withdrew her arm.

He stepped up to the tub and reached for the soap again. Her hand brushed against him—strategically—and he snapped immediately erect.

"That feels good," Lucy sighed.

He realized that he had not touched her back. Then she meant— He bent over, dipped the soap in the bathwater, and began to rub her back. Up. Down. Up again. The cleft of her buttocks was plainly visible. Homely as a heifer, he thought. She's on the edge of ugly. He continued soaping her back.

She surprised him by suddenly standing up in the tub and taking the soap from him. She bent over and began to soap her thighs with surprisingly sensuous movements. She momentarily covered her crotch with the bar of soap and then, straightening, began to move it in a circle about her navel.

Suds slid down her slightly mounded belly and into her crotch before continuing down her thick thighs.

I've had worse, he thought, knowing what he wanted to do with his hands but keeping them in stiff soldierly place at his sides.

"Oh!" Lucy cried.

"What?"

"I dropped it—the soap." She peered down into the sudsy water. She turned and bent over.

Cimarron stared at her ample buttocks and recalled a painting he had once seen. It had been hanging above the bar in a Texas town. It was of a woman who was tied to a black horse. She had buttocks almost as large as Lucy's. His hand reached out. He patted her gently.

She turned around swiftly and seized him. Her arms went around him. Her lips slammed against his. His hat fell off.

A moment later, she released him and he staggered backward, stepping on his hat. "Help me out of this tub!" she cried.

He did and she came at him in a kind of lusty frenzy.

She tore off his buckskin jacket and hurled it to the floor. She tried to remove his blue bandanna, but her

34

fumbling fingers couldn't untie the knot. She gave up on the bandanna and instead, after hurriedly unbuttoning his shirt, she practically tore it from his body.

She unbuckled his cartridge belt and dropped it. "Your boots!" she cried, her breath coming fast and shallow.

"I'll hold on to this, if you don't mind," Cimarron said, picking up his cartridge belt.

"Pull off your boots!" she commanded. "You'll dirty the sheets!" She shoved him and he sat down heavily in a chair. She had his boots off a moment later and a moment after that his jeans unbuttoned. "Stand up!" she commanded, and he did.

Down came his jeans as Lucy, on her knees, tugged briskly on them.

As Cimarron stepped out of them, Lucy's eyes widened, and, still on her knees, she gasped. "Why, it could be classified as the eighth wonder of the world!"

He was about to thank her for the compliment but he never got the chance. She rose, turned him around, and gave him a shove. "The bedroom," she whispered huskily. "First door on the right. I'll dry myself and be right there."

Wearing only his socks and bandanna, he made his way out of the kitchen. When he reached the first door on the right, he went through it and found himself in a bedroom.

There were no windows in the room. The walls were bare and unpainted. A rack stood in one corner with women's clothes draped over it. The room contained a chair and a dresser on which he placed his gunbelt. A bed.

He would have made for it immediately, but the cat he had last seen on the parlor windowsill now sat in the middle of it, its eyes on him.

"Scat!" he said halfheartedly. "This isn't a threesome. It's between me and your mistress. Scat?"

The cat bared its teeth. It hissed.

Then it lunged at Cimarron, who barely had time to cover his genitals as the cat's claws raked his chest, drawing thin tendrils of blood.

He spun around and kicked the cat, hurting his toes.

It yowled and went careening from the room.

As he lay down on the bed, he heard a door open and then close. Good, he thought. She's gotten rid of the critter.

He lay on his back, his hands clasped behind his head, and stared up at the ceiling, which showed faint traces of having once been whitewashed. He wouldn't have to look at her, he told himself. He'd bury his face in the pillow alongside her head and think of—

Belle Starr.

The name had just popped unbidden into his mind. How long had it been since he'd seen her? Nearly two years. He wondered where Belle was now and, wondering, grew even harder. He looked down at himself. He was throbbing. "You've got to learn to be a little patient," he said aloud and then laughed at the improbability of that ever happening to his ever-ready-for-action appendage.

He suddenly wondered not where Belle Starr was but where Lucy Raleigh was. How long could it possibly take her to dry herself? She'd been in one helluva hurry to bed him. He wouldn't have minded if she hadn't even bothered to try to dry herself off. He sat up in the bed, frowning, not liking the thought that had sidled into his mind.

He swung his legs over the side of the bed and called, "Lucy!"

He waited, expecting at least a giggle. He got none.

Rising from the bed, he made his way to the open door and looked out into the hall, his hands once again covering his genitals in case the cat was still somewhere in the house readying itself for another frontal assault.

"Lucy?" Tentatively. Hopefully.

He hurried down the hall, holding himself as if he were afraid something might loosen and fall off, and stepped into the kitchen—the empty kitchen.

He swore. .

She was gone.

He ran to the window and looked out. He swore again. Gone too was her horse he had earlier told her to get ready to ride. Well, it sure did look like she had readied it and was riding it right this very minute.

He released his hold on himself, looked down and snarled, "You get me in more trouble than all the rest of me put together does!"

His clothes—

They were gone.

Gone? He turned, first one way, then another, his eyes on the floor where Lucy had thrown them. They were nowhere to be seen. He ran back to the bedroom and tore the clothes from the rack.

Dresses. Undergarments. A sweater.

He placed the back of the sweater in front of himself and tied the arms together behind him. Then, after grabbing his gunbelt, he made a dash for the front door. He went through it and headed for his horse. He freed it and leaped into the saddle; as he did so, the sweater came undone and fell to the ground.

He strapped on his gunbelt and was about to dismount to retrieve the sweater when a woman standing in a neighboring yard let out a scream.

"It's all right," he called out to her. "It's just that I'm—"

She crumpled to the ground in a dead faint.

Maybe he could use his bandanna as a kind of loincloth as the men did—in Africa, was it? He was about to untie it when a man came racing out of the house next door to kneel beside the woman lying motionless on the ground.

"Did you see where Miss Raleigh went?" he yelled to him.

The man looked up at him and shook a fist.

"I'm a lawman, mister!" Cimarron yelled. "You don't answer me, I'll arrest you for obstructing justice!"

"Where's your badge, if you're a lawman?" the man yelled back, still shaking his fist.

"It's—" Cimarron began and then gave it up. He walked his horse toward the man, who leaped to his feet.

"Where'd that Raleigh woman go?" he asked, his tone sharp.

"I don't know," The man replied, fear on his face. "I never set eyes on her, not since yesterday noon, I didn't."

"West," whispered the woman who was coming out of her faint. "She was riding west." She looked up, blinked, saw Cimarron, and fainted again.

He turned the chestnut and headed up the street, trying to ignore the shouts and cries that his passage through Skullyville elicited from the town's residents as they pointed at him, and he swore under his breath because the saddle leather was cold beneath his buttocks, the March air was cold on his naked body, and his feet kept slipping out of the stirrups because his socks were wet as a result of his having stood in a puddle of bathwater the elusive Lucy Raleigh had left on her kitchen floor.

3

Cimarron, as he rode, scanned the countryside around him, peering through the stands of trees that covered the hilly, almost mountainous ground, searching the packed earth of the California Road for sign of Lucy Raleigh.

As the minutes passed and he continued riding hard, he began to despair of finding her. Maybe the woman who had told him that Lucy had ridden west had been wrong. Maybe Lucy had started out in that direction and then had cut north. Or south. Maybe she'd even doubled back and was even now riding behind him.

Then, up ahead, he spotted the cloud of dust drifting in his direction as a result of the westerly wind. Moments later, he was able to make out the figures of men moving through the dust that their mounts and wagon were raising.

He hugged the chestnut with his knees, his stirrups flapping wildly since, because his feet continued to slip out of them, he was not using them, and urged the horse on. He drew rein when he reached the posse and yelled, "Any of you men see a woman riding west?"

"Cimarron, what in the *hell* are you doing riding around like that?" Bud Billings asked him.

He ignored the question and repeated his own.

One of the men in the halted posse pushed his hat up on his head with a thumb and said, "I don't reckon the world's seen a sight like you, Cimarron, since God was a pup. If then."

"I'm after a woman," Cimarron yelled, exasperated and then furious when Billings remarked dryly, "I've no doubt about that." "She's wanted for attempted murder," he shot at Billings.

"The woman we passed a ways back," one of the men

38

said, grinning, "was in a helluva hurry. Was she the one you're after?"

Cimarron gave a rapid description of Lucy Raleigh, and the man nodded.

"Plain as pudding, she was," he said. "So that must have been her. Looked like she was hell bent on reaching San Francisco before nightfall."

"Billings," Cimarron barked, "you and your men stay put right here. I'll be back with the woman, given any little bit of luck. You can take her back to Fort Smith with you."

Ignoring Billings's protests, he rode west, slamming his heels into the sides of his chestnut, and less than ten minutes later, he spotted the fully clothed Lucy riding hard up ahead of him.

He flogged the chestnut with the reins and let it have its head.

Lucy turned when she heard him coming, an expression of astonishment on her face.

Suddenly, she turned her horse and headed up the slope of a hill into the trees covering it.

Cimarron went after her, dodging low-hanging branches, the chestnut under him skidding to avoid the trees, turning right, then left, white froth oozing from between its lips, sweat slicking its hide.

He came abreast of Lucy near the crest of the hill. He leaned over and seized her reins. He gave them a jerk, and her horse reared. She fell from the saddle, and as she did so, he jumped down from his chestnut, which ran a few paces and then stopped, its body heaving and froth continuing to slide from between its lips.

He grabbed the bundle tied behind the cantle of Lucy's saddle and ripped it open. His clothes and boots tumbled to the ground. He grabbed his hat and put it on and was jamming one leg into his jeans when Lucy got up from the ground and went running through the trees, back the way she had just come.

"Goddam her!" Cimarron muttered and drew his .44. He fired over her head. She dodged behind a tree. "You come out from behind that tree and I'll shoot your ass off, woman!" he yelled at her as he hurriedly unstrapped his cartridge belt in order to get his jeans on.

Lucy remained behind the tree as Cimarron hurriedly

dressed, and then, once his gunbelt was in place again and his six-shooter in his hand, he rounded up the two horses and led them toward the tree where Lucy had taken refuge.

"Get on your horse," he ordered her, his eyes afire with fury.

"You're absolutely scandalous!" she declared. "Riding about naked and shooting at a helpless woman!"

"Scandalous I may be. Outfoxed by you I'm not. Now climb up on that horse."

Lucy meekly obeyed him. When she was in the saddle again, she said, "You can't arrest me. You haven't got a warrant."

Cimarron's hand slid into his pocket and found no warrant. "What'd you do with it?"

"Tore it up and threw it away." She gave him a haughty smile.

"Move out. We're going back to the Road."

When they reached the California Road, Cimarron gestured brusquely, and Lucy, squaring her shoulders, rode east. He followed directly behind her, his right hand resting lightly on the butt of his revolver.

"That little glade over there," Lucy said, breaking their silence and pointing. "It's so pretty. Like something from a picture. Why don't we go over there, you and I? We could strike a bargain. This time I'll give you what you wanted back at the house. You can give me—well, you can ride on alone—afterward."

Cimarron remained silent.

"The truth is, I'd like to be mounted by a man like you. You may not believe me when I say that I was sorry I had to run off and leave you like I did after I saw— Are you listening to me?"

Cimarron felt a stirring in his groin. He glanced at the glade. "Keep moving," he said.

When they caught up with Billings and his posse, Cimarron explained to Billings about the destroyed warrant. "But take her in anyway. Marshal Upham'll write out another one."

"Irregular," Billings murmured with a curious glance at Lucy.

"I don't give a shit if it's ten times irregular!" Cimarron snarled. "Take her in with you, and be sure you don't tell

Upham what happened to me. Just tell him that I arrested Lucy Raleigh—that's her name—but I lost the warrant."

"How can I tell him what happened to you?" Billings responded innocently. "I don't know what happened. All I know is I saw you come riding toward us near to naked as an eel. Were I to tell the marshal that, he'd think this job had addled my brains. Or yours."

Cimarron, with a curt nod to Billings, turned his horse and headed west again, his stomach rumbling from hunger, his thoughts on the breakfast he should have had before leaving Fort Smith.

He rode, angling northwest, until the sun began to reach for the horizon, stopping only long enough at the Illinois River to drink from it and fill his canteen.

The Boston Mountains were far behind him and he had crossed the tracks of the Missouri, Kansas and Texas Railroad when he spotted several sage hens in the distance. He slid his Winchester from the boot, took aim, and fired once. Two of the three hens disappeared. He rode up to the one he had downed and got out of the saddle. Using a flint and steel, he started a small fire and then, pulling his bowie knife from his right boot, proceeded to lop off the head and legs of the bird. He held the carcass over the flames to singe away the feathers and then he gutted it. After hacking several branches from a nearby shin oak, he used one to spit the bird and placed it over the flames, resting the spit on two notched sticks he had stuck into the ground on either side of the fire. He hunkered down and turned the spit slowly as the sun disappeared and the fire fought the deepening shadows that soon were everywhere.

When the hen was roasted to his satisfaction, he ate it hungrily, holding the ends of the shin oak's branch in both hands, and spitting out bones which hissed and crackled as they landed in the flames.

When he had finished his meal, he moved closer to the fire and drew his buckskin jacket tighter to shut out the chill that had come with the night. He sat there, staring into the flames, thinking of Lila Kane and smiling to himself as a fox barked not far away.

Then he rose, pounded a picket pin into the ground, and tied the chestnut to it before removing his gear from the horse. He shook out his blanket and draped it over a branch of the shin oak to dry.

He pulled a handful of bluegrass and used it to rub the horse down, talking to the animal as he worked, occasionally whistling through his teeth. The horse nickered and nuzzled him. He patted its neck and ran his fingers through its mane, searching for burrs. He found one and removed it.

A nearly full moon was riding in the sky when he kicked out his fire and got his bedroll and tarp. After spreading the tarp on the ground, he wrapped the blanket around him and lay down, his .44 unholstered beside him and within easy reach.

Cimarron awoke early the next morning and sat up shivering in the cool damp air. He squinted into the dense layer of ground fog which floated everywhere and upon which hazy sunlight fell. He wiped away the moisture that had condensed on his face, got to his feet, and walked over to where he had built his fire the night before.

He stared down at the scattered bones of the sage hen he had eaten, and saliva filled his mouth. Somewhere out there in the swirling fog, he thought, is my breakfast. The fogbound landscape around him, he thought, looked like a ghostly battlefield. The trees, because of the fog drifting among them, seemed to move from time to time, tall silent sentinels. He picked up several bones and pocketed them. He found a few feathers which were not completely singed and pocketed them as well. He tried to ignore his hunger, but in his mind fat jackrabbits by the dozens bounded. Prairie quail posed and preened. A pronghorn antelope tossed its head, taunting him.

He got up and quickly had his horse ready to ride.

As the fog began to surrender to the onslaught of the rising sun, he rode northwest.

By midmorning he had reached his destination, a tributary of the Arkansas River. He dismounted and freed the chestnut to graze, its reins trailing. He pulled his shirttail from his jeans and tore a strip of cloth from it. Working carefully, he tore the cloth again, and when he had enough threads of sufficent length, he began to braid them. When he was satisfied with what he had done, he took the bones and feathers from his pocket. He cracked a bone between his fingers and then cracked it again until it was the small curved shape he wanted. He took a piece of his shirttail and, holding the feathers against the curved piece of bone, used the cloth to bind the feathers to the bone until it was almost invisible. He tied the fly he had fashioned to the fishing line he had made by braiding the threads of his shirttail and dropped it into the clear water. He jerked the line several times, and the makeshift fly looped through the water.

A few minutes later he saw something—a dark shadow—dart below the surface of the water. He leaned over and trailed the fly in the water. He jerked it slightly toward the surface and then let it drift back down. The shadow he had seen circled and then, as the fly descended toward it, it lunged.

The line in Cimarron's hand went taut. He gripped it tightly with both hands and pulled, hoping it would hold, his eyes on the grayling he had caught. Not entirely trusting the braided line, he thrust his right hand into the water as the fish rose toward the surface and then thrust several fingers into the fish's mouth. He hauled it up and threw it onto the grass bank, where it flopped and gasped its life away as he busied himself digging a firepit and then building a fire.

He placed stones in the fire and then used his knife to scale the fish. He gutted it from anal vent to gills and then, pulling on the fish's cartilage, he stripped free the gills, pectoral fins, and intestines. Using his thumbnail, he scraped out the blood lying along the spine and then cut out the anus.

When he judged the stones in the firepit to be hot enough, he cut the fish into slabs and laid the pieces on top of the stones, turning them from time to time.

When they were thoroughly cooked, he speared one piece after another with his knife and ate them, enjoying their slightly gamy, slightly smoky flavor.

When he had finished his breakfast, he sat cross-legged on the ground, watching the fire burn down to embers.

And arguing silently with himself.

He was heading in her direction. To visit her, he wouldn't have to go out of his way. But if he did visit her, he'd lose time. Hell, would a lost day or two spent dallying again with Lila Kane matter? No one had told him he had to get to the Cherokee Strip by a certain time. But neither had anyone told him he was at liberty to mix his lawman's business with his personal pleasure.

An image of Lila Kane shimmered in his mind.

How long had it been since he'd seen her? Swiftly calculating, he came up with the answer. Two years. Two years ago this month, to be exact about it.

On the way back, he told himself. I'll stop by her place on my way back to Fort Smith.

The lovely image in his mind pouted.

Well, I don't have to stay, do I? he asked himself. I can just ride up and bid her the time of day and ride right on out again.

I'm fooling myself, he thought. If she's still there it'll be more like my dismounting from that chestnut of mine and then mounting her if she'll have me at least one more time.

Would she?

There was one sure way to find out.

Even if she wasn't ready to wrassle, as she had once put it to him, she wouldn't pull any tricks on him the way Lucy Raleigh had done the day before. He thought of how close he had come to having Lucy. You're getting simple, he thought. You never had a chance of having that one, and she knew it right from the very start.

He got up and kicked out the fire.

Another fire smoldered and then burst into bright hot life within him as he continued thinking about Lila. She lived nine or ten miles north of Broken Arrow, and he wasn't far from that town now. Even if it turned out that she wasn't there anymore, had moved on, the trip wouldn't be a total loss. He could ride north the twenty or so more miles to Catoosa and spend the night in a hotel in a real bed. And, if he had any luck, maybe he'd get to share his bed with one of the women from the saloons that were as numerous in Catoosa as mushrooms after a warm spring rain.

He stepped into the saddle and moved briskly out.

He had ridden through Broken Arrow but was only a mile or two beyond it when he heard the sound of gunfire. He halted his horse and guided it quickly into the shelter of some loblolly pines. He listened.

Another shot sounded.

44

The gunfire came from up ahead, he realized. Up ahead and off to the right.

Well, lawman, he thought, get on along and cool down the tempers of whoever it is has got killing on their minds up there.

He moved out of the trees and cantered at right angles to the trail he had been following. Then he turned north and, a few minutes later, headed east, intending to come up on the fracas, whatever it might turn out to be, from a safe distance.

The country through which he rode was only thinly treed and practically uninhabited. The ground beneath his horse's hooves was almost bare except for patches of brown thatch visible here and there. Occasionally he caught sight of a hint of green where the long grass was being awakened by the warm sunny days only to return to dormancy in the cool, sometimes cold, March nights.

There they were!

When he spotted the two gunmen up ahead of him, Cimarron, dismounted. He tied the chestnut to a pine and made a run for a frost-split boulder off to his left. He crouched down behind its crumbling mass and unholstered his gun, surveying the scene in front of him.

The gunmen were firing at a plank shack in front of them. Two horses stood nervously nearby. The door of the shack was closed, and so were its wooden shutters. But someone inside was returning the fire of the two gunmen through a loophole in the wall to the left of the door.

The two gunmen, several feet apart, were crouching behind a flatbed wagon they had evidently overturned.

I've got me a problem, Cimarron thought. I don't know what the hell's going on here. Don't know which side's got the good guys and which one the bad apples.

Just then, one of the gunmen let out a yell—a name he shouted at the top of his voice.

"Vance!"

For a moment, there was silence.

Then the gunman shouted again, "Vance, you and Chief come out of there or we'll drive you out!"

"Try it!" came a harsh shout from inside the shack. "We'll kill both of you lighthorse bastards first!"

So, Cimarron thought. The boys behind the wagon are the good guys. Creek lighthorsemen. Vance and Chief are

45

the bad guys. But what we've got here is a Mexican stand-off, looks like. Well, maybe I can help to tip the balance some even though it's not my fight. The jaspers inside the shack must be Indians too, he thought, else the lighthorsemen wouldn't be after them. White men aren't their fair game out here in the Territory.

Cimarron gave a sibilant hiss. It carried, and both lighthorsemen turned, their guns aimed at the boulder behind which he crouched. He stuck the pin of his badge into the barrel of his revolver and then raised the gun above the top of the boulder. He waited a moment and then called out, loudly enough for the lighthorsemen to hear but not loudly enough—he hoped—for Vance and Chief to hear his words, "I'm a deputy marshal out of Fort Smith. Figure on giving you boys a hand. I'll move back and then circle around and come up on the shack from behind. I'll start a ruckus back there and then you two can storm the place. How's that sound?"

Neither man answered him. But both nodded before turning back to face the shack.

Cimarron pocketed his badge and then, gun in hand, made a run for some trees not far from the boulder. He reached them safely and after pausing momentarily to judge distance and his chances, he made a run parallel to the north wall of the cabin.

A bullet *pinged* past him, so he knew they had spotted him, but he kept on going and was relieved, a moment later, to find there were neither windows nor loopholes in the wall he was facing. He made his way around to the rear of the shack, halting just before he reached the end of the wall. Taking off his hat, he peered around the corner. When he saw and heard no one, he clapped his hat back on his head and made a dash for the trees which grew several yards beyond the shack.

He scooped up some debris that lay beneath them and then dropped it. Too damp. But there was a sunny spot not far from where he stood. He moved into it and felt the ground. Dry. Again he scooped up a handful of partially decomposed leaves and broken branches, which he carried to the rear of the shack. He made a return trip for more tinder and then, when he had piled it up against the unpainted boards that formed the shack's wall, he took out his flint and steel.

It took him several tries, but at last a spark caught and he knelt and shielded the tiny flame with both hands. He blew on it and it blazed up. He took off his hat and fanned the flame vigorously, stepping back as the pile of tinder *whoosshhed* into bright-red life. Smoke rose from the fire; he inhaled some and covered his mouth with one hand to muffle the cough. He spat, and his spittle hissed in the fire.

When the shack itself began to burn, he ran back under the trees and pressed tightly against the trunk of one of the largest in the small grove. He waited.

The lighthorsemen would soon see the smoke, he told himself. The men inside the shack would soon realize they were being burned out.

Nothing happened.

The smoke rose, but the wind tore at it and sent it swirling into nothingness. Occasional shots sounded. Cimarron heard no voices. He had to let the Creeks out there behind the wagon know that it was time to charge the shack.

The fire had eaten through the base of the boards of the shack's rear wall. Cimarron thought he heard the men inside talking, but he wasn't sure. He picked up a dry branch, ran forward, and thrust it into the fire. When it began to blaze, he stepped back and tossed it on the roof.

One of the men inside the shack let out a roar.

Cimarron raced back to the trees, cocking his .44.

If they tried to get out this way— But they wouldn't, he was almost certain. The wall—most of it—was burning now. Two of the boards had collapsed and lay burning on the ground. Smoke billowed along the ground, thick and black. As Cimarron watched, part of the wall collapsed in a bright display of scattered sparks, and he could see inside the shack.

Suddenly, the door of the shack was thrown open.

They've charged, he thought, catching sight of one of the lighthorsemen. He couldn't see the men called Vance and Chief. He began to wonder if they were still inside the building or if they had somehow managed to escape.

"Vance!" yelled one of the lighthorsemen. "Come on out of there! You too, Chief!"

Cimarron saw a man walk, hands over his head,

through the door and outside. It was about over, he realized. The roof was burning. It wouldn't be long before it collapsed.

He squinted, trying to see inside the shack, as acrid smoke rose from the fallen and still-burning planks, but he could see nothing now.

And then—something. Something—someone—was moving just beyond the jagged flames and seething smoke.

A man leaped through the flames, a blanket over his head. He hit the ground and rolled, the blanket flapping about his body.

Cimarron stepped out from behind the tree. "Hold it right there, mister."

He advanced, his slitted eyes impaling those of the man who was kneeling on the ground and staring up at him, his expression a mixture of hatred and contempt. The man scrambled backward, still on his knees, waving his hands in front of him as Cimarron continued walking toward him.

"Don't shoot. I surrender." Only fear was on the man's face now.

"Which one might you be?" Cimarron asked him. "Chief?"

"Vance," the man answered and lost his balance. He fell to the ground.

Before Cimarron realized that Vance's move had been a trick, Vance threw off the blanket and fired the gun which suddenly appeared in the hand he had kept hidden.

Cimarron threw himself to the ground and fired as part of the shack collapsed, sending up a cloud of smoke and dust that obscured Vance.

He sprang to his feet, his body swiveling, his gun gripped tightly in both hands as he peered into the thick smoke searching for Vance.

Slowly, the smoke cleared.

Vance had vanished.

"Lawman!"

Cimarron spun around to find one of the lighthorsemen coming around the side of the shack, which was almost completely engulfed in flames now.

"You get Vance?" the Creek asked.

"He got away," Cimarron said, angry with himself for

having let that happen, for having let himself be tricked by Vance's faked fall.

The other lighthorseman appeared with a prisoner upon whose right hip an empty holster rested.

The man, his hands held high above his head, was looking at the ground.

"My name's Lansing," the Creek who had questioned Cimarron declared, and Cimarron went up to him and they shook hands.

"Cimarron's what I'm called."

"Thanks for your help," Lansing said.

"Some help I was to you. I let Vance get away."

"I'll find him," Lansing stated flatly. He turned to his companion. "Take Chief in with you. I'm going out after Vance."

When the man Lansing had spoken to had disappeared with his prisoner, Lansing turned to Cimarron and said, "Well, one out of two's not so bad. We have a fifty percent success rate." He smiled, his dark face wrinkling, his black eyes gleaming.

A yell. A curse. A shot. All in rapid succession.

Lansing was sprinting around the side of the shack, Cimarron right behind him. They found the other lighthorseman standing with a six-gun in his hand. It still smoked.

"He made a run for it. I meant to wing him, but it looks like I got him in the chest."

Lansing knelt beside Chief's body. "Dead," he said. "Leave him here to rot. He deserves it. We'll both go out after Vance."

"What's he wanted for?" Cimarron asked.

"You name it, he's done it," Lansing answered, rising. "If it's illegal, immoral, or just plain wrong. The last charge on his list, though, is probably the worst. Him and that Creek who called himself Chief, the two of them rode up to a cabin outside of Red Fork. A young Creek couple, they'd set up housekeeping there. Just married they were. Well, to make a sad story short, they beat up the husband and abused the wife."

"Assault and rape."

"Worse. That was just the beginning of their escapade. They got bored after a time, according to the husband. They told him what they wanted him to do. He wouldn't do it. They started stabbing him here and there until there looked to be more blood on the outside of him than there was on the inside. He did what they told him to do then—to his wife. He poured coal oil on a broom handle and then, while Vance and Chief held the woman's legs apart, he shoved it up inside her and set it on fire.

"She burned to death—from the inside out. He wrote it all down after they left. When we found them—we'd been trailing Vance and Chief—he was dead too."

"He bled to death?"

"He shot himself in the head because he couldn't stand to live after what he'd done. That's what he wrote." Lansing glanced at the remains of the shack. "Did you see which way Vance went?"

"I didn't, I'm sorry to say. The smoke—I don't know which way he went."

"Thanks again. Be seeing you, Cimarron."

As Lansing and the other lighthorseman began to examine the ground for sign, Cimarron made his way back to where he had tethered his horse. He resumed his journey, trying not to think about the story Lansing had just told him, trying instead to think only of Lila Kane, a way of drowning horror with a flood of tender memories.

Later, when her cabin and three-sided shed, its back to him, came into view, Cimarron felt excitement growing within him. He halted his horse and sat his saddle, gazing at the scene before him, hoping to see some sign of life. He saw none.

But then, only a moment later, he heard the sound of metal striking metal, and he smiled. She was in the shed. At her forge. He imagined the hammer in her hand, the sparks flying as it struck the iron she was working. He saw her again as he had last seen her. In his mind, he saw the regular features of her pretty and not very far from beautiful face. Her deep-blue eyes and full lips. Her soft brown hair that was braided girlishly into two pigtails. The small firm breasts above her narrow waist and her slender hips.

He was sure she would still be wearing jeans, a man's shirt, work boots, and a Stetson just as she had been during those days two years ago when they had been briefly together.

He spurred his horse and galloped down the rise and up to the rear of the shed, where he halted.

"Hey there, you Lila Kane!" he yelled. "I got me an unshod horse out here that needs tending, so you hustle yourself on out here and have a look at him!"

"Go to hell, mister!" a woman's voice cried from inside the shed. "You want your mount cared for, you bring him around back here. I'm a working woman who don't wait on folks like you who like to give other folks orders."

Cimarron grinned. She hadn't changed. Feisty as ever. A woman more than able to whip the world into a shape that suited her. A woman worth her weight in wildcats. His grin widened.

"Lila!"

No answer. Only the sound of the hammer striking iron.

"Lila, it's me! Cimarron!"

Silence then, deep and encompassing, after the *clang, clang* of her hammer.

Cimarron's grin faded. Would she welcome him? Did her silence mean she didn't want to see him again? Did it mean she regretted what had happened between them?

He glanced to his left and saw the grave of Archie Kane, Lila's brother. Someone—Lila, no doubt—had painted the wooden cross above it a stark white. It gleamed in the sun.

She came around the side of the shed then and halted, one hand shielding her eyes as she stared up at Cimarron.

"Hello, honey," he said softly. "Was in the neighborhood and thought I'd stop by."

"Cimarron."

There was a world of meaning, of feeling, in the name she had spoken so softly that Cimarron had barely heard it leave her lips. But he could not identify the nature of the feelings or the meanings.

"Well, are you going to sit in that saddle all day or are you going to get down and give me a proper greeting?"

"I don't dismount 'less I'm asked to. Wouldn't be proper. Or polite."

"I don't remember you as being very proper. Or polite either, for that matter."

"Two years have passed, honey. Maybe they've changed

51

me." Cimarron got out of the saddle. "You've been doing all right for yourself, have you, all this time?"

Lila nodded. She dropped her hand and glanced at her cabin.

"Thought about you from time to time. Missed you."

"A wandering man like yourself, such men don't miss nothing except the water when the well goes dry."

"You're wrong, honey. I just told you the truth." Cimarron studied her. She had changed and yet she had not changed. She still wore work clothes as he had expected. Her hands were still callused, their fingernails broken. There were streaks of dirt on her face where she had wiped away sweat.

Then what was different about her?

It came to Cimarron suddenly. Her hair was undone, the pigtails gone. Her figure was fuller. She hadn't been much more than angular two years ago. But now her breasts were larger, like melons that have ripened in hot sun and warm rain. Her hips seemed to have more of a curve. There was something too about her face—it was—Cimarron didn't know at first what it was.

But then he knew with a sudden and complete certainty. The girl he had known—that girl was gone. Lila stood before him a woman grown, and it was that profound change that stirred him so.

"Cimarron!"

She had cried the name, a shrill incantation. Then she was running toward him, her Stetson falling off and lying forgotten behind her. She was in his arms and he was holding her as her hands clutched at him, drew him close, and held him tightly as if she would never let him go, and he was kissing her lips, her cheeks, her forehead, her lips again.

"Don't cry," he whispered.

"I'm not crying!" she sobbed. "Oh, Cimarron! I never expected to see you again!"

"It's real good to feel you so close to me again, honey. It's nothing but nice."

"I missed you," she whispered, her face buried against his chest. "I tried not to. I tried so *hard* not to. But, dammit, I *did!*"

Cimarron was about to speak when she drew away from him. "Come inside the cabin," she said, her eyes, though wet with tears, twinkling. "I've got something to show you."

"What might that be?" he asked as she took his hand and led him, both of them running, into the cabin.

"Him!" she said, her voice high and happy. She pointed.

Cimarron stared down at the cradle that was made from a hollowed-out log set on two curved boards which served as rockers.

From a clean nest of white muslin, a small face peered up at him. The infant's green eyes blinked solemnly. Its thumb went into its mouth.

"You had yourself a baby!" Cimarron exclaimed, delighted. "You got yourself married!" A pang of disappointment shot through him, and he tried not to let it show on his face.

"I'm not married," Lila said. "But, you're right, I did have a baby. He's just over a year old. His birthday was last January third."

"Well, now," Cimarron said, staring down at the boy in the cradle, who was still staring up at him. "You're a mother. Now, don't that beat all!"

"And you're a father. Now, don't *that* beat all!"

Cimarron turned to her, incredulous. "You mean—" He pointed at the infant. "You mean he's—"

"Your son."

For long moments, Cimarron was silent, and then, "I never thought I'd turn into a daddy, I truly never did."

"Well, you have," Lila said, and he seized and hugged her until she made him let her go because, she said, he was squeezing the very last little bit of life out of her lungs.

4

"You look about as solemn as a tenderfoot trapper skinning a skunk," Lila said as she busied herself at the stove.

Cimarron looked up at her from the chair in which he sat holding his son and said, "Being a daddy's enough to sober most men, even one as fiddlefooted as me." He paused, his eyes still on Lila. "But it's not just that that's set me to thinking."

"What else has?" Lila asked as she cracked eggs into a frying pan.

"I haven't done right by you, honey. But I never knew about—what's his name? Does he have himself a name?"

"I call him Archie," Lila answered, her voice low. "I never did learn your real name, if you've got one, and so I thought it would be nice to name him after my brother on account of how poor Archie got himself killed so young."

Cimarron's mind raced, remembering. "Archie," he said, looking down at the baby he was still afraid he might drop or break if he made a wrong or too-fast move. "That's a fine name."

"Cimarron."

He looked up again.

"You're not to go worrying about whether you did right or wrong by me. I never had any kind of hold on you. It was—we were—well, it was just one of those things. It was nice, like you said before, being together, the two of us. You remember how I was back then about—things. Still damp behind the ears, is what I was. I certainly never gave no thought to having a baby when we— Why, when I started to swell up like a balloon I thought at first I had a goiter or something like that. That's how dumb I was.

"Anyways, before I knew it Archie was here and you'd

been long gone and things, well, they worked out. I've still got my business—the forge and all. We get along fine. I traded some of my corn crop last year for a cow that'd been broken to milk. I hunt like always." She pointed to her rifle which hung on two wooden pegs above the door. "I built that there cradle for Archie."

"You had the boy all by yourself when your time came?" There was a dark undertone of guilt in Cimarron's voice.

Lila must have heard it, because she turned to him and smiled brightly. "There's an old Creek woman lives not far from here. Miz Henley. She saw me one day toward the end of my term, and she and I we got to talking. She helped me birth him. I think of her as Archie's godmother. Come and sit down to the table, Cimarron."

He got up, carefully placed Archie in his cradle, and then sat down at the table.

Lila set a plate that was practically covered with scrambled eggs in front of him and then a side dish of fried pork. She filled his cup with coffee and sat down across from him.

Cimarron suppressed a smile. Lila herself might have improved, he thought, but her cooking certainly hadn't. The eggs were drowning in grease, the pork crisped.

"Eat up," she ordered. "I got a mess of beans warming on the back of the stove for after you've ate those eggs." She looked down at her hands, which were folded in front of her on the table. "Cimarron, you mind if I ask you something?"

He was immediately wary and immediately ashamed of himself for being wary. "Ask away," he said uneasily, his mouth full of food.

"I was wondering—well, you didn't come all the way out here from Fort Smith to see me, did you? Not especially, I mean, you didn't, did you?"

Cimarron heard the note of hope in her voice, but he couldn't bring himself to lie to her. What's happened to me? he asked himself. I've lied long and loud to more women than I can count. "Nope. I was on my way up to the Cherokee Strip and I just wanted to see you again."

When Lila said nothing, he continued, "Things have happened faster'n weeds sprout in a kitchen garden since I got here. I haven't had time to sort them all out or make much sense out of them. But, honey, I—you oughtn't to be out here all alone with Archie. I mean, you got no other family. You—"

"Are you trying to tell me I got you?"

Was he? He shook his head in dismay.

"It's all right," Lila said, her eyes searching his face. "I told you. The two of us'll be fine."

"How come you never sent word to me at Fort Smith about my—our son?"

Lila poured herself a cup of coffee. "When the four of us—my three brothers and me—were just kids, those boys had a way of blaming me for everything bad that ever happened to a single one of them. They used to make me feel awful, and it was a long time before I caught on to the game they were playing. If one of them fell in a creek, it was my fault because I hadn't pointed out a slick stone to him before he tried crossing it. If one of them—and Archie was the worst of the three—if he caught a cold it was because I forgot to tell him to wear a muffler."

"You told me when we first met all about how you raised your brothers after your ma and pa were killed. But, honey, what's what you just said got to do with what I just asked you?"

"Suppose I had sent word to you about Archie. You'd think I was blaming you for what happened."

"I wouldn't've!"

"You'd have run."

"Not me."

"Even if you didn't run and you and me got together again for any length of time it wouldn't be long before you wouldn't be able to stand the sight of me. You'd start hating me for tying you down. I know you, Cimarron. Maybe you don't think I do. But I do. You're a man who likes living free as the wind and wild as any old tomcat. Now you know why I didn't send you word."

Cimarron finished the last of his eggs.

"Beans next," Lila said and got up from the table.

Cimarron looked at them lying on his plate when she returned from the stove. Dry as dust and overcooked. He forked some into his mouth. "Delicious," he said, and Lila beamed at him.

He managed one more mouthful before putting his fork

down. "You and me, honey, we've got to decide what we're going to do."

"What are you talking about?"

"Well, we should get married to start things off with. I could quit my job and move out here. Or you could move into Fort Smith and I'll stay a lawman."

Lila placed her hands on her hips and stared down at him, her lips pursed.

"What's the matter? Did I go and say something wrong?"

"Do you think I'd marry up with a scar-faced stallion like you?"

"Well, I thought— I mean there's Archie to think of. I thought—"

"Stop thinking!"

"Honey, I know you don't love me, but I've got a responsibility where this whole thing's concerned. A woman can't—"

"A woman can't what? I don't know what woman you're talking about but as far as I'm concerned, I can do any damn thing I set my mind to. I don't need a man underfoot messing up my cabin, plowing crooked furrows, like that."

"I know you're able to look after yourself and all, but I thought a woman—a woman with a baby—would want—need—a man to—"

"To what? Make an honest woman of her? Well, I might not have any fancy paper that makes me legal in the sight of the law, but I damned well don't need one. I'm a good woman and I've been being a good mother to Archie without you around. Look at him! He's as fat and saucy as a cat lapping cream. You think maybe I've not done right by the boy?"

"No, honey, it's not that. Maybe you're right. Maybe I'd just be in the way—your way. Make a mess of things. Truth to tell, I don't know the first thing about being a daddy and I sure as hell don't know how to go about being a husband to a woman as fine as yourself."

Lila made a strangled sound, and then her tears came.

Cimarron leaped to his feet and put his hands on her shoulders.

Her head was bent and her hands covered her face.

"What've I done now to hurt you, honey?"

"N-nothing," Lila moaned, her body trembling. "It's just that you didn't know what you were saying, I guess."

"What'd I say that I didn't know?"

"Before when you said you knew I didn't love you or anything like that. Well, you were wrong. I do love you now like I started doing not long after we first met. Only I didn't ever tell you so."

Cimarron took her in his arms and then gently caressed her hair. "I'll do right by you, honey—by both of you. You can count on that."

"We'll talk about it. Some other time." She wiped her eyes and drew away from him. "I promised myself I'd never—if I ever saw you again, I wouldn't—" The tears began again.

Archie awoke and began to howl, his tiny fists pummeling the air.

Lila went to him and picked him up. She hushed him by rocking him in her arms. She placed him against her shoulder and patted him.

He burped.

"He's a handsome little devil, isn't he?" Cimarron grinned.

"Just like his daddy," Lila said. "Only I hope he don't grow up to be the ruin of good women, as some folks would put it, like his daddy has been." She smiled.

"You're not ruined one bit. Fact is, you're better than new. Look at you." He reached out and took her arm. He led her across the room to the cracked mirror that hung on the wall. "Look. See that lovely lady looking back at you? Skin softer than rose petals."

"My hands, they're all callused."

"Don't interrupt. Hair that shines like the sun's got caught in it."

"I brush it every night."

"Don't interrupt. A figure so fine that if Solomon had ever once spotted it, he'd have sent Sheba packing."

Lila wiped away the last of her tears with the back of her free hand. "Then you're not mad?"

"Mad? At what? You?"

"About what happened. I know you didn't plan on this happening. But then neither did I."

"Honey, I haven't had me even the thinnest slice of what you could call a family for so long I can't even

58

remember what it was like to ever have had one or been part of one. But once—one Christmas when I was a boy—though we were dirt-poor and having one helluva hardscrabbling time of it—I got a present from my ma and pa. An orange that tasted sweeter'n sorghum. I was the happiest kid in the whole of Texas that Christmas, I can tell you. Happier'n a kid pulling a pup's ears is what I was. But I never got a better present than this here one that you've gone and given me and kept a secret from me for so long."

"You mean Archie?"

"I mean Archie." Cimarron reached out a hand to his son, and Archie seized his index finger. "This boy of ours, he's got himself a regular grip of iron, he has. He's going to grow up to be a champion prize fighter!"

"He will not! He's going to be something respectable. A storekeeper!"'

"A cowboy who'll turn the town of Abilene on its ear!"

"A minister maybe!" Lila practically shouted, trying to drown out Cimarron's laughter.

"A hell-for-leather, horse-forking, high-living, and far-riding man!"

"Oh, I just know he will!" Lila, surrendering, cried with delight. "He's bound to with a daddy like you. It's in his blood and there's just no denying or getting around it!"

Cimarron took Archie from Lila's arms and placed him back in the cradle. Then he turned back to her and she moved into his arms.

Neither of them spoke. They stood close together, their bodies touching, Cimarron's head spinning because of the way his world had so suddenly changed. "If I were a praying man," he whispered in Lila's ear, "I'd be down on my knees right now thanking the good Lord for what Him and you have gone and done for me. But I reckon if it's true that He knows a man's mind and can read what's in a man's heart then there's just no need for me to tell Him what He like as not already knows about how I feel."

"I'll clear away," Lila said and went to the table, where she began to gather up the dishes.

"I'll lend a hand," Cimarron said and reached for a dish.

"You could fetch some water from the creek," Lila told him. "The bucket's there—in the corner."

Cimarron picked up the bucket and went outside. He made his way to the creek and filled the bucket with water which was tinted orange by the slanting rays of the sun. Won't be dark for hours, he thought as, whistling, he started back to the cabin. But that old sun will slip out of sight all in good time, and then Lila and me . . .

A son, he thought. I've got a son. He stopped whistling and laughed out loud, throwing his head back, happy that he was here and alive and that Lila loved him and Archie would come to do the same once he got old enough to know him. We're a family, he thought, the three of us. The beginnings of one, anyway. Maybe the next one'll be a girl who'll grow up to be as pretty as her mother, he hoped, unmindful of the fact that he was almost running back to the cabin and causing the water to slosh out of the bucket.

"I'm back!" he declared as he entered the cabin.

Lila stood facing him on the far side on the room, her face pale, her eyes haunted.

"What's wrong, honey?" He looked down at the cradle. Archie was sound asleep, his tiny eyes squeezed shut.

"Nothing's wrong," a male voice said from behind Cimarron as he crossed the room. "Everything's as right as rain."

Cimarron started to turn.

"Hold it right there, mister! Hands up high!"

Cimarron heard boots on the wooden floor and then felt his gun being drawn from its holster. He raised his arms, his eyes on Lila.

Her words came in a rush. "He came in just after you went down to the creek and hid behind the door. He's got a six-gun."

"Who are you?" Cimarron asked, his fingers clenching into fists.

"Turn around," the male voice commanded.

Cimarron did and found himself facing Vance. He remembered what Lansing had told him about what Vance and Chief had done to the Creek couple whose home they had invaded. "The lighthorse are trailing you, Vance."

"Not anymore they're not. I hid out and then went

60

back to the shack thinking to catch up with Chief and set him free. Found him dead. Trailed those two lawmen. Caught up with them. Shot 'em both in the back. They never knew what hit them. Now, mister, whoever you might be, it's your turn. If it hadn't been for you, Chief and me would have held off those two fool Indians till the last trump."

"Let's go outside," Cimarron suggested. "You're gunning for me, not the woman. She's got no part to play in this."

"She your woman, is she?"

Cimarron nodded. "Let's go, Vance." He took a step forward, but Vance shook his head.

"Chief was blood kin of mine. My nephew. He's dead on account of you." Vance's eyes drilled into Cimarron's. Then they softened and he smiled. "Chief, he was more than just blood kin to me. We were as close as two coons hiding in a hollow log. He wasn't too bright, Chief wasn't, but that worked out in my favor. It made him easier to teach, and, believe it or not, after a while he got to liking what I did to him and what I talked him into doing to me from time to time. I tell you, Chief was as good spread face down on the ground as any woman I ever had, and what's more that boy got so skilled I swear he could have sucked the sun right out of the sky!

"But don't you go and get me wrong, mister. I like women too, and when I finish you off I'm going to busy myself liking that blue-eyed woman of yours over there. It's just that out here in the Territory women's as scarce as sinners in church, and that, like I said, is where Chief came in nice and handy on those long trails we traveled and lonely nights we shared."

Cimarron had heard Lila's gasp when Vance mentioned her, and now, his thoughts racing, he was trying to decide how he was going to take Vance. He had no doubt that he would take him. But how?

"There a back door to this place?" Vance asked.

"No," Lila said, her voice low.

"You stay put, missus," Vance told her. "Your man and me's going outside. But I'll be right back, so you get yourself ready, you hear?" He stepped to one side and waved with his free hand.

Cimarron stepped forward, went past Vance, and on

outside. He heard Vance behind him. He leaped to one side, turned swiftly, and as Vance fired, he brought both fists down on the wrist of Vance's gun hand.

But the revolver remained in Vance's hand.

Cimarron lunged for his own gun, which Vance had stuck in his waistband, but before he could get his hands on it, Vance gave him a vicious kick which Cimarron thought, as pain shot through his leg, felt as if it had broken his shinbone.

Vance ran a few paces, spun around, and raised his gun.

Cimarron threw himself through the open doorway, dropped to the floor, and was about to slam the door shut when flame flared from the barrel of Vance's gun.

Cimarron slammed the door just as Lila gave a strangled cry. He turned swiftly toward her and saw her stagger, her back to him. He wanted to go to her, but he had to take care of Vance first.

He reached up and seized her rifle from above the door. He checked it quickly. It was loaded. He dashed to the window.

Vance was running toward some trees at the base of the ridge.

Cimarron fired and missed. He threw open the door and fired again.

Vance went down.

Lila moaned, and Cimarron turned to find her slipping to the floor.

He ran over to where she was kneeling on the floor, her body bent forward, and he saw the bloody hole in the left side of her back.

With his free hand, he gripped her shoulder. "I'll help you lie down," he whispered.

She looked up at him, her eyes glazing. "Archie," she murmured, and only then did Cimarron notice that she had taken the child from the cradle and was still holding it, a bloody and obviously lifeless bundle, against her breasts.

He swallowed hard and fought against the nausea that had suddenly engulfed him. His hand tightened on Lila's shoulder as he tried to tear his eyes away from the tiny corpse she was holding in her arms.

"Cimarron," she said, a plea. She held Archie out to him.

"Cimarron," she said again and then coughed. Blood gushed from her mouth and spattered what little remained of Archie's skull. She fell forward, dropping the infant as she did so. She lay still on the floor, and Cimarron sobbed once and then bit his fist until blood flowed from it.

A great wordless cry of anguish was torn from him. He threw back his head and howled, hearing again the sound of Vance's shot, which had missed him but had entered Lila's body, passed through it, and gone on into the body of Archie, killing them both.

His howl subsided into a whimper and then it was gone completely. Slowly, he got to his feet, his right hand clenched on Lila's rifle. And then he was running. To the door. Through it. Vance—where? He scanned the still-sunlit landscape.

There!

Vance was dragging himself along the ground, heading for the trees. There was a gun still in his hand—his own.

Cimarron, as he raced toward Vance, saw his own gun lying on the ground, where it must have fallen when he had dropped Vance. He shifted his rifle to his left hand and picked up his .44 as he ran on without breaking stride.

Vance, when he heard Cimarron coming, fired at him.

But Cimarron dodged the bullet by veering to the right and then ran relentlessly on.

"I don't want to shoot you," he told Vance, when he reached him, feeling grateful that the man had only suffered a flesh wound in his right thigh. "So don't move."

It was true. He didn't want to shoot Vance. But he did want the man to die. Slowly. And in agony. Already, he knew what he was going to do to Vance, and a dark joy welled up within him, blotting out the sun and bringing an awful end to the world.

After tying Vance to one of the trees the man had hoped would afford him shelter, Cimarron went into the cabin and carried Lila's limp body out into the open and carefully placed it on the ground. Then, steeling himself for his next task, he returned to the cabin and picked up the broken body of his son and carried it outside. He placed the infant next to its mother.

"What're you fixing to do to me, mister?" Vance yelled at him.

Cimarron neither answered him nor glanced in his direction. He made his way to the three-sided shed and began to place coal in the forge, avoiding any green coal in order to build a clean coke fire. He went outside again and pulled several handfuls of thatch and then, using his flint and steel, he started his fire. As it began to burn to a depth of nearly nine inches, he scoured the shop for what he needed.

A horseshoe. An iron wagon-wheel rim. Several piggin strings that were hanging from a nail and had once belonged to somebody's saddle.

He set the piggin strings and horseshoe to one side and then cleaned the face of Lila's anvil. He chose a stout hammer from the array of tools lining one wall of the shed and then he used a bellows on the fire until it was blazing brightly.

With a pair of tongs he held the wheel rim in the fire and waited, watching it slowly turn red, then white. He placed it on the forge and hammered it until it snapped. He continued working on it, using the chipping block, until he had a length of iron that suited him. He returned the two-foot-long piece of metal to the fire, and, when it was once again glowing whitely, he placed it on the face of the anvil and hammered it on both edges and on one of its ends.

It took him some time to achieve the result he was seeking. When he was at last satisfied, he held the tongs out in front of him, examining the sharp edges and equally sharp point on the metal spear he had forged. He plunged the weapon into a barrel of briny water that stood near the anvil and hardly heard its hissing as the metal cooled, because his thoughts were thundering back and forth between what had just happened and what was about to happen.

Picking up the piggin strings and horseshoe, he carried the spear, which was hot in his hand, outside. He went over to where the two bodies lay, their lifeless faces gilded by the last rays of the setting sun.

He gazed down at them for a moment, the heart within him as shattered as Archie's small skull and just as cold, and then he knelt and buried the horseshoe, points down,

64

in the dirt until only a low metal loop remained above the surface of the ground.

Vance stared at him, his eyes wide, his lips parted.

Cimarron broke branches from a tree and pounded two strong stakes into the ground only inches apart. He straightened and tied several lengths of piggin strings together until he had formed two single strands, each about two feet long. Then, using the tongs as a shovel, he dug a deep hole and placed the blunt end of the spear in it. He filled in the hole. When he was finished, the spear protruded more than a foot above the surface of the ground. It sprouted like some deadly flower.

"You stay away from me!" Vance yelled as Cimarron walked over to him.

Cimarron reached out and grabbed his prisoner by the throat with both hands. He slammed Vance's head against the tree. Twice. The second blow rendered Vance unconscious.

Cimarron untied him and then pulled off the man's boots and tossed them aside. Working quickly, he tied Vance's ankles to the two stakes he had driven into the ground and then tied one length of piggin string around each of Vance's wrists.

Vance lay unmoving on the ground, his body curled up as if to avoid the spear jutting up from the ground.

Cimarron ran the free ends of the piggin strings through the horseshoe loop and then sat down just beyond it to wait for Vance to regain consciousness, keenly aware of the corpses lying near him which would be well within Vance's range of vision when he awoke.

Uncounted minutes passed before Vance finally groaned and then stirred. His eyes flickered. They opened. "What the hell—"

Cimarron pulled on the piggin strings in his hands.

Vance's body was dragged toward the spear. "Hey!" he yelled.

Cimarron, sitting cross-legged on the ground, waited for Vance to figure out what he had to do to avoid the spear. It didn't take Vance long. He scrambled up just before his body touched the spear and, bracing his hands on the ground between the spear and Cimarron, arched his body so that it was curved above the blade.

Cimarron estimated that there was a good four inches

65

between the sharp point of the spear and Vance's midsection.

"What're you trying to do to me?" Vance yelled, his head hanging down toward the ground as he stared at the sharp metal that seemed to be reaching up in an effort to slice into him. "Let me loose!" he roared.

Cimarron sat motionless.

Time passed. The sun set. Shadows crept across the land. Cimarron had not moved when the nearly full moon appeared in the sky.

But Vance had. He had struggled to tear the two stakes from the ground to free his feet. He had dragged his hands along the ground beneath him, trying to reach the spear, apparently intending to try to rip it from the ground. All his efforts failed. He groaned and raised his head. He looked at Cimarron, who was staring at him in silence. He started to speak, but only spittle slid from between his lips.

Cimarron drew the piggin strings toward him, wrapping their ends around his fists.

Vance let out a cry as the point of the spear touched his body.

Cimarron's hands became still as he watched the few drops of blood, made shiny by the moonlight, drip from Vance's gut. He loosened his hold on the piggin strings and Vance's body arched upward, almost a pyramid now, Vance's buttocks its apex.

The night grew older.

Cimarron alternately let the piggin strings go slack and then, after an interval that varied in length each time, he tightened his grip on them, pulling Vance's hands along the ground toward him and thereby lowering his prisoner's body toward the deadly blade.

Twice it entered Vance's body. Twice Vance screamed for a long time. Twice Cimarron let him live.

"*Damn* you!" Vance screamed at the top of his voice. "Damn you to hell!"

Cimarron stared at the blood sliding down the length of the sharp spear.

"It was an accident!" Vance cried, swinging his head from side to side like a demented animal. "It was you I meant to kill!"

Vance's blood on the spear looked black to Cimarron.

66

"No!" Vance screamed as Cimarron drew the piggin strings toward him and Vance's hands slid along the ground. "Oh, sweet Jesus Christ, please *don't,* mister! I'll do anything you say. I'll make it up to you somehow. I will, I promise you, as God's my witness, I will! Only don't do this to me no more. I can't stand it!"

Cimarron's fingers moved. The piggin strings slid through the iron loop toward him.

Vance's howl tore through the night.

Coyotes yipped in the distance as if in response.

Sweat dripped from Vance's face, although the night was cold. He tried to hurl himself to one side and succeeded only in driving the spear deeper into his gut. He screeched in anguish, but there was only Cimarron to hear him.

"My arms!" Vance cried. "My legs! They can't take any more of this. They're giving out on me. I can't hold myself up, not one more minute I can't! Oh, mister, please. You want me to beg you? All right, I'm begging you. You hear me, mister? I'm begging you to let me loose from here. You can hit me. I won't fight back. Kick me. I won't lift a finger against you. But don't do this terrible thing to me. I'm bleeding to death bit by bit. Look! *I am!*"

Cimarron suddenly leaned forward and let the piggin strings dangle, but he did not release his hold on them.

Vance's breath shot from his heaving chest as he pulled his hands along the ground and was able to draw his body up and away from the blade beneath him.

"You're a devil, mister, not a man!" Vance muttered, his voice weakening. "Only some unholy demon would do me this way."

Cimarron slowly drew the piggin strings toward him. He gathered them in a fraction of an inch at a time.

Vance's body began to straighten. Guttural sounds issued from his throat that had been meant to be words. He moaned, his head hanging down.

Cimarron continued to draw the piggin strings toward him, still slowly. He knew when the spear entered Vance's body. The man's anguished cry told him. He continued to pull on the piggin strings, watching Vance, listening to his screams.

Vance's body convulsed. His hands slid out from under him and he fell.

Cimarron let go of the piggin strings. He sat there as the minutes and then the hours passed, listening to Vance, watching the gutted man die.

He was still sitting there when the first gray light that preceded the dawn filled the sky. Only then did he get up. He stood looking down at the bloody spear that protruded from Vance's back for a moment, and then he went to the shed to find a shovel so that he could dig graves for Lila and his son.

He intended to leave Vance where he was for the coyotes, wolves, and green-necked buzzards which would surely come to feed on the carrion that Vance was in death just as he had been in life.

5

Cimarron rode north into the Osage Hills, pausing now and then to rest his chestnut, a man alone and yet not alone.

Lila rode with him, Archie in her arms, laughing sometimes, silent other times. He felt her presence and that of his son. But then he'd turn his head and they were not there, had never been there, he knew, and his features would set and harden.

He rode doggedly on, because he had a job to do and he intended to do it. It was a wonder to him that the world around him didn't stop and the sun refuse to rise. But the sun did set as it always had. The world went on. One man's pain, however great, his loss, no matter how profound, could not break the laws the world obeyed, he realized with resignation. Somehow it seemed to him that that fact diminished a man. Or maybe, he thought as he got down from his chestnut and watered it at a stream, it shows a man how small he really is in the vast scheme of things. Makes him know his place and learn to bear his pain and go right on living.

A hard row to hoe.

The phrase had leaped unbidden into his mind.

"Most of the people in this life have themselves a hard row to hoe."

You said it more than once in my hearing, Ma, he thought, and I knew what you said was true by the time I was ten. He got back into the saddle and walked his horse through the hills, keeping a loose rein on the animal as he sought out draws to make the traveling easier on the chestnut and choosing the lower hills to climb when no draws were to be found.

He passed small Pawnee settlements off to his left from time to time. He made camp each night in sheltered gullies, and on only one of those nights did he go hungry because he failed to bring down any game. Riding on in the mostly empty land, he fell asleep in the saddle more than once, and, upon awakening, cursed himself for his carelessness, because he was moving through country which was roamed by men like Vance, to whom a lone rider meant easy prey, prey from whom could be taken money, a horse and its gear, guns, a pair of boots, life itself.

The sky had been spitting snow at him when he crossed the border into Kansas and the air had been cold. The morning sun had been lost to sight in the storm that had sprung up so suddenly and turned the sky to slate.

But the sun was blazing again now and Cimarron saw buds about to burst on trees and bushes as he rode into Hunnewell, Kansas, and dismounted in front of the first saloon he came to. He tethered the chestnut to the hitch rail in front of the saloon and went inside. At the bar, he ordered whiskey, and when a bottle and glass were set on the bar in front of him, he partially filled the glass, emptied it, poured more whiskey into it, and promptly drank again. He stood, his left boot hooked on the brass rail, both hands gripping the edge of the bar, staring down at his glass and resisting the impulse to fill it a third time.

His resistance lasted less than a minute. He poured and drank. He felt the whiskey singing in his blood, a warm song. He heard the words of the song reverberating in his mind, and they were wild words, words of hate and fury. His hands tightened their grip on the bar. But it's over, he reminded himself. You did what you had to do and now it's all over and done with. So set it aside and move on. Let it go.

But he couldn't let it go.

That small hole in Lila's back—almost tiny. But it wasn't the hole through which her life had leaked that had killed her. It was what had gone on inside her where she was torn and so badly hurt—that's what had taken her from him.

Archie—

He squeezed his eyes shut, trying to banish the awful image of his dead son from his mind where it blazed so bloodily.

"Have some of these oysters, stranger."

Cimarron opened his eyes to find the bar dog standing

70

in front of him and holding out a bowl. He looked down at the oysters in the bowl. He shook his head.

"They're on the house."

He shook his head again.

"Haven't seen you in here before, have I?" Without waiting for an answer, the bar dog continued, "I'm willing to bet you're one of those that's planning on helping to open up the Territory. You've got that hungering look about you, if you don't mind my saying so. The lust for land gives a man that kind of look. 'Course one or two other things can also stamp that look on a man's face fast. A pretty woman, for one."

It was time to get on with it. The bar dog's words had jolted Cimarron, reminding him of why he was here and of what he had to do. "You happen to know where I can find a man by the name of Bill Lee Lomax?" he asked.

"There you go!" the bar dog exclaimed, shaking a finger at Cimarron. "Didn't I just say you were one of those land seekers? Lomax, though—you'll have to hustle to catch up with him. Him and his flock's headed west. From what I hear they're fixing to cross the border at Kiowa."

"And break the law."

"What's that?" the bar dog asked, but Cimarron didn't repeat his words.

A boy stepped up to the bar. "Where's Mr. Lomax?" he asked the bar dog.

"Like I was just telling this fellow here, he's headed west to the town of Kiowa."

"Dammit to hell! Well, as long as I'm here I guess I'll have some of that whiskey before I move on." He reached for the bottle sitting in front of Cimarron.

Cimarron's hand shot out and gripped the bottle. "You got no manners to speak of, that's plain to see," he said coldly, his eyes riveted on those of the startled boy. "How old are you? Fourteen?"

"I'm sixteen. Sixteen and a half, and mister, if you don't let go of that bottle, I'll bust your skull for you."

"You will, will you? Well, let me warn you. My skull's as hard as stone and you don't look like any stonemason to me. Too skinny. Arms like pipestems."

"Now, no trouble, gents," the bar dog whimpered.

The boy swung his right fist.

Cimarron grabbed it, jerked it, and the boy stumbled toward and then past him. He fell to the sawdust-covered floor. Cimarron put a boot on his chest and pinned him to the floor.

"Let me up! Damn you, let me—"

"Stop that!" cried a woman as she came storming into the saloon and up to Cimarron. "You take your great clumsy foot off him or I'll—" She raised two small fists.

On the floor, the boy's hands seized Cimarron's boot but failed to dislodge it. He squirmed beneath it.

Cimarron pressed down harder, and the boy gasped.

The woman's fists landed on Cimarron's chest with the impact of immature apples torn from a tree by a gust of wind.

He reached out and caught the woman's wrists in one hand and held tightly to them as she too tried to squirm free of him.

He found her attractive enough, with her red hair and eyes which were as green as his own. She had an oval face with high cheekbones. Her lips, parted now as she breathed heavily as a result of her struggle, were full, and her nose, slightly uptilted, gave her a faintly impish look. Her hair was naturally wavy, and now, as she twisted and turned, it flew about her face. She was as tall as Cimarron, with a solid womanly figure beneath the floor-length gray dress she wore, which was buttoned at the throat and reached to her wrists.

She kicked him, and as he momentarily lost his balance, she cried, "Get up, Brendan!"

Brendan rolled out from under Cimarron's boot and came up fast but awkwardly, both fists flying.

Cimarron took a glancing blow on the right shoulder before he was able to reach out with his free hand, grab Brendan's arm, and twist it deftly, turning the boy's back toward him.

"You're hurting him!" the woman cried. "Let him be!"

Cimarron thrust Brendan's arm upward, causing the boy to bend forward. He raised a knee and slammed it against Brendan's buttocks, sending him careening along the length of the bar. Turning to the woman, he said, "You go look to him. Try teaching him not to meddle with a man who's minding his own business." He released his hold on her wrists.

72

She gasped.

Cimarron, alerted by her gasp, turned and ducked, and the spittoon Brendan had thrown went over his head to smash against the far wall.

He ran down the length of the bar and slapped Brendan's raised fists aside. Brendan lunged forward and bit Cimarron's arm. Cimarron swore, picked the boy up, tossed him over his shoulder, and strode out of the saloon. He stood the sputtering boy on his feet and then grabbed him from behind and upended him, dropping him headfirst into the partially filled rain barrel which stood at the corner of the saloon.

"Oh, help us do, holy Mary, Mother of God!" the woman cried as she came running out of the saloon and over to the rain barrel. She overturned it and then helped the dazed Brendan to his feet. "He's just a boy!" she screamed at Cimarron, her eyes blazing. "And you came close to killing him!"

"If I'd wanted to kill him, I would have, no two ways about it," Cimarron told her bluntly, and then, turning to the dripping Brendan, he said, "You want to fight like a dog, which is what you were doing in the saloon, you ought to wait till your teeth grow stronger and your claws a whole lot longer."

Brendan glared at him. "You had no right to put your hand on my mother."

"Oh, it's his mother you are," he said, turning again to the woman who stood with her hands fisted at her sides and her eyes still blazing. "Well, I can tell you what you whelped is a vicious little critter that'll have your hands full turning into a man that measures up to his betters."

"How dare you, sir!" the woman cried. "Brendan didn't—"

"He did. You ask him, Mrs.—"

"O'Malley. Mrs. Theresa O'Malley. Brendan, what happened in the saloon?"

"Nothing."

Mrs. O'Malley seized her son by the hair and shook him. "Tell me now or it'll go poorly with you!"

"I wanted a drink. He had the bottle and wouldn't give it up so I tried to take it away from him."

"A drink, is it?" Mrs. O'Malley declared. "You'll drink the good Lord's water and be content with it. That's all

73

the drink you'll be having while I'm still around to lay down the law!"

Cimarron sensed that the wind had shifted. He glanced at the wet and forlorn-looking Brendan and watched as Mrs. O'Malley gave her son one final shake and then released him. When Mrs. O'Malley turned back to him, she said, " 'Tis an apology he's owing you, Mr.—"

"Name's Cimarron."

"Brendan, you have something that needs to be said to Mr. Cimarron," she prompted.

"I guess I'm sorry," Brendan muttered, his head hanging down and water dripping from his hair.

"You guess!" Mrs. O'Malley snapped.

"I'm sorry," Brendan said hotly, unable to meet Cimarron's gaze.

"So am I," Cimarron said. "I'm a peaceable man most of the time. I try to avoid feuds and fussing as much as I can." He held out his hand to Brendan.

Brendan looked down at it as if he had never seen a hand before, and then he shook it.

Mrs. O'Malley smiled, her lips turning up at the corners and her nose seeming to tilt even more impishly than usual. "Brendan, did you find out where Mr. Lomax is?"

"Heading west," Brendan answered sullenly. "To someplace called Kiowa."

"Oh, dear," Mrs. O'Malley sighed. "He was supposed to be here in Hunnewell, and we've come a long way."

Cimarron thought she looked to be on the verge of tears. "As it happens, Mrs. O'Malley, I happen to be heading for Kiowa myself."

"Oh, you are, are you? Then perhaps we could travel together. I'll confess that I'd be much more comfortable having a man along, although I've done without one so far on our journey."

"Your husband's not with you?"

She shook her head. "Mr. O'Malley died two years ago."

"I'm sorry to hear of your trouble."

"Where's your wagon, Mr. Cimarron?"

"I've no wagon. Just that horse standing over there at the rail."

"Then you're not a homesteader?"

74

"Nope, I'm not. But I take it you're fixing to be, seeing as how you're looking for Bill Lee Lomax."

"Oh, yes, we came all the way from New York City to homestead. I happened to receive one of the letters Mr. Lomax sent out describing how marvelous the Oklahoma lands were and all free for the taking, and, well, I said to myself, Tess, now you put your sorrows behind you and you take Brendan and go west. There's a new life waiting for you there. A place where Brendan can grow up brave and free. I was afraid at first, to be truthful about it. But then my fear began to fade in the face of the hopes I soon found myself cherishing. The next thing I knew we were on our way. And now, here we are!"

Here you are, all right, Cimarron thought, as Mrs. O'Malley twirled in a tight circle, her skirt flying up around her shapely ankles. Here you and your boy are with both of you heading for trouble sure as water's wet.

"Brendan, be about getting the wagon ready to travel," Mrs. O'Malley said, and Brendan started away.

"Mrs. O'Malley—"

She smiled at Cimarron and said, somewhat shyly, "Since we'll be traveling together, let's dispense at once with the formalities. Since I was a wee child, everyone's always called me Tess."

"Tess. Not Theresa?"

She shook her head. "The only one who ever called me Theresa was our parish priest. I think he thought it would help to make a lady of me, but I fear it never did. I was rather unruly as a child, what my mother called the devil's own spawn, though she loved me dearly and on her deathbed told me that though I might be the devil's own spawn, she was glad that some of old Scratch's spunk had rubbed off on me."

Tess smiled, again rather shyly, and added, "You saw the terrible temper I have. But if you'll travel with us, I promise you'll not see it unleashed again. I'll be quite prim and proper."

"You just be the woman you are, Tess. That'll be more than good enough for me. And just call me Cimarron— no Mr."

Tess blushed, surprising Cimarron, because she seemed so open, almost forward. But evidently she harbored a reserve of modesty which was suggested by her blush and

75

occasional shy manner. He found himself, as she talked on while they waited for Brendan to arrive with the wagon, listening carefully to the muted music of her voice, which was lightly touched with the trace of a brogue. Tess O'Malley intrigued him. What, he wondered, had brought a woman and her young son more than halfway across the country? There were homesteads to be had farther east. Why had she not remarried after the death of her husband?

"Ah, here comes the boy now," Tess declared, pointing to Brendan, who was driving the wagon up the dirt street.

"If you'll excuse me for a moment, ma'am," Cimarron said and crossed the street. He went into a general store, and when he emerged he was carrying two flour sacks loaded with provisions.

"You can store those in our wagon, Cimarron," Tess called out to him as he approached.

He did and then helped Tess up onto the seat beside Brendan. He untethered his chestnut and swung into the saddle. When the wagon moved out, he rode beside it.

Tess reached behind her and found a sunbonnet, which she put on and tied beneath her chin. Brendan, beside her, never glanced in Cimarron's direction.

When Hunnewell was far behind them, Tess said something to Brendan, and he halted the wagon. They changed places and Tess picked up the reins and moved the two horses out again.

Cimarron watched her. Within minutes, he was convinced that she would be able to handle her team in fire or in flood. She had a sure hand on the reins and a feeling for the horses. She didn't drive them and she didn't indulge them. She seemed to have a way of making the animals move at what they probably thought was a pace of their own choosing. She's a woman, Cimarron thought, who knows what needs to be done and how to do it.

Without realizing it, he had ridden abreast of the team, and it suddenly occurred to him why he had done so. Looking back from time to time, he was able to see Tess's face. The smiles she gave him were bright and pleasant. He felt as if he had known her for days, not just hours. Her friendliness and her vivacity flowed readily from her and enveloped him. That's her way, he thought. That's how she is. She'd be the same with any man. He dropped back, thereby avoiding the scowls Brendan had taken to giving him, but he did miss Tess's small smiles.

They nooned beside the Chikaskia River, and Cimarron relished the food Tess prepared, remarking on the fluffiness of the biscuits she baked and the tastiness of the stew she cooked. "My mother, God rest her," Tess remarked, "always said that if you breathed a prayer on the dough the biscuits would be light and the right amount of salt in a stew made even runty vegetables taste as good as spring grass to a goat."

"It takes more than the right amount of salt to make a stew as tasty as this one," Cimarron commented as he ate heartily. "I know. I've cooked many a stew in my time, most of which I'll allow were enough to make a man's hair fall out."

Brendan poured himself a cup of coffee and asked, "What business have you got in Kiowa?"

"Like you and your ma," Cimarron answered, "I'm on my way to look up Bill Lee Lomax."

"Are you now, Cimarron?" Tess put down her empty plate. "But you said you weren't a homesteader, so—" She looked down at the ground. "Sorry. I shouldn't pry."

"I'll tell you why I'm going to Kiowa to talk to Mr. Lomax. You'll likely as not find out sooner or later anyways. You may not know it, but what Lomax is fixing to do—cross the border into Indian Territory—is against the law, and I happen to be a lawman. I've been sent out to keep him up here in Kansas."

"I don't understand," Tess said, frowning. "Mr. Lomax's letter said the Outlet lands were public and that everyone had an equal right to settle on them."

"Saying it don't make it so, Tess. There's a lot of folks want the Territory opened to settlement. So they argue that the land's public land. It's not. It belongs to the Indians, and white people aren't allowed in without a permit from the tribe on whose land they plan to live."

"A lawman," Brendan said and glanced meaningfully at his mother. "You sure know how to pick your friends," he added bitterly.

"You got something against lawmen, boy?" Cimarron asked.

"Lawmen aren't good for much except stepping on the

toes of other people. Always telling them what they can and can't do."

"You don't like that?"

"Brendan—"

Cimarron glanced at Tess, and she fell silent. "A land needs law, boy," he said to Brendan. "Without it, there's those who'd savage other people with no one at all to stop them."

"That's just it!" Brendan cried heatedly. "It's only the weak who need the law. The strong—they've got their own laws. They *are* their own law!"

"I've heard similar sentiments expressed before," Cimarron admitted. "Don't know, though, as how I hold with them."

"Cimarron's right, Brendan," Tess said firmly. "A society can't live without laws and men to enforce them."

"Against the weak."

"You got it wrong, boy," Cimarron said mildly. "A lawman—a good lawman—he goes after whoever breaks the law as it's written down. Let me ask you something. You think a man's strong because he takes what rightly belongs to somebody else who's not able to fight for what's his?"

"Sure I do. Don't you?"

"Nope. There's all kinds of ways of being strong and weak. You just haven't lived long enough yet to become acquainted with them all. A boy who gets himself upended in a rain barrel by a man half again his size isn't necessarily what I'd call weak. Foolish, maybe, but not weak. What you call weak, why, I might just call inexperienced."

Tess gave Cimarron a grateful look, and her eyes told him that she had understood what he had been saying to Brendan and that she understood too what he had understood about Brendan.

"It's about time to be on our way," Cimarron said, rising. "Brendan, you know how to sit a horse?

Brendan's face lit up. He hesitated.

"There aren't that many horses in New York City, Cimarron," Tess said.

"I can ride a horse," Brendan insisted. "Sure I can. Why?"

"Well," Cimarron said, "I thought you might want me to take over the driving of your wagon for a spell. To do that, you could sit in the back of the wagon and I could tie my horse to it. Or you could ride my horse."

"Is it a gentle animal?" Tess asked.

"Gentle enough. But should your boy fall off it, well, he'll just pick himself up, dust himself off, and climb right back on. Won't you, boy?"

Brendan nodded eagerly and headed for Cimarron's chestnut, which was grazing near the wagon.

"Hold on there!" Cimarron yelled to him and went over to where Brendan was trying to mount the horse from the right side. "White men climb into the saddle from the left. Only Indians do it from the right. A horse gets to know what to expect, and since I'm a white man— Come on around here to this side, boy. Now put your left foot in the stirrup. Up you go!"

Cimarron spent the next fifteen minutes teaching Brendan how to handle the reins and how to stay steady in the saddle. By the time he was finished, he had decided that given enough time, Brendan just might make a good horseman.

Later, as he drove the wagon, with Tess seated beside him, she said, "Brendan's really a good boy."

He made no comment, wondering why she had felt it necessary to make the statement. Because of the fight in the saloon? The boy's surliness during their nooning?

"He's one of the reasons I wanted to come west," she continued. "New York City—it was no place for him. He'd been getting into trouble there the same as his father did before him, and I didn't want to see what happened to his father happen to Brendan."

Cimarron waited for her to go on.

"John—my husband—was shot and killed in a gang war there. It was over some territory that was being disputed by two gangs of Irish thugs. John ran with one of them. They took protection money from shopkeepers. They thieved. A thoroughly bad business it was. But John justified what he did because of the hard times we were having. It brought money home, he said. He couldn't find a decent job, he said, so what was a man to do under the circumstances?

"Brendan idolized his father, and that was the root of the trouble. He wanted to be just like him, and he was well on his way to being so when my husband was killed. Brendan was heartbroken, as was I. It wasn't long afterward that Brendan took his father's place—as much as a boy his age could do so—with the gang. He was arrested twice and spent time in prison once. Thirty days. He was proud of that fact, can you believe it? Well, then Mr. Lomax's letter arrived and soon afterward I made up my mind to come west.

"Perhaps now you can understand why Brendan takes a rather dim view of lawmen. He considers them his enemy. I pray all that will change."

Cimarron remained silent as he drove on, his eyes on the young would-be outlaw cantering up ahead of the wagon.

They arrived at the camp, which was situated north of the town of Kiowa, the following morning.

Cimarron drove the wagon into it and then halted it, surveying the scene before him. There were more than fifty wagons in the camp, he estimated, many of them with slogans crudely painted on their white canvas: *Oklahoma or Bust* and *Never Turn Back.*

People were everywhere—men and women tending campfires or visiting with one another. Children played noisily, their shrill cries splitting the air. A dog barked in the distance.

"We're here," Tess said and sighed. "We made it. We finally made it! There were times on the trail, I can tell you truthfully, when I thought we never would see this day. Oh, I'm so happy to have arrived at last!"

Cimarron wondered how long her happiness would last. He wondered how long it would take him to ruin her happiness and just exactly how he would go about doing that. Take the first step, he told himself. Find Lomax. "I'll be leaving you now, Tess," he said as he climbed down from the wagon. "I'll get my horse and be on my way. It's been a pleasure."

"Will we see you again, Cimarron?"

"I expect so." He touched the brim of his hat to her and then, after finding Brendan and retrieving his horse, he rode through the camp, noting how many of the men had weapons and guessing that there were other men who kept their rifles and revolvers out of sight.

"Where might I find Mr. Lomax?" he asked a man who was repairing one of the wheels of his wagon.

The man straightened and pointed south. "See that there army tent? That's Lomax's."

"Much obliged." Cimarron turned the chestnut and headed for the tent. When he reached it, he dismounted and called out, "Lomax!"

A moment later, the tent flap flew up and an attractive young woman wearing a severe black skirt and unadorned white blouse appeared. "I'm Mrs. Lomax. May I be of some help to you, sir?"

"It's your husband I came to see, ma'am. Now, if you'll just call him out here—"

"I'm afraid there would be no point in doing that, because my husband is in Kiowa at the hotel meeting with some gentlemen there. But he'll be returning shortly, I expect. May I ask who you are, sir? I don't believe you're a member of our little group. I don't recall having seen you before."

"Folks call me Cimarron, Mrs. Lomax."

"What a strange name. Oh, forgive me, I didn't mean to be rude. You have business with my husband?"

"I do." Cimarron's eyes dropped to Mrs. Lomax's breasts, which filled the blouse covering them. To her hips, which the black skirt covered without hiding their seductive curves and provocative flaring. He looked up. Mrs. Lomax's face was a study in primness. Her lips were almost pursed as she studied him. Her cheeks were flat planes. She had a straight nose, and her equally straight blond hair was pulled back from her forehead and gathered in a tight little bun at the nape of her neck. Her eyes were as brown as acorns. She looked to Cimarron as if she was trying to hide something, but he wasn't sure what that something might be. There was a tightly coiled quality about her. Even her voice was steady and controlled.

"Is there anything I can do for you, since my husband is not available at the moment?" she inquired.

Cimarron's sudden thought must have shown in either his eyes or his face, because Mrs. Lomax blushed. He felt a need to apologize to her, a foolish need to say he was sorry. "I'll come back a little later," he said and gave her a curt nod. As he rode away, he couldn't resist the impulse. He looked back. She was there, staring after him. A lightness he hadn't felt since he had ridden up to Lila's

81

cabin seized him and he began to whistle through his teeth.

He stopped whistling when he heard the angry shouts coming from the far end of the camp. Men were arguing there, but he couldn't make out their words. He spurred the chestnut and rode toward them. Maybe it'll turn out to be interesting, he thought. Maybe I'll learn something from the ruckus up ahead. One thing's sure. All is not peace and harmony in this camp of eager homesteaders.

He found two mounted men—one white-haired with a heavily seamed face in which two deeply set blue eyes blazed and one much younger who had curly blond hair, a raw-boned face, and uneasy gray eyes—who were surrounded by a crowd of men and women on foot.

The elderly man shook a fist at them. "I'll stop you, you interloping bastards! Me and my riders will!"

"Who are you, mister?" Cimarron asked the elderly man.

"Rodney Carlisle, that's who. I thought everybody in this camp knew who I was by now."

"I just came to the camp a little bit ago," Cimarron said. "What's your stake in what's going on here?"

It was the younger man who answered Cimarron's question. "My father owns the RC Ranch down in the Strip. We run over two thousand head of cattle down there."

"And we'll not have any sodbusters taking over our range!" Carlisle thundered, shaking his fist again, this time at Cimarron.

"We got as much right south of the border as you do!" a man shouted from the crowd, and there were mutterings of agreement from the others gathered around him.

"Carlisle's correct," Cimarron told the man, hooking his left leg around his saddle horn. "Which means, as I understand things, he's got no right at all. Unless, of course, Mr. Carlisle's got himself a permit from Cherokee Nation to graze cattle in the Strip. You have a permit, do you, Mr. Carlisle?"

"Don't need any damned permit from any damned Indians!" Carlisle roared. "Next thing you know, some uncivilized sonsabitches'll be claiming I need a permit to take a shit!"

There were shocked murmurs from the women in the crowd.

"Pa," the younger man said, "there's ladies—"

"Shut up, Dean! When I want your advice, I'll ask you for it."

"You might be wanting *my* advice, Mr. Carlisle," Cimarron offered.

"Why would I want the advice of some saddle tramp?"

"You take me for a saddle tramp, do you? Well, now, can't appearances be deceiving? Or is it that your eyes aren't as good as they used to be, Carlisle? I'm no saddle tramp. I'm a lawman and an officer of the federal court in Fort Smith which has jurisdiction over the Territory—the Cherokee Strip included. My advice to you is go get yourself a permit for your RC Ranch or get the hell out of the Strip."

Carlisle tried to speak but could only splutter, his furious eyes on Cimarron, his hand heading for the six-gun holstered on his left hip.

"Don't, Carlisle," Cimarron said coolly. "An old man like you has no business trying to turn himself into a gunfighter. Besides, I'm willing to bet I'm a whole lot faster than you are."

Dean reached out and put a hand on his father's shoulder.

Carlisle's eyes narrowed. "Listen, lawman. You leave me and mine alone, you hear? You don't, you're asking for trouble."

"Then I'm asking, Mr. Carlisle."

A cheer went up from the crowd.

A woman called out to Cimarron, "You tell him, Deputy. Tell him we got our rights to the land too."

"Sorry to contradict you, ma'am," Cimarron said, without taking his eyes off Carlisle. "But I told you all before. None of you have got any rights in the Strip, which is Cherokee land, and I'm here to see to it that you, Carlisle, get out of it and you folks"—he waved a hand, encompassing the crowd—"stay out of it. You all don't, I feel it's fair to tell you, you'll find I can be meaner'n a lost soul with hell let loose for recess."

Cimarron turned his horse, and as he made his way back the way he had come, he caught Tess's eye. He was about to nod to her, but she turned her back on him and walked swiftly away.

6

As Cimarron rode away from the crowd surrounding Rodney and Dean Carlisle, catcalls and derisive hoots followed him.

I've not exactly endeared myself to those folks, he thought. Not the homesteaders standing on their side of the fence nor Mr. Carlisle standing over on his. Well, I've got a job to do, and in my line of work doing it makes me more enemies than it does friends.

But what was bothering him this time was the fact that he was not dealing with hardcases wanted for murder or rape or whiskey-running. The homesteaders were decent people looking for a way to turn their dreams into reality. Cranky old Rodney Carlisle? Well, the man had probably put a good part of his life into building up his RC Ranch and he wasn't about to sit still and have some young lawman come along and go tramping on what he considered his right to live where he wanted and to run his business the way he saw fit.

Cimarron rode out of the camp, heading for Kiowa.

Once he reached it, he went directly to the hotel, which stood, square and squat, in the middle of the town's main street. He went up to the desk and asked the clerk behind it if he knew where Mr. Bill Lee Lomax could be found.

"That's Mr. Lomax right over there, sir," said the clerk, pointing to a man lounging in an upholstered chair and speaking animatedly to two other seated men who were leaning toward him.

"Much obliged." Cimarron stood still for a moment, watching Lomax.

He was a wiry man who looked as if he could move fast if he had to. As he talked, his hands cleaved the air. His black hair was thinning on both of his temples. His eyes were also black, and they darted back and forth between his listeners as he talked.

Cimarron didn't like the looks of the man. There was something feral about Lomax. It showed in his nervous activity and in the way his eyes continually flickered as if he were constantly on the alert for danger. He had an unhealthy look about him. His skin was pale and waxen as if it had never felt the sun.

Cimarron went over to him and, at the first pause in Lomax's torrent of words, said, "I'd like to have a talk with you, Mr. Lomax, if that's convenient."

"I'm engaged," Lomax shot back, barely glancing up at Cimarron. His voice was as edgy, Cimarron thought, as the man himself.

"Then I'll just stand by and wait till you're free," he told Lomax, seating himself in a nearby chair.

"When exactly?" one of the men, who had a smooth round face and round eyes, asked Lomax.

"Soon, very soon."

"It had better be," said the other man, whose brown hair was parted in the middle and whose chin was almost nonexistent.

"Fallon," Lomax said to the nearly chinless man, "and you too, Randolph—now both of you have to be patient as I've been patient with both of you. I was expecting to hear from you while we were still at the rallying point in Hunnewell. An operation like ours doesn't run on goodwill and gratitude, you know." Lomax smiled benignly.

"I want to know exactly when you're planning to move south," Fallon stated flatly.

Lomax hesitated a moment and then, clearing his throat, said, "Tomorrow. We were planning on holding a dance tonight at the camp. It'll be the perfect time to make the announcement that we're moving out. Especially in light of the fact that more than a few families have been growing restless and muttering about moving into the Strip on their own. We did have five other families due to arrive in the next few days, but they'll just have to look out for themselves. You can tell your clients, Fallon, that we'll head down into the Strip first thing tomorrow morning."

"I wouldn't do that were I you, Mr. Lomax," Cimarron

85

said. He crossed his legs and folded his hands over his stomach, meeting Lomax's startled eyes.

"I beg your pardon?" Lomax blurted out.

"See no need for you to do that," Cimarron said.

"Who is he, Lomax?" Fallon inquired.

"I never saw him before,"

"Name's Cimarron." He reached into the pocket of his jeans and pulled out his badge, which he held out to Lomax. "My name's not so important, but that star is, if you take my meaning."

"Then she was right, by God!" Randolph exclaimed. "I took her statements as nothing more than idle threats. But, by God, she did go to the federal court to try to stop us!"

Cimarron's thoughts raced. "You wouldn't be talking about my good friend Miss Victoria Littleton, now, would you, gents?"

"Damn her to hell!" Fallon muttered.

Lomax shifted position in his chair. "Cimarron, the Strip and the Unassigned Lands will one day—and soon, I do believe—be public lands, so—"

"Hold on there, Lomax," Cimarron interrupted. "Maybe you're right in what you say. Personally, I think you are. But that's not the point, is it? The point is, as I see it, that right now those lands belong to Cherokee Nation and anybody trespassing on them's got the court in Fort Smith to answer to. And I am—out here right now—that court. Its legally appointed officer, is what I mean to say."

"I've a mind to go up to Miss Littleton's room and thrash her within an inch of her life!" Randolph cried in exasperation.

"Hold on, Charles," Lomax said, and then, turning back to Cimarron, he said, "I'm sure we can work out some sort of satisfactory arrangement with this lawman, gentlemen. He looks like a reasonable man."

"Oh, I'm reasonable enough unless I happen to get riled by land grabbers or the like."

Lomax smiled and put out a hand to restrain Fallon, who was rising from his chair, his face flushing. "A joke, gentlemen. The lawman, I'm pleased to note, has a sense of humor. I hope he also has a sense of self-preservation."

Lomax paused, his eyes flickering, the oiliness of his voice seeming to thicken the air in the lobby.

"That's a threat, Lomax?" Cimarron asked mildly.

"Not at all, not in the least," Lomax assured him. "I was about to suggest right now that Mr. Randolph and Mr. Fallon, and myself, of course, would be more than happy to see to it that you haven't traveled all the long way out here from Fort Smith in vain. Perhaps you failed in your mission to find me and the families I've gathered together outside of town. But you would perhaps consider your mission a success nevertheless were you to return to Fort Smith with a great deal more money in your jeans than when you set out."

Cimarron leaned back in his chair. "I found you, Lomax."

"Perhaps I didn't make myself clear, Cimarron. I—"

"You made yourself clear, no perhapses about it. But I'm not about to let you cross the border."

"And just how do you propose to stop the good citizens who have gathered here to open up the Outlet to settlement?" Randolph asked snidely.

Smirking, Fallon asked, "Do you have a posse with you?"

"I came out here alone," Cimarron replied. "But make no mistake about it. I'll stop you, Lomax."

"He fancies himself a one-man army!" Fallon declared haughtily.

"Maybe I do at that," Cimarron admitted. "So you gents, you all'd better watch out when you next see me coming, 'cause if you put so much as a toe over the border, well, you can get ready for Armageddon! Now I'll be bowing out of this little discussion. Want to go visit with Miss Littleton for a spell. I much prefer the company of such as her than that of the lawless likes of you, even though you do wear such fine store-bought duds and, in the case of Mr. Fallon there, reek of hair pomade."

Cimarron rose and headed for the desk, where he got the number of Victoria's room from the clerk. As he began to climb the stairs, he was aware of the eyes of the three men boring into him. Good thing that looks can't kill, he thought as he found Victoria's room, or I'd've been dead and maybe buried by now.

He knocked on the door.

When Victoria opened it a moment later, she exclaimed, "You!"

"It's me, all right. Mind if I come in?"

"No, I don't mind one bit. Come in, please do."

He went past her and sat down in a chair beside the bed without being asked as Victoria closed the door and turned to stare at him. Hungrily, he thought. Or am I just hoping, he wondered. Hoping I'll get to have her and that maybe having her'll help me forget. . . .

He fought to banish the images of Lila and Archie that flitted through his mind. He forced himself to keep his attention focused on Victoria Littleton. She's quite a woman, he thought. Woman enough to arouse any man's hopes, not to mention mine. . . . Never mind, he warned himself. Nothing she could do to me or me to her'll make me forget what happened to Lila and Archie. Besides, I'm here on business. "Miss Victoria," he began.

"I'm so glad to see you again, Cimarron," she declared as she came over and sat down on the bed. "I'd been hoping that you would get here. That nothing would happen to change your plans. Or to you."

"I'm fit," he assured her. "I was kind of surprised to find out you were here."

"How did you find out?"

"Some fellow downstairs mentioned your name."

"Fallon? Randolph? Or was it Bill Lee Lomax?"

"One of them mentioned you. I forget which one exactly. Who are Fallon and Randolph?" He tried to catch her eye and failed, and then he realized where she was looking as if mesmerized, and he slowly spread his legs, his hopes rising anew. "Miss Victoria," he prompted when she didn't answer his question.

She looked up at him. "What—oh, yes. You were asking about Fallon and Randolph. Fallon is a lawyer who represents a conglomerate of railroad interests—men who are very eager to see their lines crisscrossing the Territory, because where the railroads go, people follow and settle. That is where Charles Randolph comes into the picture. He's a wholesale merchant from St. Louis, and settlement in the Territory means a vastly enlarged market for his goods."

"That explains why they were hustling Lomax so hard, trying to herd him and his people down across the border." Cimarron watched Victoria's tongue slide between her teeth and moisten her lips as her eyes roamed down his torso and came to a halt below his belt.

"You'll stop them, won't you, Cimarron?" she asked. "I mean we will, won't we?"

"We can give it a good try."

"I believe them to be very dangerous men." Victoria looked up at him and asked. "Doesn't your wife worry about you when you go out on such dangerous missions?"

"Nope."

"Oh, I'm sure she must."

"I haven't got me a wife."

"Oh, what a shame! Then you must be a very lonely man."

"That's a fact," Cimarron said soberly, deciding to play her game in the hopes that they might both win it in the end. "But if I had me a wife—well, a good woman can do wonders for a man, and chasing loneliness till it tucks its tail between its legs and runs for cover is just one of those wonders." Another, he thought, is helping a man forget his hurts, the ones that come from losing. . . . Lila, he thought. Archie, he thought, and his jaws clenched.

"Of course, you're speaking of a western woman. We eastern women—I'm sure we're far too tame, not to mention timid, for a man like yourself who—" She paused and slowly licked her lips again, her eyes on Cimarron's.

"You don't look tame to me, Victoria," he commented, deliberately dropping the "Miss."

"What do I look like to you?" She tried a bantering smile. It didn't work.

"Any man can spot a fire that's burning bright. It takes a certain kind of man to spot one that's smoldering."

"A man like you?"

"A man like me." He decided to chance it. After all, what did he have to lose? "I had you figured the night we first met back in Fort Smith. Figured you might have more than one reason for coming out west."

"I came because of the CCR."

"The CCR?"

"I mentioned our organization to you. The Champions of Cherokee Rights. But you're right. I'll admit it quite freely. I came west to see what it was like out here. The land. The people."

"The men?"

She hesitated and then nodded once.

It was enough. Cimarron got up. He put his hands under her arms and brought her to her feet. He wrapped his arms around her, pressing the tips of his fingers against the base of her spine. He moved his hips slightly and then kissed her.

"Please," she whispered, pulling away from him. "Don't."

Time to test her, he decided. He pulled his pelvis away from her and loosened his grip on her without entirely freeing her.

"Don't," she repeated.

"Wasn't all that sure what you meant at first," he said with a smile and thrust himself against her until her hand began to move downward. When it slid between his legs and then closed on him, he knew she had passed the test. His. And her own.

"That's real nice," he murmured and kissed her again. He cupped her right breast in his hand.

"The men in the New York office of CCR," she said in a tone that was barely audible, "they're all totally dedicated to the cause, of course, but—but they just drive me crazy, every last one of them, with the way they behave toward ladies like myself. Respect. Courtesy. Even chivalry."

"Those things have their place," Cimarron murmured and ran his tongue lightly along her neck.

She shuddered. "You must think I'm awful."

There it was. Why, he wondered, did women have to be convinced that they weren't awful for feeling anything as natural as lust? Well, there were a lot of answers to that one. "You must think the same thing about me. The way I just up and grabbed hold of you like that."

"No, it's—you're— Oh, I feel so strange."

"The way I rammed it up against you like I went and did." He pressed his hardness against her again.

She shook her head, and her fingers tightened on him.

"It was plain awful of me not to hold myself in check. Why, if I don't let go of you, and I mean right now, you'll start yelling, 'Rape!' And then what a fix I'll find msyelf in."

"I wouldn't. I won't!"

A few minutes later, he had her undressed, and after she had quickly helped him undress, he laid her down on the bed and she was staring up at him and her hand was reaching out. . . .

He wasted no time. He was within her and plunging and she was moist and receptive and she lurched beneath him, her head turning rapidly from side to side, sweat on her face and in her hair, matting it.

"I've never been to New York City," he grunted a moment before his orgasm, his hands tightly clasped on her shoulders.

"I've never been—had like this before." She cried out as he flooded her and then she was convulsing beneath him, alternately sobbing and laughing, her arms wrapped around him, her legs encircling him.

He remained within her until she quieted and then slowly withdrew from her.

"Oh, God!" she moaned.

"You've gone and forgotten my name already," he teased, although his tone was hurt and wounded. "Tomorrow—why, even before this day is done, I'll just be a memory in your mind, if that."

"That's not true," she protested as he lay down beside her and ran a finger around and between her breasts. "But it all happened so fast."

"I told you I was awful."

"You weren't. You were wonderful." She propped herself up on her elbows and looked down at him. "Again?"

"Glad to oblige," he said and rolled over on top of her.

This time, when her juices were flowing freely and he was sucking first one breast and then the other, she pushed his hand away and seized him. He let her guide him into her, and when her legs went around him, he began moving, but slowly, leaning on his forearms and watching her face.

As her lips parted in a silent cry, he increased the pace of his thrusting but held himself back until he had brought her to climax. Then, slowing his rhythm, he watched with pleasure as she began again to ascend to the heights with him. Judging by the lunging of her body as it rose to meet him and by the way she began to tremble, he let himself go, and their bodies lay quivering together in rapture.

"That was a toe-twister, now, wasn't it?" he asked her a moment later.

She sighed. "Whatever it was, I loved it," she said, her eyes closed. Suddenly, they snapped open. "I just had a horrible thought."

"No one will ever know but you and me."

"No, no, it's not that. I just thought what if you hadn't come."

"But I did. Twice."

"No, I meant come *here*," she said as he pulled out of her and flopped on his back on the bed.

"The nice things you say, they sure have a way of making a man feel real fine."

"And what do you have to say about me?" she replied.

"You were wild and wanton. Just the way I like my women."

"You've had—many women?"

"I don't keep count."

Victoria sighed and stretched as Cimarron got up from the bed and began to dress.

"Cimarron, what are we going to do about Lomax and his people? I mean, how can we stop them from crossing the border?"

"Well, I've got me one or two ideas on that score. First off, I want you to give me Marcus Doby's address back in Tahlequah so I can send him a wire."

"You won't have to do that. He's here in Kiowa."

"Well, now, it begins to look like luck's on my side. He's here in the hotel?" When Victoria nodded, Cimarron, as he pulled on his boots, said, "Let's go see him."

When Victoria was dressed, they left the room and she led the way to a door at the far end of the hall and knocked on it.

"Yes? Who is it?"

"Marcus, it's Victoria."

"And Cimarron," she added as Doby opened the door.

"You're a welcome sight, Deputy," Doby said heartily and shook Cimarron's hand. "Please come in."

"Mr. Doby—" Cimarron began.

"Marcus."

"Marcus, I want you to send a wire to Washington. I take it you know some powerful people there, seeing as how you're a big man in Cherokee Nation's legislature."

"I do have a few friends in Washington, yes. Congressmen. A Senator or two. I've even met twice with President Hayes on matters of concern to the Cherokees and the other tribes in the Territory."

"Good. What you'd best do is wire President Hayes. What you tell him is this." Cimarron outlined the message he had in mind.

"Do you think he'll help us?"

"He will if you do like I told you to. Make it an urgent matter. Tell him—oh, hell, tell him it's a matter of life and death. Lie if you have to. But get him to do what we want."

"I'll send the message immediately," Doby said.

As he rose to leave the room, Cimarron said, "I'm as hungry as a horse lost in a desert. Victoria, what say we find ourselves something to eat?"

"You'll join us later, Marcus?" Victoria asked politely but without any enthusiasm.

"When I've sent the wire, my dear."

They left the room, and Doby went to send his message while Cimarron and Victoria headed for a restaurant which, she said, was the best in town.

"In fact, the only one," she added and smiled ruefully.

As they walked up the boardwalk, Cimarron caught sight of Dean Carlisle in the distance. He was emerging from a one-story building on the far side of town.

"What's the matter, Cimarron?"

"That fellow up ahead. I not only have to deal with Lomax and his lot but with him and his daddy too." He explained to Victoria who Dean was and told her about his encounter with the father and son back at the camp.

"Then what you're saying is that the Carlisles and the would-be settlers are at each other's throats and we're right in the middle of the fray."

"Couldn't have said it better myself." Cimarron thoughtfully stroked his chin. "Come on. I've got me another idea." He took Victoria by the hand and hurried her up the boardwalk. "Carlisle!" he yelled, and, as Dean came up to him, he said, "This lady's a friend of mine—Miss Victoria Littleton. Victoria, this gentleman is Dean Carlisle."

"I'm pleased to meet you, sir," Victoria said.

Dean, staring at her, said, "An honor, I'm sure, to make your acquaintance."

"Dean," Cimarron said, "let me buy you and Miss Littleton a drink."

"I could use one after just meeting up with Lomax and his cronies up at the—" He caught Victoria's eye.

Is he blushing? Cimarron asked himself, not believing what he saw.

"Mr. Carlisle," Victoria said pleasantly, "you needn't fear embarrassing me. I'm aware of the nature of the establishment you just left." To Cimarron, she explained, "It's the town's bordello. Oh, Mr. Carlisle, there's no need for you to be abashed. I'm a woman of the world. Come along and we'll have that drink Cimarron suggested."

They took a table near the door of the saloon, and Cimarron brought Victoria the beer she had requested and a bottle of whiskey and two glasses for Dean and himself. He sat down and poured from the bottle and then raised his glass. "Here's hoping we can stop those sodbusters from coming down into the Territory like a plague of locusts."

"Cimarron, what—" Victoria cried and he kicked her ankle.

"They'll plow up the land until there's not a free foot of grass for cattle to graze," he continued forcefully, almost angrily.

"You think you can stop them?" Dean asked.

"I intend to. But I could use all the help I can get. Say, Dean, I've got an idea. Maybe you could lend me a hand. I'm willing to bet that you don't want to see a shooting war with your daddy and his boys on one side and all those homesteaders on the other, now, do you?"

"I don't. But Pa, he's bound and determined to protect his range rights."

Dean's last word echoed in Cimarron's mind. He let it go.

"If you and me could put a halt to their migration, Dean," he said, "your daddy'd be mighty proud of you, I'll wager."

"He thinks I'm good for nothing much more than line-riding and calf-counting."

Cimarron had his answer. He pressed his advantage.

"Now, I don't want to see bloodshed neither. What we need is a way to put a stop to what Lomax is planning without anybody getting hurt in the process."

"Do you know of a way?" Dean asked, emptying his glass.

"Here's what I've got in mind," Cimarron answered and proceeded to describe the plan he had begun to formulate only seconds after spotting Dean leaving the whorehouse.

He interrupted what he had been saying when he caught sight of Mrs. Lomax as she entered the saloon and looked around. "Excuse me, Victoria, Dean. Be right back. You two get to know each other, since you're on the same side of this matter we've been discussing." He rose from the table and went over to Mrs. Lomax. "Nice seeing you again, ma'am. I take it you're looking for your husband?"

"Yes, I am. Do you know where he is?"

"I do. He and his businessmen friends are visiting up the street a ways. Come outside. I'll show you." He led her out onto the boardwalk and pointed. "They're up there. See that little place at the end of the street?"

Mrs. Lomax's face reddened. She stamped her foot and then went running up the boardwalk.

Cimarron stood watching her, a grin on his face. "Give Mr. Lomax my regards, ma'am!" he yelled after her.

He returned to the saloon, feeling fine. Any trouble he could cause for Bill Lee Lomax—any kind of trouble at all—was one more drop in the bucket of trouble he had begun to fill up for the man.

Once back at the table, he sat down and glanced from Dean to Victoria. "You two been getting acquainted?"

"We have," Dean said eagerly. "Miss Victoria and I—it seems we share a number of interests."

"Mendelssohn," Victoria said dreamily.

"What's that?" Cimarron asked.

"The theater," she said as dreamily.

"Oh," Cimarron said. "I see." He glanced again at Dean. He looks a little green around the gills, he thought.

"I hope you'll come to the ranch to visit," Dean said.

"I'd like to, Dean," Cimarron said sincerely. "But first, we've got that job we discussed to take care of if you're still game."

"I was talking to Victoria," Dean said without taking his eyes from her face.

"Let's go," Cimarron said, rising.

When Dean didn't move, he reached out, grabbed Dean's shoulder, and shook it. "Let's go," he repeated.

"What?" Dean looked up at Cimarron, who was bending over him. "Oh. Yes. All right." He got up from the table.

Cimarron started for the door of the saloon. When he realized that Dean wasn't with him, he looked back.

"Well, I'll be damned!" he said softly as he watched Dean take Victoria's hand in his own, bow from the waist, and kiss her fingers. *"Dean!"*

Dean scurried away from the table, looking back over his shoulder and, Cimarron thought, grinning as foolishly as a cat caught up in a tree with no way to get down.

That night, while the dance was in progress, Cimarron and Dean stood on the edge of the camp listening to the music and watching the dancers.

On the improvised wooden platform on the opposite side of the camp, torches flared and a fiddle, accompanied by a man playing a Jew's harp, filled the night with music. The caller of the square dance stood rather precariously on an upended cracker barrel, stamping his foot and occasionally clapping his hands as he extemporized rhymes and jingles for the dance that was in full and rousing progress.

> *"Salute partners. Lady on the left.*
> *Eight hands up and circle to the left;*
> *Circle right back and don't you stop,*
> *But break in the center and spin the top."*

"You ready?" Cimarron asked Dean.

"I'm ready."

"You work to the left. I'll work to the right."

"If we don't get every wagon—"

"We'll get as many as we can. If you can't manage a wheel, work on the hounds where they're bolted to the reach. Let's do it!"

Crouching down in the shadows beside the wagon on his right, Cimarron began to turn the bolt that held the wheel to the axle. At first, it wouldn't budge. He persevered and it finally began to turn. When he had given it several turns and tested the wheel, he moved on to the next wagon. The caller's voice was raucous in the night.

"Swing your partner round. Left hand lady round.
Right hand to partner, round and round.
Come to the pretty girl,
Watch her close.
Come to the pretty girl,
Double the dose."

Cimarron removed the cotter pins from the two wheels on the right side of the second wagon and replaced them with brittle twigs. He moved on to the next wagon and then the next, keeping to the shadows and avoiding the flickering light that was being cast by the torches lighting the dance platform.

He had just unscrewed a bolt from one of the hounds on the next wagon when he heard a startled gasp from behind him. He tensed and accidentally banged his head on the wagon bed. He got out from under the wagon and stood up to face the girl—she looked to be no more than sixteen—who stood facing him, her eyes wide with wonder.

To keep that wonder from turning into alarm, he took off his hat and said, "Sorry to disturb you, miss. I was looking for my watch. Dropped it, I did. Now, why isn't a pretty little thing like yourself over there at the dance?"

"Papa says I'm to stay in the wagon because I took a chill this morning. You won't tell, will you?"

"That you sneaked out here to watch the festivities? Not on your life, I won't. Goodnight, miss." He moved around the wagon and away from it, rolling his eyes and vowing to be more careful from now on.

He had worked on nine more wagons and was expecting to see Dean coming around to meet him at any moment when he felt the barrel of a gun bite into the small of his back.

"What do you think you're doing out here, mister?"

Cimarron's hands quickly undid the buttons on his jeans. He turned quickly and said, "You caught me in the act, mister. I didn't even have a chance to put it back in my pants before you threw down on me."

"Do your pissing up against somebody else's wagon. Get out of here!"

"I'm going, mister," Cimarron said, buttoning his jeans. "Mister, I'm *gone!*"

He hurried around the wagon and then around the next one, where he stood rigidly, listening and hearing only the music and the voice of the square-dance caller.

> *Treat 'em all alike;*
> *Second lady out to the right.*
> *Swing Mrs. Jinks,*
> *Then Captain Jinks,*
> *And now the dude of the army."*

Cimarron went to work on the wagon beside him. Moments later, he moved on to the next one. He swore as a sharp-edged bolt cut his finger.

> "Three hands round and the gent cut a caper.
> Chase the possum, now the coon,
> Then the pretty girl round the moon."

"Cimarron, that you?"

"It's not Victoria Littleton," Cimarron snapped and began to suck his bleeding finger.

"Isn't she something wonderful?" Dean whispered in the darkness.

"High-toned ladies like her tend to turn me skittish. You get all your wagons?"

"All but one. Some old geezer was sitting outside it whittling. Can you imagine? Whittling while that dance is going on over there?"

"He must have been a real old geezer. Let's get out of here. I've got to make camp for the night."

"No, you don't. I mean, you could come home to the ranch with me."

"I'm not so sure your daddy would welcome the sight of me."

"We'll tell him about the wagons. I'll tell him that it was your idea."

"No, you'll tell him it was your idea and I just lent you a hand. Well, let's ride. Let's go tell your daddy what we just went and did."

7

The Carlisle ranch stood alone on the plains. As Cimarron and Dean rode up to it, Dean commented, "Carlisle's castle."

"Yours, you mean?" Cimarron asked. He had caught the note of bitterness in Dean's voice.

"Pa's," Dean answered and dismounted.

As they tethered their mounts to the hitch rail, Cimarron studied the building in front of him. It was well built, he noticed, of wood and stone. The wood, he reasoned, must have been hauled down here from Kansas. Maybe some of the stone as well.

The main part of the building connected with two short wings which jutted out at right angles to it to form a square C. The windows were of glass and were bordered by heavy wooden shutters with loopholes cut into them. The front door was made of raw oak and had a hammered brass handle.

Not a castle, Cimarron thought as he followed Dean up to the door. More like second cousin to a fortress. Maybe the old man thinks the Cherokee'll come thundering down to drive him off into the night.

As Dean opened the front door, Cimarron thought at first that it had creaked, but then he realized he was hearing the sound of the windmill that stood at the rear of the house among a scattering of barns, a tack shed, and other outbuildings.

As he followed Dean into the house, Cimarron found himself in what appeared to be the main room of the house. It was ruggedly furnished with heavy tan leather chairs and an enormous pine table flanked by wooden chairs. Books filled the shelves which lined the wall opposite the door. A lamp with a dull-green shade burned on the table. There were no curtains on the windows. An elk's head was mounted above a stone fireplace, and a number of rifles stood upright in a glass-fronted locked case next to it.

Two doors, both closed, could be seen at either end of the room.

One opened and Rodney Carlisle came into the room. He halted when he caught sight of Cimarron and Dean. He thrust his hands into his pockets. To Dean, he said, "You're still a nighthawk, I see. How long has it been, boy, since you swapped your bed for a lantern?"

"Pa, this is—"

"Don't you think I know who that is? Knowing who he is poses no problem to me. What the hell's he doing here?"

"I asked him to come," Dean replied. "He's spending the night."

"Boy, you got no more sense than a calf suckling a sow. Get him out of here. I won't have any enemy of mine spending the night under my roof."

"He's not our enemy, Pa," Dean protested, giving Cimarron a sheepish glance. "You should have seen what we did to those sodbusters tonight."

Carlisle's eyes narrowed. "What did you do? There was gunplay?"

"Mr. Carlisle," Cimarron said, "you sure do jump to some awful bloody conclusions."

"Shut up, you! Dean—"

"Carlisle!" Cimarron barked, and when the old man's eyes were on him, he said, "You can tell your son to shut up. You can tell your hired hands to shut up. You can tell your horse when it nickers to shut up. Me you don't tell to shut up. Now, I hope you got that. Have you?"

Carlisle's eyes burned into Cimarron's.

"Have you?" Cimarron repeated.

"You telling me what I can and can't say in my own home?"

"Nope, I'm not telling you that at all. I'm telling you how you better not try talking to me."

"You're a spunky sort," Carlisle observed grudgingly.

"Pa," Dean said, "Cimarron and me were in the sodbusters' camp tonight and we—"

Cimarron held up a hand, and Dean fell silent. "Save

your story, Dean. He can see the fruits of our labors to-morrow morning, if he's a mind to."

"See what?" Carlisle grumbled, one hand rising to rub his chest. "What are you two talking about?"

"Doing in the sodbusters," Dean said as Cimarron simultaneously said, "Trying to keep trespassers out of the Strip."

Carlisle eyed Cimarron suspiciously. "You've come over to my side?"

"I'm on the law's side. You know that, Carlisle. So if you've any objections to me spending the night here, you speak up and I'll fork my horse and ride right on out of here."

"I'm not the one who invited you here, so I reckon I won't be the one to send you packing." Carlisle gave Dean a fierce glance.

"You mind if I take a look at your books, Mr. Carlisle?"

"You can read?" Carlisle's tone was, if not incredulous, at least skeptical.

Instead of answering, Cimarron went over to the shelves and began to scan the titles of the books which rested on them. He took down a book and began to leaf through it.

"I'll get the whiskey," Dean volunteered. "You want a drink, Pa? Cimarron?"

Neither man answered him, and as he left the room through the door on the right, Carlisle moved closer to Cimarron until he was able to see the title of the book in Cimarron's hand.

"Marcus Aurelius," he commented. "You've read him?"

"Nope. Never even heard of him. But it looks like he's got some pretty slick things to say from what I've seen so far."

"You look and talk like a ranchhand," Carlisle commented. "Or maybe a farmer. Yet you find Marcus Aurelius interesting."

" 'He that walketh with wise men shall be wise: but a companion of fools shall be destroyed.' "

"That's from the Bible?"

"The Book of Proverbs, yes." Cimarron replaced the book.

"Last one of the day!" Dean declared as he returned to the room carrying a tray on which rested a crystal decanter and glasses along with a bottle of whiskey. He put the tray down on a table and poured three drinks. He handed one to his father and one to Cimarron and then raised his own glass. "A toast. Here's to our success in keeping settlers out of the Cherokee Strip!"

"I'll drink to that!" Carlisle declared emphatically and did. "Now I'm going to bed," he announced gruffly. "I've been feeling poorly all day." His hand rose, and again he massaged his chest. "You'd best sleep with your gun handy, boy," he told Dean. "I know I intend to do just that what with the likes of him"—Carlisle jabbed his index finger in Cimarron's direction—"here in the house."

" 'Boy,' " Dean repeated when Carlisle had gone from the room. "He'll be calling me 'boy' when I'm fifty years old."

Cimarron seated himself in one of the large leather armchairs.

"I can't do anything to suit him," Dean complained bitterly. "Nothing I say—he never listens to me. Sometimes he looks right through me like I wasn't even there. I hate that old man!"

"Do you?"

"God knows I try my best to please him, but my best isn't near good enough for him."

"Why don't you try living to suit yourself?"

"I do! I have! But it seems—it's like I'm a boomerang. I go off on my own for a spell and do for myself but before long I get drawn right back here and it all starts all over again. He turns on me and I turn right back on him. We're like two pumas trying to prove which one's the strongest. At each other's throats morning, noon, and night, we are. I tell you, Cimarron, it's tearing me to pieces!"

"Love has a way of doing that to people."

"*Love?*" Dean cried, the word sounding like an epithet. He sat down opposite Cimarron. "He doesn't love me. And I hate him, the old bastard! I could see him lying dead in a ditch and my heart would go forth rejoicing!"

"I don't believe you," Cimarron stated quietly.

"Ever since my mother died, it's been this way. And that means since the day I was born almost. She died not long after. Fever took her. There was no doctor around. He nursed her best as he could, but she died anyway. I guess he was sorry he was left saddled with me. Whatever it was, he paid me no attention for the longest time. Turned me over to housekeepers, cooks, and the like. When I'd try to talk to him or to show him something I'd learned to do, he had no time for me and no interest in me. He acted like I was—"

"The cause of your mother's death."

Dean stared at Cimarron. He started to speak. His lips closed. He ran a hand through his hair. Then, "You think that's it? My God, do you think he's been blaming me for her death?"

Cimarron shrugged. He'd said enough. He'd tossed the fat into the fire, and now he'd wait to see if it sizzled.

"But I didn't kill her!" Dean argued with himself. "It was the fever that did. How could Pa go and blame me for what happened?"

Cimarron said nothing.

Dean was silent for several minutes before remarking, "It doesn't make any kind of sense to me, and yet—and yet if he did blame me, if he thought her dying was my fault, well, that would explain how much he hates me, wouldn't it?"

"It might explain how hard it is for him to let himself love you, maybe. And there's another angle to all this, it seems to me. You lose somebody you love the way your daddy lost his woman, a man might find it hard to let himself love anybody else. *Anybody* else," Cimarron repeated for emphasis. "Another woman. Or his own son. That way a man wouldn't risk losing somebody he loved a second time and getting hurt all over again."

"Christ in the counting house!" Dean exclaimed and dropped his head into his hands. "What you say makes sense to me." He raised his head and stared at Cimarron. "But you could be wrong, you know."

"I could be and that's a fact."

"I'm tired," Dean announced abruptly. "Tired right down to my toes. Let's go to bed. The bedrooms are through that door over there—in the west wing."

The following morning, as Cimarron came into the kitchen in the east wing of the house, he found it empty.

He made himself coffee and fried two eggs he found in the buttery which was just off the kitchen.

When he had finished his breakfast, he went back to the west wing and knocked on the door of Dean's bedroom. He received no answer, so he knocked again.

"Stop that infernal racket!" Carlisle shouted from behind the closed door of the room on the other side of the hall. "Let a man sleep in peace!"

Cimarron turned and opened Carlisle's door. "Sorry to disturb you. I was trying to rouse your son."

"He's not here."

"Where is he?"

"How should I know?" Carlisle, hunched up in bed against his pillow, glared at Cimarron. Then, relenting, he said, "He told me he was riding into Kiowa. Something about some woman."

"Victoria Littleton?"

"That's the one. He wanted her to see whatever it is that's going to happen to Bill Lee Lomax's brood. He said you could meet him later at the campsite."

"He had himself a good idea, Dean did. You want to ride with me and see what'll come of it?"

"I will if you'll get out of here and let a man dress himself in private." Carlisle swung his legs over the edge of the bed and started to stand up.

Cimarron moved quickly as the old man staggered. He reached him before Carlisle could fall and helped him to sit down on the bed. "You sick, Carlisle?"

"It's nothing." Carlisle tried to wave Cimarron away.

Cimarron placed a hand on Carlisle's forehead. "Maybe you'd better stay in bed today," he suggested. "You've got a spring fever."

"I'm no sissy. No spring fever's going to keep me from witnessing what that boy of mine has engineered."

"Carlisle, how old is Dean?"

"Thirty-two. Why?"

"He's no boy."

"He acts like one what with his drinking and his whoring. He has no sense of responsibility, none."

"Maybe you won't let him take on any real responsibilities here at the ranch. Maybe you want to keep him from becoming a man."

104

"You're not making any sense a-tall. Why would I want to do those things you accuse me of?"

"I'm not accusing you of anything. I'm just suggesting an idea or two for you to turn over in your mind, that's all. And while I'm at it, though I'm not a man to meddle in others' affairs, why won't you let him get close to you? That much I've seen for myself. Why in the hell won't you let him love you? He does, you know, but if you're not careful, Carlisle, you'll take that love and twist it around until it turns into hate."

"I don't hate the boy."

"I believe you. Only not hating's not the same as loving somebody." Cimarron turned on his heels and left the bedroom.

When he heard Carlisle call his name from outside sometime later, he opened a window and yelled, "Come on into the kitchen, Carlisle."

When the old man appeared, Cimarron said, "Sit down."

"What's all this?"

"Where I come from it's called breakfast. Sit down and eat, Carlisle."

"I'm not hungry."

Cimarron pulled a chair out from the table.

Carlisle hesitated and then sat down. "You have a helluva nerve taking over a man's house like you owned it and minding his personal business for him too," he grumbled as he began to fork fried eggs into his mouth.

Later, as they rode north toward the border, Cimarron slowed his chestnut to match the gait of Carlisle's horse.

Carlisle coughed, a wet racking sound.

"You sound sicker'n I took you to be," Cimarron told him.

"It was those damn eggs of yours. Fried stiff as boot leather they were. A piece must have got caught in my windpipe."

They rode on, both men silent, until the camp came into sight.

"Over there," Cimarron said, pointing to the right. "We can take up a position on that little hilly spot. From there we'll have ourselves almost a bird's-eye view of what's in store for those settlers."

Carlisle followed Cimarron to the hill, which was little

more than a hummock, and the two men sat their horses and watched the activities taking place in the camp.

Wagons were being loaded and fires put out. Women scurried about in search of children, who, when found, were boosted into the wagons. Men were putting their teams into their traces.

Leather creaked. Harness jingled.

"They look like they're planning to move out," Carlisle said. "You brought me here to see them move down into the Strip?"

"I did."

"Damn you, Cimarron, I—"

"Hold on, Carlisle. Don't damn me till you see what's about to transpire."

"What *is* about to transpire?"

Cimarron didn't bother to answer the question. He stood up in his stirrups and waved his hat above his head to signal Dean and the two riders with him who were approaching the camp from the east.

Dean caught the signal and veered south, the two riders, whom Cimarron recognized as Victoria and Doby, following him.

"Morning, Pa," Dean said as he came abreast of Cimarron. "This is a friend of mine, Miss Littleton. And her friend, Mr. Doby."

Carlisle merely harumphed.

Dean turned to Cimarron and said, "Victoria wanted Mr. Doby to come along too. She thought he ought to see what I told her would happen here this morning."

"Marcus, did you send that wire?" Cimarron inquired.

"Yes, I did."

"Any answer?"

"Not so far."

"Well, if President Hayes won't order troops into the field to hold back these people," Cimarron mused, "we're going to have our hands full, that's for certain."

"Look!" Victoria cried. "There's Lomax."

"Fallon and Randolph too," Doby said.

Cimarron watched Lomax climb up on a flatbed wagon and begin talking to the people in the camp. He concluded his speech quickly, his words inaudible to Cimarron, and dramatically pointed south.

Shouts of joy from the settlers reached Cimarron's ears.

106

He sat his saddle and watched the first of the wagons start south.

Carlisle muttered something and then coughed, bending forward in the saddle.

Time passed. The wagons rolled on, side by side, some trailing, one racing ahead of all the others.

"There goes the first one!" Dean shouted gleefully. "Look at that, Pa!"

Cimarron watched the rear right wheel of the wagon go wobbling to the ground.

The wagon listed, its axle dragging. The team continued trying in vain to pull it until its driver halted his horses.

Another wheel came off another wagon. The wagon tilted and then, as the second wheel on the same side slid off its axle, it fell on its side, knocking one of the wheels off the wagon traveling next to it and bringing that wagon to a halt.

People were thrown to the ground. Supplies and household goods which had fallen from the crippled wagons lay strewn across the plain.

Men cursed and women cried. Both ran about aimlessly, colliding with their neighbors as they sought to retrieve their lost wheels. A sunbonneted little girl picked up a broken doll from the ground, stared at it a moment, and then let out an anguished wail.

Lomax rode into the confusion and began shouting orders, but no one paid any attention to him. Fallon and Randolph rode up to him, and there was a hurried conference among the three men.

"You and the boy did that?" Carlisle asked Cimarron, indicating the disabled wagons.

"Dean and me did, yes."

Carlisle apparently caught the significance of Cimarron's use of Dean's name. "Good for you—son," he said to Dean.

Dean smiled at his father and then glanced at Cimarron, whose face remained impassive.

"They've been stopped!" Victoria cried. "Oh, Marcus, we stopped them!"

"We didn't do it," Doby corrected her. "Cimarron and Dean did."

"Well, you know what I mean," Victoria responded,

obviously flustered. "It's just that I think of us as—as a sort of team."

"The game's not over yet," Cimarron reminded her. "In fact, it's just started. We haven't won it. Not yet we haven't."

"Oh, but we will win it!" Victoria cried confidently.

"Maybe," Cimarron said. "Maybe not."

A young girl ran up to Lomax and shouted something. Then she turned and pointed at Cimarron.

Lomax turned and looked back at Cimarron. He heeled his horse and, followed by Fallon and Randolph, rode up to Cimarron.

"You did this!" Lomax accused him.

"Don't deny it!" Fallon bellowed. "That girl said she saw you in our camp late last night during the square dance."

"I'm not denying anything, Fallon," Cimarron said. "Nor am I admitting anything either."

Randolph hallooed the girl, and she came running up to them. "Missy, is this the man you saw?" Randolph asked her.

"It's him all right. I saw him. I spoke to him. He said he'd lost his watch and he was hunting for it under our wagon."

"But you weren't looking for any watch, were you, lawman?" Randolph inquired, his tone tense. "You were monkeying with the wheels of our wagons."

"Maybe this girl," Cimarron said, "had a nightmare and I was part of it."

"You know that's not true!" the girl cried. "I saw you just as plain as day I did!"

"I saw him too!" shouted a man who had come up to the group along with some of the other settlers. "He said he was pi—he said he was emptying his bladder." The man glanced covertly at Victoria, his face reddening. "But he wasn't pi—emptying his bladder. We all know now what he was doing! He pulled cotter pins and unscrewed bolts so the wheels would fall off our wagons."

An elderly bald man with the long white beard of a patriarch stepped out of the gathering crowd and pointed an accusing finger at Dean. "I spotted that skinny blond jasper last night. I was sitting outside my wagon whittling. Just whittling and whistling in the way I have, and I saw

108

him skulking about. I didn't think nothing of it at the time. Had my whittling on my mind. I was working a tricky little piece of pine, you see, and I—"

"You stand accused by these three people," Lomax said, and the man he had interrupted murmured, "I've been whittling on and off since I was knee-high to a short horse."

"You're good at it by now, I'll bet," Cimarron said to the old man, ignoring Lomax.

"I'm the very best!" the whittler declared, his eyes bright and his beard wagging. "Here, let me show you this—"

Carlisle's laughter boomed out of his throat. He slapped his thigh. And coughed.

Cimarron caught movement out of the corner of his eye. He turned his head and saw Tess O'Malley shouldering her way through the angry crowd, Brendan not far behind her.

"Did these people do this to us?" she cried, her angry eyes on Cimarron.

"Those two did," Lomax answered, pointing first to Cimarron and then to Dean. "They sneaked into camp last night and damaged our wagons."

"May you rot in hell, both of you!" Tess screamed, and tears began to run down her cheeks. "My dishes—they belonged to my mother, and nearly every one—*broken!*"

A man in the crowd came up to Tess and put an arm around her, and as he did, she buried her face against his chest.

"You can always get yourself some new dishes," Cimarron said, his eyes on her and the man who was trying to comfort her.

Tess spun around and shouted, "The ones I had—they were an heirloom!" Furiously, she wiped the tears from her face. "You had no right to do this to us. People have been hurt. Someone might have been killed!"

As the man who had joined Tess put his arm around her, Cimarron said, "Point is you folks have no right down here south of the border. Now, I suggest you get your wheels back on your wagons and turn them around and go on back to Kansas where you belong."

"We won't!" Tess screamed, shaking both of her fists at Cimarron.

"Oh, yes, you will!" Victoria said sharply.

Tess hesitated only a moment, and then she ran forward and seized Victoria, pulling the surprised woman from her horse.

Both women hit the ground. They rolled over and over, dust and thatch flying up around them. Tess pulled Victoria's hair, and the pins flew from it. Victoria retaliated by slapping Tess's face. Tess let out a cry of fury and began pummeling Victoria, who then pummeled Tess just as energetically. Both women's skirts billowed, revealing petticoats and, in Victoria's case, frilly lace.

"Give it to the hussy, Mrs. O'Malley!" a woman shouted from the crowd.

"Let's *all* give it to her!" another woman shouted, and she ran forward to join the fray, followed by the woman who had just urged Tess on.

Cimarron leaped from the saddle and shoved both women out of his way, toppling one and causing the other to try unsuccessfully to slap his face. He seized Victoria and Tess by the hair and hauled both of them to their feet.

"I do declare," he told them, "you two shame the gracious image I've always had of womanhood." He gave them both a shake and then thrust them in opposite directions before turning to Lomax. "Get your people out of here," he ordered. "Before the shooting starts."

"Let it start!" roared a male voice from the midst of the crowd of people.

Cimarron's .44 cleared leather instantly and, as if his action had been a signal, Dean's and Carlisle's revolvers appeared in their hands.

Lomax backed up and bumped into Fallon, who swore.

A shot went winging past Cimarron's head. He fired at his assailant, deliberately aiming high, and the man dropped his gun and threw up his hands. Cimarron scanned the faces of the people in the crowd. "Anybody else want to throw down on me?"

"These are peaceful people!" Randolph roared. "Let them be!"

"I'm willing to do just that very thing," Cimarron replied, his eyes roving among the crowd. "I didn't fire first," he added significantly.

The women were the first to start back toward the wag-

110

ons, some of them herding children before them. Then, the men, grumbling and casting backward glances, followed their women.

Brendan remained where he was. He did not move when his mother, walking among the women, called his name.

"Lomax," Cimarron said, indicating Brendan with a curt nod, "you take that lost pup of yours and put him to work fixing wagon wheels."

"I'm not fixing any wagon wheels," Brendan said sharply. "It's you I'm going to fix."

"You might be biting off more than you can chew, boy," Cimarron warned him.

"Come on, son," Fallon said to Brendan and put an arm around his shoulder. "I'd like to have a talk with you and some of the other men in camp."

Brendan, obviously pleased at being referred to as a man, let Fallon lead him back toward the broken wagons that were littering the plain.

"You won the first round, lawman," Lomax snarled at Cimarron. "But this fight's only just begun."

"Reckon you're right about that," Cimarron admitted, holstering his revolver and indicating that Dean and his father should do the same. "Be seeing you, Lomax. You too, Randolph."

Both men turned and hurried after Fallon and Brendan, who, as they walked back to the wagons, were busily engaged in earnest conversation.

As Cimarron watched, Fallon summoned several men to his side and then several more as he walked on in the midst of them.

"They're plotting something, you can bet on it, Cimarron," Dean declared.

Cimarron nodded, and then his head snapped to one side as Victoria came out of nowhere and slapped his face. "Hey!" he yelled and made a grab for her.

She eluded his grasp and said, "Just who do you think I am? The way you manhandled me, you'd think I was a common trollop!"

Cimarron reached out, and this time he caught her. He pulled her close to him and, speaking in a low tone so only she could hear him, said, "I had the impression you kind of liked being manhandled by me."

"That was different!" she muttered, matching Cimarron's low tone. "You just made a public spectacle of me in front of all those people!"

Cimarron pushed her away from him. He ducked as she swung on him again. As he came up, he said, "You were doing all right on your own on that score. But I didn't want all those other biddies joining in your fracas, so I had to do something or things would've gotten way out of hand."

"I didn't start it!" Victoria cried. "It was, that O'Malley woman. She *attacked* me!"

Cimarron was about to say something when Carlisle began coughing again, one hand pressed against his chest while sweat beaded on his face and forehead.

"What is it, Pa?" Dean asked. "You sick, Pa?"

Carlisle tried to speak but couldn't. He tried to spit but was unable to do so.

Dean slapped him on the back, which served only to intensify his father's coughing.

"Take him home, Dean," Cimarron ordered. "Get him into bed under lots of covers. He's real feverish. Try to sweat it out of him, whatever it is that's ailing him. Give him hot drinks."

"Let me help you take care of him," Victoria said to Dean. "I'll be glad to do whatever I can."

"Pa and me would both appreciate anything you could do to help, Victoria," Dean said, obviously pleased by her offer.

Victoria gave Cimarron a wicked glance as she got back into her saddle. "The two of us will take care of him, Dean," she said.

Cimarron read the message she was sending him in her eyes. It was both simple and straightforward. *And I'll take care of you, Dean.* He shrugged and watched Carlisle ride off, flanked by Dean on one side and Victoria on the other.

"Do you think President Hayes will send troops out here to the border, Cimarron?" Doby asked, concern evident in his voice and a worried expression on his dark face.

"It would be a blessing if he did," Cimarron replied. "Dean and me, we can't keep harassing those people for-

112

ever. If we do there's bound to be bloodshed sooner or later."

"But if troops come won't there be bloodshed?"

"I'm counting on Lomax backing down once the troops get here—if they do. His people aren't really outlaws. They're ordinary folks, and I'm hoping the troops, if they get here, will make them see the error of their ways so that they'll all go on back to wherever it is they came from."

"I feel so helpless," Doby lamented. "There doesn't seem to be anything I can do to alter this rather alarming and potentially dangerous situation."

"Sure there's something you can do, Marcus. You can ride back to Kiowa and send President Hayes another wire. Tell him what happened here this morning, only make it sound a whole lot worse than it really was. Send a wire to Judge Parker in Fort Smith while you're at it. Tell him to wire Hayes too. Tell him it's his judicial duty and if he doesn't do it he's liable to wind up minus one deputy marshal, namely me."

"I'll do it!" Doby said enthusiastically.

"There's something else you might do to help iron things out around here, Marcus, if you've a mind to."

Cimarron told him. He concluded by remarking, "It's asking a lot of you, I know. But maybe you'll give the matter some thought."

Doby was silent, his expression thoughtful for a time, and then he said, "I'm not sure whether I can arrange it. But I'll try. If I can arrange it, everyone will benefit."

"That's the same way I see it, Marcus."

"What's your next move, Cimarron?"

"I'm thinking it might be a good idea for me to have another little talk with Lomax. By this time, after what's happened here this morning, he might be willing to listen to reason."

"Lomax strikes me as a hothead, Cimarron. You'd better be careful in your dealings with him."

Cimarron grinned. "I appreciate your concern, Marcus. I'll be as careful as a barefoot boy walking in a pasture full of cow flops."

8

Cimarron got out of the saddle in front of the army tent and yelled, "Lomax!"

A moment later, Mrs. Lomax threw back the tent flap and came outside. "It's you again."

"Your husband here, Mrs. Lomax?"

"No, he's not. You do have bad luck trying to locate him, don't you?"

"Sure looks that way, now don't it?"

"Is there anything I can do for you?"

"A pretty woman such as yourself—yes, there's one or two things you could do for me. But I'd best not mention them. Wouldn't want to spook you."

"I'm not easily spooked, as you put it, and I do know exactly what you mean. You are not a subtle man, Mr.—I don't believe I caught your name."

"Didn't throw it your way when I was here yesterday. It's Cimarron." He couldn't resist the impulse that suddenly seized him. "Your husband—you think he might be back in town at that place I pointed out to you when last we met, Mrs. Lomax?"

"It's likely," she admitted matter-of-factly. "May I ask you a personal question, Cimarron?"

He waited for it.

"That scar on your face."

His fingers rose to touch it.

"What happened to you?"

"I was raked by a branding iron my pa was using when I was but a boy. He got mad when I let a calf get away from me and he started yelling and waving his branding iron about and this messed-up face of mine is the result of his letting himself get all upset."

"It must have been a very painful experience."

"It smarted some for a spell, yes. But I got over it.

114

You're not the first woman who's asked me about it. It does seem to have some fascination for women. They lose that fascination fast though once they find out my scar didn't come from a knife or bullet or anything like that but from a plain old branding iron in the hands of the hot-tempered man that was my pa."

"It gives you rather a sinister look, I think. Perhaps you shouldn't tell people like me the truth when they ask about it. Perhaps you should tell them that you were scarred during a fight with—oh, with an Indian. An Apache! Or that you were knifed by an outlaw who had you at his mercy all tied up and helpless and in his cruel hands."

"Do you think that would make me a more interesting sort of fellow to the ladies?"

"I do. Not that you are uninteresting as a result of your having told me the truth about your scar."

Well, now, Cimarron thought. So I'm not uninteresting to the lady. And Lomax isn't around. He gave Mrs. Lomax a smile.

She gave him one of her own. "Would you like to come inside the tent and wait? My husband might return soon, although I don't know that for a fact."

"After you, Mrs. Lomax."

"Orajean," she said before ducking down and entering the tent.

"Orajean," he repeated as he followed her into the tent. "First time I ever met a woman by that name."

"It's the first time I've met a man named Cimarron. It's a name as interesting as your scar, and I'm sure it too has a story behind it. Does it?"

"It does. But it's not one I'm keen on telling, nor is it one you'd want to hear."

"My!" Orajean exclaimed. "You are a man of mystery. I know nothing about you except your name and the story of how your face was scarred. I'd like to know more." She seated herself on a wooden chair. "Sit down, Cimarron."

He seated himself on one of the two canvas-slung pole beds in the tent. "Mrs. Lomax—"

"Orajean."

"Orajean, how'd Bill Lee become interested in herding a bunch of settlers down into the Territory?"

Instead of answering his question, Orajean asked one

of her own. "Why are you interested in my husband's activities?"

"I'm a deputy marshal. It's my job to stop Bill Lee from breaking the law by trespassing on Indian lands. In this case, on land belonging to Cherokee Nation."

"You're not going to arrest him, are you?"

"I am if he persists in what he's planning."

"He'll go to jail?"

Now how the hell, Cimarron asked himself, did I wind up answering instead of asking the questions? "He'll go to jail maybe. Or get a fine. Or maybe both."

"It would serve him right if he had to spend some time behind bars!" Orajean declared hotly, surprising Cimarron.

"You want him to land in jail? How come?"

"I want him to suffer as I have suffered because of him!" she replied vengefully. She hesitated a moment and looked down at the ground. Then, after sighing, she said, "You might as well know. Almost everybody else already does. In fact, you do know, come to think of it."

"I know what?"

"You told me Bill Lee was in the bordello in Kiowa, so you know that he is neither chaste nor faithful to me. But what you don't know," she continued, her voice rising and her cheeks flushing, "is that he is diseased as a result of his lustful behavior.

"I suppose part of the problem is my fault. That is to say, I would have nothing to do with Bill Lee for some time because of— My husband is not a very considerate man. He is—was—in bed—often brutal to me. It seemed that only by behaving so brutally could he achieve—satisfaction.

"Now that he is diseased," she went on, looking up at Cimarron, "I will never have anything to do with him, and he knows that because I've told him so many times. I have been living a celibate life since he—since he was stricken. But, as God is my witness, he deserved what he got. I suppose it was as inevitable as each day's sunset that he would become promiscuous since I refused to share his bed.

"Perhaps I should actually be relieved because of the way things have turned out. It certainly was not very pleasant being with him—as a dutiful wife. In fact, it was horrible. He *hurt* me! But I've already alluded to that fact and shall say not another word about it. I suppose you think I was wrong to refuse to honor my obligations as a wife. I suppose you think I should have suffered in silence and simply let him have his way with me."

"Orajean, why don't you stop all your supposing about what I think? As far as my thoughts go on the matter you've been talking about, well, the way I see it a woman's got just as much right as any man to look out for her own well-being in the best way she can. The thing is, though, she ought to just go ahead and do it without looking around for anybody else to tell her she's doing the right thing."

"You're a very quick-witted man, Cimarron. It's true. I feel guilty about what I did to Bill Lee. I feel that I'm the one who drove him into the—arms—of those awful women in those houses."

"Not all of those women are awful, as you call them. I've known a few in my time that I thought real highly of."

As if she had heard nothing of what Cimarron had said, Orajean continued, "What is most difficult about the situation between Bill Lee and myself is the fact that I feel so guilty about my own terrible desires. About the mere fact of having them boiling up inside me and threatening at any moment to spill over."

Time to go, Cimarron told himself. Get while the getting's good. He stood up.

"You're leaving?" Orajean got to her feet and smoothed her skirt. "I thought you wanted to talk to Bill Lee."

"I do and I will. But some other time." Cimarron took a step toward the tent's entrance.

Orajean, her skirt rustling, suddenly appeared between him and the tent flap. "It's been a time of torment for me, Cimarron," she whispered. "Can you understand that?"

"Reckon I can. A healthy woman like yourself needs looking after." But not by me, he thought. I want no part of being caught between a sex-starved woman and the man she's married to. Maybe Bill Lee Lomax will turn out to be a sharpshooter, and then where'd I be?

"You don't find me attractive." Orajean's statement was a taunt.

"It's not that."

"Then what is it?"

Cimarron caught the edge of anger in her tone.

Before he could say anything more, she said, "Are you afraid of me? Or of Bill Lee and what he might do to you if he found us together?"

"I'm not the least bit afraid of you, honey, but—"

"Oh, say it again, Cimarron. *Please!*"

"Say what again?"

"You called me 'honey.' It's been so long since a man—a real man like I know you to be—spoke so sweetly to me." She threw herself upon him, her arms encircling him, and kissed him fiercely. "Oh, Cimarron, it's been so long. I've yearned for—I've dreamed about—no, that's not true. I must tell the total truth to *someone* or else I'll simply *explode! I've lusted!* At night sometimes, when I'm alone in bed and Bill Lee is out after a woman, I touch myself, and since we met yesterday—last night when I was alone again, I thought about you—your face, your body, your—"

Cimarron gently disengaged himself from her. "I'm real sorry, Orajean. But I reckon another man's wife is best off being none of my business, and though you're a tempting plum it'd be a pleasure to pluck—"

Orajean drew back from Cimarron and delivered a stinging slap to his face.

"Orajean!" Lomax cried as he came into the tent. "What did you—did he—"

Standing with her back to her husband, Orajean swiftly pulled down her bodice and let out a wail. "Bill Lee! Look what he just did to me!" She spun around to reveal the breasts she had just bared to her husband.

"Goddam you, Cimarron!" Lomax roared. "First you foul our wagons and now you try to foul another man's wife!"

"Hold on, Lomax!" Cimarron said quickly. "I didn't—"

"You did! You think I'm blind? I'm not blind, and by God in His heaven I intend to make you pay for shaming poor Orajean!"

Orajean began to weep noisily, but Cimarron could see no tears on her cheeks, could hear only her sobs, could not miss the triumphant glance she shot in his direction as Lomax lunged at him.

118

He stood his ground and shoved Lomax's clenched fist aside and then he seized the man, turned him, and sent him hurtling toward the tent flap. "Get out of here, Lomax! When you cool down some, you come on back and I'll tell you what really happened here!"

"Bill Lee!" Orajean cried. "Don't let him get away with the awful things he did to me!"

Lomax, as if his wife's words had been a thrown lasso that had roped him, spun around and once again came lunging toward Cimarron, who suppressed a sigh, clenched his right fist, and landed it on Lomax's jaw, snapping the man's head to the side.

Cimarron's left arm shot out and his fist sank into Lomax's gut, causing Lomax to grunt loudly.

Lomax seized a chair and threw it.

Cimarron ducked and the chair sailed over his head and into the tent wall, bulging it and pulling free one of the tent's stakes. The canvas wall leaned and then partially buried Orajean, who cried out and began to flail her arms wildly to free herself. She fell forward.

Lomax shoved her away from him and went for Cimarron again, his fists raised, his stance stiff. He danced around Cimarron, his eyes slitted and his fists fighting the air in front of him.

Cimarron slowly circled, keeping Lomax in sight and waiting for the man's next move.

When it came, he was ready for it. As Lomax flung a fist at him, Cimarron ducked down under it and came up fast. He landed a smashing blow to Lomax's gut, just below the man's rib cage, and followed it up with a rapid left uppercut, then another body blow.

Lomax staggered about the tent and collided with Orajean, who turned him around and sent him stumbling toward Cimarron, who caught him, turned him, and seized him by the scruff of the neck. He walked him toward the tent flap, but before he could throw him through it, Lomax rammed an elbow into Cimarron's ribs and then kicked backward, catching Cimarron in the shin just above his boot top.

Angry now, Cimarron released his hold on Lomax and, when the man turned toward him again, slammed his right fist into the man's face.

"My nose!" Lomax cried as blood poured from it. "You've broken it!"

Cimarron pulled back the tent flap and then seized Lomax again and hurled him through it. He went outside and, before Lomax could recover himself, threw a hard and high overhand left which caught Lomax on the side of the head, and then he systematically clubbed him with both fists in the ribs and kidneys.

It was his overhand left that did the most damage. Lomax went down and lay motionless not far from Cimarron's boots.

Cimarron, his knuckles aching, turned and went back inside the tent.

"Get out of here!" Orajean screamed at him.

"You satisfied now, are you? Now that you've used me to set your husband to hurting? Your cheap little trick set us up so that you'd win no matter what happened or which of us got the worst of it in that fight. Do you try to do in every man who turns you down that way?"

"Get out of here or I'll—"

Cimarron waited for her to finish her threat. When she didn't, he said, "I'm not getting, so you do whatever it is you feel you ought to. I came here to ask some questions of your man. I can't ask them of him now. But I can ask them of you and I figure you'll answer them. Because if you don't, I'll do for you the way I just did for him."

"You wouldn't dare strike me!"

"Oh, I'd dare, all right. You want to test me, you just refuse to answer when I ask you what I want to know. Now then. What part are Fallon and Randolph playing in your husband's settlement scheme?"

"None of your damned business!"

Cimarron reached out and grabbed Orajean. He sat down on the cot and threw her over his knee. He pulled up her skirt and spanked her, unmindful of either her struggles or her cries.

"I'll stop now so you can answer me," he told her and did, but he didn't let her get up.

She was silent.

His right palm slapped her buttocks twice.

"They're paying him!" Orajean screeched. "Let me up!"

120

"How much are Fallon and Randolph paying your husband?"

"A flat rate of fifty dollars a head for every damn fool he can entice into crossing the border and settling in the Territory."

"Lomax is just doing all this for the money?"

"What else? He doesn't give a baked bean about those fool settlers. Let me *up*!"

"What's his next move—your husband's?"

"I don't know."

Slap, slap!

"He's—they're going to get you! I heard them talking and they believe they'll have free sailing once you're out of their way."

"So you knew more about me than you let on before with all that talk about my scar and my name."

"Is this the abnormal way you take your pleasure with a woman?" Orajean cried.

"Honey, you'll just never know how I go about getting my pleasure with a woman, because were I to show you I might wind up with a knife in my back—one you'd hide under your pillow."

He pulled her up by the hair and then got up himself. "You tell your husband when he comes to that if he tries to take me, him and his friends, it's him and them that might get took." He ducked down and went outside.

He had expected to see Lomax still lying on the ground, but the man was gone. He shrugged and went to his horse.

Before he could step into the saddle, he felt hands on his shoulders. He shook them off and turned quickly.

A fist flew into his face.

Another glanced off his shoulder.

Then, before he could make a move, they were on him. He wasn't sure how many men there were in the mob that had come down on him so quickly, but he knew there were many, perhaps as many as a dozen. His knees buckled and he went down as countless fists and a club in an anonymous hand began beating him senseless.

Just before he lost consciousness, he caught a glimpse, through the forest of booted legs that surrounded him, of Orajean. She was standing in front of the tent clapping her hands and shouting, "Kill him! *Kill him!*"

Sound. The jingling of harness. A horse blowing.

Smell. That of a horse's sweat and the unwashed clothes of a man.

Cimarron heard and smelled them and then—pain. Not much but enough. His hip hurt. Evaluating what he had heard and what he had smelled and linking all of it to the pain in his hip, he knew where he was and what was happening as consciousness slowly returned to him.

Somebody's got me tossed face down over his horse like a sack of grain, he thought, and his saddle horn's worrying the hell out of my hip. My gun—cartridge belt—they're gone. So's my horse. My hat too.

He swore silently and looked down at his hanging hands as the horse walked on, flanked by the horses of other men.

He raised his head slightly and then quickly let it drop again as the barrel of a six-gun touched the nape of his neck and a voice from above him said, "Don't you move, mister, or I'll shoot you dead."

"How much farther we taking the lawman, Lomax?" someone riding to the rear of Cimarron called out.

Cimarron saw a bay moving close to the horse over which he had been thrown. He saw a boot kick free of a stirrup and then that boot's toe was under his chin and it was raising his head.

"He's awake, Mr. Lomax!"

Cimarron twisted his head away from the boot and looked up at the rider who had just shouted his message to Lomax.

Brendan O'Malley.

Brendan stared down solemnly at Cimarron.

Cimarron, the gun barrel pressing against his neck, resisted the impulse to reach out, yank Brendan's boot, and unseat the boy.

Brendan swung his foot and the side of his book struck Cimarron's cheek.

Then, as Brendan's bay moved out of sight, Cimarron speculated about where his captors were taking him and why. Where probably doesn't much matter, he thought. Why, though, now that definitely does.

They may be fixing to kill me, but I'm sure enough not yet ready to die. Got me lots of living, not to mention loving, to do before the day comes when I lay down and death creeps up to catch me napping.

He tried shifting position to ease the pain in his hip, but the unknown man who had the gun in his hand tapped Cimarron's skull with the barrel and said, "Told you, mister. You stay still now or this six-shooter's liable to go off and take a hefty part of you with it."

Cimarron let his body go limp. He ignored the pain in his hip and the harsher pain scampering around in his skull where the mob had landed many of their blows during the attack at the camp.

The rider looming up there above me, he thought. Would he really shoot me if I tried something? Not if I were real sneaky in the trying and he never noticed I was trying, he wouldn't.

He waited impatiently, hope dwindling. But then, as the party of mounted men moved out over a stretch of grassless ground and their horses kicked up clouds of dust which swirled smokily through the air around them, he made his move.

Working covertly and quickly with a minimum of motion, he loosened the cinch strap of the horse beneath him and then, as the saddle slid to the left and the rider seated in it let out a startled yelp, Cimarron slid with the rider down the side of the horse to the ground.

As the man fell on top of him, Cimarron grabbed his gun, and a moment later the man pulled its trigger. A futile move, because Cimarron's right hand tightly circled the cylinder, preventing it from turning. He jerked the gun out of the man's hand and sprang to his feet.

Two riders were bearing down on him.

He shot the horse in the lead and the animal screamed and went down, throwing its rider. He swung the gun up and aimed at the second rider, an older man, he noticed, and the man abruptly turned his horse and galloped away.

He heard the sound of pounding hooves behind him. He spun around, knees bent, both hands on the gun as he aimed it at the man riding toward him.

"*Get him!*" he heard Lomax shout in the distance.

"I'll get him!"

Cimarron, as he recognized Brendan's voice, roared, "I'll kill the first sonofabitch that's fool enough to come within range of me!" He fired once and the rider bearing down on him dropped his gun and seized his suddenly bloody shoulder.

Before he could fire again, the other riders drew rein and sat their horses in a semicircle, staring at him.

"Now you gents just ride away from here," he ordered. "I'm not a back-shooter, so you're safe. Go on now. Move!"

They didn't.

Something's wrong, he thought. What? He didn't know. But he noticed that most of the men were not looking at him but over his head. From their mounted positions, he quickly realized, they're looking down at something— somebody—behind me!

He spun in place but he was too late.

Brendan threw the flat stone he held in his hand and it crashed against Cimarron's skull to light a red fire in his brain which totally, if only momentarily, consumed him. He felt himself sink to his knees, his arms rising to protect his head from another blow, his blurring vision on the gun he had dropped, which was well out of his reach.

"Get up!"

He warily raised his head and saw Lomax looking down at him. Shakily, he got to his feet, aware of the blood that was flowing from his scalp and into his right ear.

"It's time we took care of him," someone in the crowd of mounted men said. "We don't, he might try another trick or two."

"I'm more than willing," Lomax said. "Take him over there to that tree."

Someone gave Cimarron a shove, and as he went stumbling toward the tree that Lomax had pointed out, he thought of the gallows standing in the stone-walled compound in Fort Smith. "Shit," he muttered aloud. I escaped hanging in Fort Smith, he thought, and now it looks like I might be going to hang in wherever the hell this is that I'm at.

"String him up like we planned," Lomax ordered.

A man dropped a noose around Cimarron's neck and tossed the other end of the rope over a limb of the tree. He glanced at Lomax, who nodded.

"Give me a hand, boys," the man said, and then, when Brendan O'Malley and another man also gripped the free

124

end of the rope, Cimarron found himself hauled up into the air.

He gagged. His fingers tore frantically at the noose around his neck.

A moment later, as his boots struck the ground his knees buckled under him. Regaining his balance, he fought to loosen the noose, but before he could do so, one of the men grasping the free end of the rope yelled, "Heave!" and he was hauled up again and left dangling, the rope cutting off his breath.

He swung helplessly, his body turning, his fingers clawing in vain at the rope that was choking him.

He hit the ground hard, and this time there was enough slack in the rope to allow him to lie crumpled and gagging on the ground.

"Tighten up on that rope!" Lomax yelled.

But before Brendan and the other two men could do so, Cimarron succeeded in slipping the noose from around his neck.

He started to rise, but several men jumped him and held him down as Lomax yelled, "Tie the bastard's hands this time!"

In less than a minute, Cimarron's hands were bound behind his back and he was standing on his feet again, gasping for air, the noose taut around his neck.

He saw Lomax smile and wink at Brendan and the other two men. He felt the rope tighten. He stood on the tips of his boots, stretching his body, his head thrown back.

"Just a little bit more," Lomax said.

Cimarron was lifted off the ground to sway in the breeze. He gasped and the sun spun in the sky above him.

Suddenly, his boots hit the ground again and he heard himself—no, someone else, gagging. Blinking to clear his vision, he saw Brendan, no longer holding the rope, bending over and vomiting.

Lomax said, "Lawman, maybe by now you've learned your lesson. I hope you have. Get out of here and leave us alone. Or next time we won't be content with teasing you. Next time, we'll really hang you!" He gestured and the two remaining men hauled on the rope.

Cimarron's throat burned and his vision blurred. The world around him reeled as he fought to remain conscious. He opened his mouth, gasping in vain for air. In his chest his heart hammered against his ribs, and his eardrums roared. Darkness came to drown him.

When he regained consciousness, the rope was gone from his neck. It took him several seconds to realize that it now circled his wrists, which were high above his head. He looked up to where it looped over the limb of the tree above his head and then ran down and around the trunk of the tree, where it was firmly knotted in place. He looked down. He was standing on the toes of his boots.

He hung suspended in a world of pain. His ankles screamed in agony as they tried to support his weight. His toes felt as if they were broken. His arms were trying to tear themselves from their sockets. His throat burned. On the skin of his neck was a red rope burn.

But he could breathe, although it was painful for him to do so.

He took short and shallow breaths. His eyes began to water.

He looked up, blinked several times, and estimated the distance from the ground to the tree limb above him.

He began to swing his body, trying to ignore the pain the movement brought to his arms and shoulders as he did so. It took him some time to gain any momentum at all, but then, as he swung backward in a wide arc and then forward again, he brought both of his legs up. They failed to reach the branch above him.

He gritted his teeth and tried again, unwilling to lose the momentum he had gathered, and this time the heels of both his boots slammed down on the tree limb. He hung there, his breath coming in ragged bursts as he sucked cool air into his mouth and down into his lungs.

Then, keeping his boots locked in place on the tree limb, he gripped the rope with the fingers of both hands and drew himself up, bit by slow bit, until his hands circled the branch. He slowly eased his body up and then around the branch until he was lying flat upon it. He lay there motionless and sweating profusely, his body trembling with the efforts he had just made to free himself.

He pulled himself along the limb, and when he finally was sitting upon it with his back braced against the tree's trunk, he slid his knife from his boot and severed the rope that bound his wrists.

He stiffened as he heard the sound of a rider approaching. Automatically, he reached for his gun and found only his empty holster. But he had his knife.

Brendan O'Malley rode up to the tree and drew rein. He looked up at Cimarron in amazement. "How did you get up there?"

Cimarron tried to speak and succeeded only in uttering a series of rasping unintelligible sounds.

"They shouldn't have done what they did," Brendan said.

Cimarron closed his eyes and leaned his head against the tree trunk.

"They didn't give you a chance to fight back. It's not like this back in New York. There you fight man to man. You didn't get a fair chance."

"What—want?" Cimarron managed to get out.

"I dropped back," Brendan answered, "and rode here. I was going to cut you down."

Cimarron opened his eyes and looked down at Brendan. "Why?"

"You needed help."

"—still do."

Brendan, obeying Cimarrons guttural commands, helped him climb down from the limb.

"Where are we?" Cimarron asked as he stood on the ground and leaned against the tree trunk.

"Due south of Kiowa. About six or seven miles."

"Will you help me get to the Carlisle ranch?"

"Sure. We can ride double. Just show me the way."

9

"What happened to my gun?" Cimarron asked Brendan as they both rode Brendan's horse over the plains.

"One of those men took it."

"My horse?"

"They ran him off."

Cimarron was silent for a moment. Then, "I appreciate you coming back to lend me a hand."

It was Brendan's turn to be silent.

"If those men—Lomax especially—find out you set out to help me, they'll turn on you sure, you and your mother both."

"I really wanted to help those men get you good," Brendan admitted. "I mean, I did until I saw what they did to you. I couldn't stomach it. But at first—my mother, she's been dreaming for so long about us having a place of our own somewhere out west here. She doesn't want it just for herself. It's for me she really wants it.

"She's not had an easy time of it since my father died. Even before he died things weren't so good for us as a family. My father was—he wasn't—"

"Your mother—" Cimarron's throat constricted, and he gagged. He swallowed twice. "She mentioned your pa to me."

"He was good to us. It wasn't all his fault what he did. He had to do it, or at least he thought he had to. When he was killed I tried to take his place, but it didn't work out. Maybe my mother told you about that too."

"She did. I can understand you wanting to be like your pa. Most boys do. Sometimes though it only brings a man trouble when he sets out trying to follow a trail that's not his own but belongs to somebody else."

"I get all mixed up sometimes. You talk about follow-

128

ing trails. The trouble with me is I don't have a trail of my own to follow."

"You're just sixteen. Some trails take time to find. Out here . . ." Cimarron waved an arm to encompass the plains. "Well, you'll find one you want to travel."

"How did you find yours?"

"It more or less found me," Cimarron answered and said no more.

As they rode on in silence, his mind became filled with all too familiar memories. The bank that day down in Texas. He remembered kneeling in front of the iron safe and scooping up the money. He saw again the sheriff enter the bank on the run, his gun drawn. He saw himself turn swiftly, fire, and then run with the money for the door. Past the sheriff lying dead on the floor he ran. Then he halted abruptly. Turned. Looked down at the face he knew so well, the face he had not recognized in the instant before firing his snap shot. The face of his father.

He heard himself questioning the terrified patrons of the bank and learning that his father had come to the small Texas town after the death of his wife, and after they had gotten to know him well they had asked him to be their sheriff.

He felt again the chill that had settled on him then and had never really left him even when he rode beneath the fiery furnace of a mid-July sun.

He saw himself running from the bank and tossing the money he had helped to steal to one of the outlaws he had been riding with and then leaping into his saddle and galloping away alone.

He'd been alone ever since. He was alone on the day he became involved in the events that led to his imprisonment in the Fort Smith jail. He recalled his trial and how close he had come to hanging.

There were times even now when he could not quite believe the way things had turned out for him. That he was now a federal lawman. That he had accepted Judge Parker's offer to work for the court, knowing it might be a way to atone for the terrible crime that still haunted him and caused him to awaken sometimes from sleep soaked in sweat and shuddering as the ghost of his father trailed him and cried out to him to explain the unexplainable—the unforgivable act he had committed.

"Is that it?" Brendan asked.

Cimarron stared at the Carlisle ranch in the distance. "That's it." The smoke coming from the stone chimney, he noticed, was not rising. It did clear the top of the chimney but then it drifted away and down toward the ground. He looked up at the sky.

Clouds were gathering. "Snow blossoms."

"What?"

"See those clouds up there? They look like white blossoms with a bluish tinge. Folks call them snow blossoms."

"But the sun's shining."

"For now it is." Cimarron dismounted and tethered Brendan's horse to the rail beside two other horses. "Notice how these mounts are stepping about instead of standing still? Critters—people too—get nervy when a storm's coming."

He went to the door and knocked on it.

Dean opened it a moment later, and Cimarron noticed the man's face seemed haggard and drawn. "Cimarron! I wasn't expecting you. Come on in." Dean opened the door wider, and Cimarron and Brendan stepped inside.

"This here fellow's named Brendan O'Malley," Cimarron told Dean. As the pair shook hands, he added, "Brendan's mother is one of Lomax's recruits." He gingerly lowered himself into a chair.

"What's wrong, Cimarron?" Dean asked. "You look peaked."

Cimarron told him what had happened.

Dean let out a low whistle. "So Lomax has started playing rough, has he?"

"I can play rougher. But, yes, he's getting his dander up, and no wonder. He's got a lot to lose if his scheme falls through on him. He's collecting fifty dollars a head for every settler he gets to come down here into the Territory."

"He's getting paid to bring us down here?" Brendan inquired, surprise in his tone.

Cimarron nodded. "You didn't think he was doing it all out of the pure and unadulterated goodness of his heart, did you?"

"I guess I didn't think much about why he was doing it," Brendan replied.

"Who's paying him?" Dean asked.

"Fallon and Randolph," Cimarron answered. "Dean, you said I looked peaked. You look a little wan yourself."

"Haven't had much sleep. Been sitting up with Pa."

"How is he?"

"Not good. He——"

Before Dean could complete his remark, Victoria emerged from the west wing and hurried across the room. "Dean, I'm worried about your father. He seems much worse, and I don't have any idea what to do for him."

Cimarron said brightly, "Hello there, Victoria."

She gave him a curt nod and continued staring up into Dean's eyes, her hand on his arm.

Dean shook his head, a gesture of weariness mixed with resignation. "There's no doctor anywhere near here."

"I'll go take a look at him," Cimarron volunteered. He rose and made his way out of the room, the others following close behind him.

He found Carlisle lying flat on his back in his bed. The old man's eyes were closed and his breath wheezed through his partially open lips. His color reminded Cimarron of the snow blossoms he had pointed out to Brendan.

"Pneumonia," he said bluntly. "He's got a double dose, looks like to me."

"You're sure?" Victoria asked him, her hand tightening on Dean's arm.

"No, I'm not. But I've seen pneumonia before, and I think I'm seeing it now. Open the window wide."

"Open the——" Victoria repeated stupidly.

"The cold air'll make him worse, won't it?" Dean asked. "The temperature outside's not far above freezing."

Cimarron went to the window and opened it as far as it would go. "Victoria, you go get blankets—lots of them—and throw them over him. Dean, you help me shove the bed over closer to the window. He'll maybe be able to breathe a little easier now."

Victoria returned to the room with an armful of blankets. She shook each one out and draped it over Carlisle. She shivered as a cool breeze blew into the room.

"Get some kind of hot soup into him if you can," Cimarron ordered her and then turned to Brendan. "I want you to do something for me, if you're willing."

"Sure, Cimarron."

"Ride into Kiowa." Cimarron shoved a hand into the

pocket of his jeans, withdrew a roll of bills, counted out several, and handed them to Brendan. "Buy me a six-gun. A Colt if you can. Caliber .44 or .45, don't much matter which. Cartridges. Go to the livery and get me as good a horse as you can and a saddle and bridle."

In the bed, Carlisle coughed, his body shuddering as he did so. His eyes remained closed.

Cimarron went over to the bed and placed the back of his hand against the old man's forehead. "Fever." He noticed that Brendan was still in the room.

Brendan stood looking down at the money in his hand. Then he looked up and met Cimarron's eyes.

Cimarron said, "Maybe some owlhoot'll try to steal that poke I'm trusting you with, so you be careful with it, hear?" His eyes held Brendan's for a moment, and then, when the faint trace of a smile appeared on Brendan's face, he said, "Go fork your horse, boy. Ride fast so's you'll not get caught in the storm that's coming."

After Brendan had left the room, Victoria asked, "Who was that young man?"

Cimarron told her. "You may not recognize the name O'Malley," he added. "But you'd recognize the boy's mother. She's the red-haired one who went and hauled you off your horse."

Victoria's eyes widened. "What was he doing here?"

"He's a friend of mine. We just did a little bit of riding together."

His explanation, which he knew was no explanation, nevertheless seemed to satisfy Victoria.

"There's some soup on the stove," she said.

"I could use some if there's enough to go around," Cimarron said.

"There's enough," Victoria assured him.

Cimarron and Dean followed her to the kitchen, where they both sat down as Victoria placed wood in the stove. She moved a large pot to the front of the stove and began to stir its contents.

Later, as she placed bowls full of chicken soup in front of them, there was a knock on the kitchen door.

Dean rose and opened it. "Howdy, Cal. What can I do for you?"

"Thought I ought to tell Mr. Carlisle what I seen," said the man standing outside.

"Come in, Cal," Dean said, and when the man stepped into the kitchen, he asked, "What news have you?"

"I was coming in from line riding when I saw them, Dean. There were a whole lot of troops. They were heading northwest toward the border. They must have come up from Fort Supply. I don't know that it means anything, but they were riding across Carlisle range, and I thought the old man ought to know about it."

"Oh, that's good news!" Victoria declared. "Those troops will keep the settlers from crossing the border."

"Maybe they'll also keep a few of them from seeing the sun rise tomorrow or the next day," Dean commented. "Thanks, Cal. I'll tell Pa what you saw once he gets over being sick."

Cal left and Dean resumed his seat.

Victoria placed bread and cheese on the table. "I'll take some soup to your father."

Dean stood up. "I'll take it. You sit down, Victoria. You've been on your feet practically since you got here."

Dean overruled Victoria's protests and left the kitchen carrying a bowl of steaming soup.

She sat down at the table and leaned back in her chair, her hands limp in her lap. She closed her eyes, and a sigh slid past her lips. Then, straightening, she looked over at Cimarron. "Oh! What happened to your neck?"

Cimarron told her. "I suppose you're too tuckered out to try comforting me to help me forget all I've just gone through."

She remained silent.

He noted her strained expression, and his mood darkened. Was she feeling guilty about having been with him? Or was she just too tired to respond to his prodding? His speculations were interrupted by Dean, who burst into the kitchen, his face pale.

"Pa's real sick!" he cried. "I think he's dying!"

Cimarron was on his feet at once. He went racing out of the kitchen and across to the west wing. As he entered Carlisle's bedroom, he heard the wordless sounds the old man was making, mumblings that seemed to come from under water.

As Dean and Victoria hurried into the room, Cimarron went over to the bed. He noted the bluish tinge to Car-

133

lisle's face, which, even as he watched, deepened into gray and then turned almost black.

"What can we do?" he heard Victoria cry from behind him, and he heard Dean moan instead of answering.

Carlisle, he knew, couldn't help himself. The old man was too weak. As he stirred feebly on the bed, trying desperately to lift himself up, Cimarron went up to the bed, knelt on it, and seized the old man. Swiftly, he turned him over so that he was lying on his stomach.

Victoria let out a cry of protest Cimarron ignored.

He grabbed Carlisle's hair in his right hand and pulled the man's head back.

"No!" Dean yelled and was on Cimarron, his hands gripping Cimarron's shoulders as he tried to drag him from the bed.

Cimarron shook him off and jerked Carlisle's lower jaw open with his left hand. He pulled out Carlisle's tongue and then shook the old man's head vigorously.

Nothing happened for a moment, but then, as he shook Carlisle's head a second time even more vigorously, Carlisle spat out a quantity of phlegm and then gasped for air. Cimarron tightened his grip on Carlisle's tongue, ignoring the slime and mucus covering his left hand. Again he shook Carlisle's head, with the result that Carlisle spewed forth more phlegm, and then continued gasping.

"You're hurting him!" Victoria cried, and again Cimarron ignored her.

He kept up his rough treatment for more than a minute until he saw Carlisle's color begin to return. The man's face slowly paled. His breathing, almost nonexistent earlier, was now shallow. He continued to kneel on the bed a moment longer, and then he released his hold on Carlisle's tongue and wiped his hand on the top blanket covering the bed. He lowered Carlisle's head and let go of the man's hair. He lifted Carlisle, and as the blankets fell to the floor, he said, "Get that stained blanket off the bed. Pull the others down."

When Victoria and Dean had obeyed his orders, he gently placed Carlisle on his back in the bed and drew the blankets up to his chin.

Carlisle's eyes were open, the wild look that had been in them earlier fading now. He stared wordlessly up at Cimarron.

"Get me a cloth of some kind—a wet one," Cimarron said, and Victoria handed him one moments later. He used it to wipe the sweat and slime from Carlisle's face and then dropped it on the floor.

"You—" Carlisle murmured, still staring upward.

His breathing was deepening, Cimarron noted with relief.

"I was—next door to dead," Carlisle whispered. His hand rose and trembled inches above the blankets.

Cimarron reached out and gripped the old man's hand. He sat down on the bed.

"I owe you, Cimarron."

"Dean, does your daddy always talk such a blue streak when he ought to be resting so's he can get back enough strength to move out of the neighborhood?"

A frown appeared on Carlisle's face. "Neighborhood?"

"Dammit, Carlisle, don't you understand anything? You just told me you were next door to dead, and that's no kind of neighborhood for any man to stay in."

The frown deepened, and then, as understanding came to Carlisle, he smiled faintly.

Cimarron, as the old man's fingers tightened on his hand, returned his smile. "Go to sleep," he told him, "I'll be seeing you again soon." He let go of Carlisle's hand, which dropped weakly onto the blanket, and got to his feet. Turning to Victoria and Dean, he said, "Sorry about the mess I made."

Dean giggled foolishly, and then his giggle became wild laughter that bounded about the room. " 'Sorry,' he says. He's sorry he saved my pa's life. *Sorry!*"

Cimarron went up to him and put a hand on Dean's shoulder. "Take it easy. Chances are good he'll get better now. That stuff was clogging his lungs, and it would have choked him to death if he hadn't—"

"If *you* hadn't rid him of it," Dean interrupted. "Cimarron, I can't tell you how grateful I am to you. If there's ever anything I can do for you you've got to promise to holler down the hill and I'll come up it on the run, I swear to the good God I will."

"You're either a liar or a fool. Maybe a little bit of both."

Anger flashed in Dean's eyes for an instant. "What do you mean by that remark?"

135

"You told me you hated the old man. You said you wished he was dead."

Dean lowered his head.

Cimarron squeezed his shoulder. "The true fact of the matter is that sometimes a man just don't know his own mind, let alone his lots more complicated heart."

"We're both grateful to you, Cimarron," Victoria said softly.

He looked at her with interest, arching one eyebrow.

Victoria looked away. "I'll sit with Mr. Carlisle. You two—go finish your soup."

Cimarron, when he was seated again at the kitchen table, spooned soup into his mouth, unmindful of the fact that it was cold. "She's being a big help to you," he commented.

"Victoria?" Dean smiled. "Wonderful woman. I never met an eastern lady before. She's a marvel."

"Pretty as a new-painted fence too."

"So refined."

"The kind of woman a man wouldn't mind marrying." Cimarron pushed his empty bowl aside.

"This man wouldn't," Dean agreed heartily.

"You going to?"

Dean stammered something.

"What say?"

"I said a woman like her would never have the likes of me. She's the kind to marry a schoolteacher. Somebody with brains and fine manners."

"You're not addled, are you, Dean?"

"No, but—"

"You don't spit on the floor or keep pigs in the kitchen, do you?"

Dean studied Cimarron for a moment before asking, "You think maybe I've got a chance?"

"I think she's taken with you."

"You do? You really do? How can you tell?"

"Well, a couple of ways. I had my eye on her, I'll admit that straight out. But she won't give me so much as the time of day or directions to the outhouse. On top of that, I noticed her looking at you from time to time. Her eyes were all bright and almost as feverish as your daddy's. Now, the way I see it, you've just got to move fast and sure. Before I try my luck."

"Is there anything between you two, Cimarron? I mean, if there is, well, I'll back off. It wouldn't be right."

"I already told you she don't pay me no mind. It's sad but it's also true. What that lady needs is somebody who can talk her language—about culture and things like that. Somebody who's also a real man. You qualify, seems to me, on both counts."

"Maybe I should go and sit with her. She's been on the go practically since the minute she got here."

"You do that, Dean. Me, I think I'll go stretch out on that sofa in the other room and try to nap till Brendan gets back with my new gun and horse."

Cimarron awoke at the sound of the front door closing. He sat up on the sofa as Brendan came up to him and said, "I got you a horse and gear. A gun too."

"That's good news to hear." Cimarron stood up. "I'll have a look at them."

Brendan followed him outside. He took a revolver from one of the saddlebags and handed it to him.

"The Peacemaker's a good gun," Cimarron commented. "This sorrel looks sturdy, if a mite swaybacked."

Cimarron checked the Texas saddle on the horse to be sure the double-cinch rig was secure. "Secondhand, I take it," he said to Brendan.

"How'd you know?"

"Boots have been in these stirrups. That's steam-bent wood those stirrups are made out of, and they show wear."

"It was the only one the man in the livery had for sale."

"I'm not complaining, Brendan, just noticing. Noticing's a habit of mine that sometimes stands me in good stead."

Brendan took a cartridge belt from the saddlebag, and Cimarron took it from him and strapped it on. He holstered the Colt and then pulled it free. He holstered it again. The holster was new, its leather too stiff to suit him, but he made no mention of that fact.

Brendan handed him a box of cartridges, and he promptly loaded the .45 and placed the remaining cartridges in the loops of the belt.

"What now, Cimarron?"

"I'm riding into Kiowa to have a talk with a friend of

mine who's staying in the hotel there—Marcus Doby. You know him. You saw him with me when the settlers tried to cross the border."

"He's an Indian, isn't he?"

"A Cherokee, and you needn't look like you just swallowed some vinegar without any molasses in it. He's a fine man and, like I said, a friend of mine. You might as well ride along with me so you can get back to your mother. She must be wondering where in God's great creation you've wandered to by now."

"She worries about me too much."

"No need to be annoyed about that. Take it as a compliment."

"A compliment?"

"Her fretting shows she cares what happens to you. It's nice for a man to have someone who cares whether he gets lost, stolen, or he strays."

As Cimarron swung into the saddle of the sorrel, Victoria came out of the house and said, "I saw you through the window. Are you leaving?"

"I am. Going to have myself a talk with Marcus. Victoria, I'd be obliged to you if you'd say my goodbyes to Dean and his daddy for me."

He touched the brim of his hat to her, turned his horse, and rode away from the ranch with Brendan.

By the time they crossed the border, snow had begun to fall.

"It's dry," Cimarron commented, referring to the flakes swirling around them as they rode into Kiowa. "It'll stick." He halted his horse in front of the hotel and turned to Brendan. "You be sure and give my regards to your mother."

"I will," Brendan said and rode north.

Cimarron got out of the saddle, tethered his horse to the hitch rail, and strode into the lobby. Moments later, he was knocking on the door of Doby's room.

Doby opened it almost immediately.

As Cimarron entered the room, his eyes went to the wires lying clustered on a table next to the bed.

"There are troops camped south of the border," he told Doby.

"Then they've come?"

Cimarron nodded. "Those wires—they're from your friends?"

138

"Most of them, yes. One is from Judge Parker. He wants to know if you're making any progress."

"What did your friends say, Marcus?"

"Three of them declined. Two are agreeable. I myself, of course, am willing to participate in your plan."

"So that makes it three and three. Not bad, though it could have been better."

"Some of us—well, you know that many Cherokees are violently opposed to the presence of whites on Cherokee lands, and they have good reason to be, I suppose."

"Marcus, you stay put right here, will you do that?"

"Yes, if you think I should. What do you plan to do now?"

"I'm going to talk to the man in command of those troops I told you about. I'll tell him what you've arranged and then I'll go talk to the settlers, and when I'm done doing that maybe this powder keg we've all been sitting on won't blow up under us after all.

"I'll want you to put in an appearance at some point to back me up, which is why I want you where I can find you real quick."

"I'll be here. If I have to leave the hotel for any length of time, I'll leave word at the desk."

"Be seeing you."

Cimarron left the room and then the hotel. He shivered with the deepening cold, and it was the cold that he used as a reason for seeking the drink he wanted anyway.

He went into the saloon that was near the hotel and was on his way to the bar when a woman yelled, "Hey there, you!"

Cimarron ordered whiskey, but before his order could be filled, someone seized him by the arm. His hand dropped to the butt of his gun.

"I was talking to you," Orajean Lomax, a glass in her free hand, declared. "Didn't you hear me?"

Hey, there, you!

"You went and forgot my name already," he accused her with mock chagrin.

"Names don't matter. Actions do. Sit down over there with me." Orajean led him to a nearby table. She slumped into a chair and waved him into one, spilling some of the whiskey in her glass as she did so.

"What're you doing here in town?" Cimarron asked her.

139

"Shelebrating!"

"Shele—celebrating what, if you don't mind my asking?"

"Bill Lee, that's what! I ran him off once and for all and then *I* ran off. What do you think of that?"

Cimarron didn't know what he thought of that, so he said nothing.

"That sonofabitch!" Orajean exclaimed and refilled her glass from the bottle that sat on the table in front of her. "I'm now a free woman. Free to do what I want with whoever I want whenever I want, and I assure you I intend to be *willful* from now on!"

"Last time I saw you you were calling for that mob to kill me quick."

"Let's let bygones be bygones! Have a drink!" Orajean thrust the bottle toward Cimarron.

He raised it to his lips and drank.

"Down the gullet, cowboy!" Orajean whooped, waving her glass in the air. "Puts power in that thing you got tucked in your pants!"

Cimarron lowered the bottle and stared at Orajean in genuine amazement.

"Hey, I didn't mean to inshult you. What I meant was that redeye will put *more* power in that thing you've got in your pants, though you probably don't need it." She drank from her glass. "Do you? Need it?" She giggled.

"It's done right well by me so far, honey."

"Will it do right by *me?*"

Cimarron thought of the troops south of the border. He glanced through the window at the thickening snow. "Come on, Orajean. I'll rent us a room."

"No." She shook her head vehemently from side to side with the studied intensity that was born of her drunkenness.

"I must have got you all wrong," he told her, frowning. "I thought you wanted—"

"I do and I'm going to get it. But I've already got a room." She swayed to her feet. "Let's go!"

He took the glass from her hand and set it down on the table.

Orajean hooked her arm into his as they left the saloon and headed back to the hotel.

140

10

As Orajean bent down and tried to insert her key into the lock on her door, she swayed, and she would have fallen if Cimarron hadn't caught her in time.

"That lock won't stand still for me!" she whimpered, the key in her hand wavering.

As Cimarron took the key from her and inserted it in the lock, a door opened at the end of the hall and Doby came toward him.

"Marcus," he said. "I didn't expect to see you again quite so soon." He opened the door and handed the key to Orajean, who took it and then grabbed his wrist.

As she hauled him into the room, Cimarron gave Doby a sheepish grin, and then Orajean slammed the door shut.

"Drop your pants," she ordered as she flopped on her back on the bed. She struggled with her clothes, pulling her skirt up, her drawers down.

So, Cimarron thought, this is to be a fast one, faster'n hell can scorch a man's skin, looks like. He took off his jacket and cartridge belt and then dropped his jeans around his boots. As he climbed awkwardly onto the bed, he was hard and more than ready.

"You'll be the third man I've had since I got here," Orajean informed him happily. "Hope you turn out as good as the first two were. What're you waiting for?"

Cimarron didn't know the answer to her question, if there was one, so he lowered his pelvis and plunged into her.

She was tight, he discovered. Dry.

But only a moment later, she loosened up and became moist and he found the going easier.

Orajean yawned.

An insult?

He kept at it, his face partially buried in the pillow.

Orajean stretched beneath him and flung her arms out

to her sides. "I wish Bill Lee could see me now!" she cried. "I just wish Bill Lee could see *you* now! Know what? His is no bigger than a just-born pup's compared to yours. Sometimes I wasn't even sure whether or not he was in me."

Cimarron continued his eager thrusting, trying to banish the name of Bill Lee, which was echoing in his mind while he wondered if he was measuring up to the standards of the other two men Orajean had mentioned.

"When I think of all the time I wasted!" Orajean gushed and then wiggled her hips, sending a tremor through Cimarron's body. "I should have left Bill Lee years ago. But I didn't know myself then like I know myself now. Cimarron, you want to know something?"

"Honey, we can talk afterward if that's all right with you."

Orajean yawned. "I could use a drink."

Cimarron plunged into her as far as he could, and she raised her arms above her head and stretched luxuriously. "Are you about ready, honey?"

Orajean answered his question with another yawn.

To hell with it, he thought, and a moment later erupted, his body shuddering as wave after wave of pleasure washed over him.

He lay trembling on top of Orajean until he felt himself becoming flaccid, and then he pulled out of her and asked, "Did you—"

He stared down at her, his question unfinished.

Orajean was sound asleep.

As he got up from the bed, she began to snore.

He pulled up his jeans and buttoned them before strapping on his cartridge belt and putting on his buckskin jacket.

He was about to leave the room when a knock sounded on the door. He hesitated. Doby? He started toward the door. Bill Lee Lomax? He glanced at the window.

He hurried over to the bed and pulled up Orajean's drawers and then lowered her skirt.

The knock sounded again.

He opened the door to find Brendan standing outside in the hall. "What the hell are you doing here?"

"I came looking for you. I remembered you said you

were coming here to the hotel to see Mr. Doby." Brendan shifted position and glanced into the room.

Cimarron moved to block his view of Orajean.

"I found Mr. Doby downstairs buying a newspaper. The room clerk pointed him out to me. Mr. Doby said you were up here."

"What do you want with me?"

"It's my mother."

"Your mother? What about your mother?"

"She's gone. From the camp, I mean. Her and our wagon. She left a message for me with a man back there. He said she told him to tell me she was heading south to find us a place to settle."

Cimarron went to the window and looked out. The snow was heavier now. He turned to Brendan. "That damn fool woman—sorry, Brendan. She went sashaying across the border in this snowstorm?"

"The man she left the message with said she left before the snow started. But she must be caught in the storm now, and I didn't know what to do—I guess I should have gone after her myself, but I figured you knew the country around here a whole lot better than I do, so I came to ask you if you'd help me find her."

"I'll help you, Brendan. Let's go."

When they reached the lobby, Doby, who was seated in a chair reading a newspaper, looked up.

Cimarron nodded to him and started for the door. He halted when he heard the wail of a woman pierce the air. He turned and looked up to find Orajean standing disheveled at the top of the stairs.

"Cimarron!" she screeched and shook her fists at him. "Get back up here! Now! This minute!"

"Can't," he yelled up to her.

"You heard me. We have unfinished business, you and me!"

"I finished. Sorry you didn't, honey."

Orajean began to bound down the steps.

"Marcus," Cimarron said quickly, "tell her I've—tell her I'm heading for the Carlisle ranch south of here."

Before Doby could say anything, Cimarron was through the door and hurriedly untethering his horse. He climbed into the saddle and pulled his hat down low on his forehead to help shield his eyes from the flakes of snow that filled the air. "You ready?" he asked after Brendan had mounted his horse.

Brendan nodded and they rode out of Kiowa.

Snow covered the ground now, Cimarron noted, pleased. It would make tracking a wagon and the wrongheaded woman driving it easier. But the snow showed no signs of stopping, and that worried him. "Your ma," he said to Brendan, "she tell that man you mentioned exactly where she was headed?"

Brendan shook his head.

"Cimarron!"

Cimarron squinted into the storm in the direction from which the man's voice had come and made out a blurred figure riding toward him. A moment later, he recognized Dean Carlisle.

"Looks like nobody, including you and me," he commented to Brendan, "has got sense enough to come in out of this storm."

"Cimarron," Dean said as he rode up to them, "I'm glad I ran into you. I was heading for Kiowa because Victoria told me you were going there to the hotel to talk to Mr. Doby. Pa wants you."

"Does he now? What might he be wanting me for?"

"He didn't say. He did say it was important that he talk to you."

"I've got other business to tend to at the moment, Dean. You ride on back. I've got a woman to find somewhere out there." He pointed south.

"A woman?"

Cimarron explained.

"I'll go with you," Dean volunteered.

"No need," Cimarron told him. "We can manage, Brendan and me."

"Just like Pa," Dean muttered angrily.

"What's that?"

"You probably think I wouldn't be of any help to you. Maybe you think I'd just get in your way."

"Dean, I'm not your pa and I don't think any of those things you just mentioned. I just don't see any reason why you should stay out here in this storm when you could be home where it's warm. With Victoria," he added.

"Mrs. O'Malley might be hurt. Anything might have

144

happened to her. I might be of some help to you—to her too, depending."

"Let's go then, Dean. Three sets of eyes'll be better than two in this weather, I reckon."

Cimarron pointed west and then turned his horse in that direction.

"Ma's headed south!" Brendan protested.

"She'll have driven around the western edge of Kiowa, if I remember rightly where she had her wagon parked. We'll ride on a bit and then turn south."

They did, while Cimarron silently cursed the falling snow that had thoroughly and completely obliterated any sign that might have been made in the ground beneath it. He rode on, squinting into the white distance, cold snowflakes striking his face and melting upon it. He reached up and buttoned the top button of his jacket. Getting colder, he thought.

They had covered little more than a mile when Dean suddenly called out, "Looks like cattle bunched up ahead there."

"Not cattle," Cimarron said. "Tents." He headed for the low triangular shapes of the soldiers' bivouac.

As he rode up to the camp he was challenged by a guard.

"I'm a deputy marshal from Fort Smith, Arkansas," he said in response to the challenge. "I want to talk to your commanding officer."

"First tent at the end of the left line, sir," the private said and pointed. "That one is Captain Soames's, sir."

"Much obliged."

When Cimarron reached the tent, he called out, "Captain Soames!"

A moment later, a man bundled up in a long army overcoat appeared. "I am Captain Soames."

Cimarron identified himself and then asked, "We're looking for a woman driving a wagon—this fellow's ma." He indicated Brendan. "She was heading south before the storm struck. Did you happen to spot her by any chance?"

Soames shook his head. "I'm afraid I did not."

Brendan's face, Cimarron noticed, fell at the news.

"Captain," he said, "after I find that woman I'm after and I get her settled—"

Interrupting, Soames said, "Settlers are not allowed down here in the Territory."

"It was just a manner of speaking, Captain," Cimarron said. "What I'd been about to say was I plan on coming back here to have a talk with you.

"As a federal lawman and officer of Judge Parker's court, I've got jurisdiction here in the Territory. In fact, I was sent up here to see if I could keep anybody out who's got a mind to sneak down into the Territory. Now, I've been doing some talking and some listening and it may just be that I know a way to talk those people out of their plans for trespassing, and if I'm right, you and your men won't have to fire a single shot in their direction and they won't any longer be a thorn in your side. Or in mine."

"What do you have in mind?"

"I haven't got the time to sit down and spell it all out for you right now, Captain. But I'll be back after I find the lady I mentioned and dig her out of the drifts she'll most likely have driven into. Be seeing you, Captain."

Cimarron rode away from the tent with Brendan and Dean following close behind him. He estimated that they had covered several miles when he felt his sorrel stumble under him. He patted the horse's neck and spoke softly to it. The horse stepped out smartly, its steamy breath shooting from its belled nostrils. "There's rocky ground underfoot," he remarked to Brendan. "See to your horse. Don't push him. There's no need."

They rode on, and a few minutes later, Cimarron veered to the right and then halted his horse and got out of the saddle.

"You find something?" Dean asked him as he rode up beside him.

Cimarron bent down to a small snow-covered hummock. He thrust his hand into it and came up with a wooden bucket that had caused the hummock to form. He turned to Brendan. "You recognize this, by any chance?"

"It's a bucket."

"When you and your ma were heading west did you ever have any trouble with your wagon wheels? They squeak?"

"Once in a while. Ma fixed them."

Cimarron nodded thoughtfully. "How?"

146

"She used the bucket hanging from our rear axle. The grease bucket."

Cimarron held up the bucket, which contained a mixture of wax and tallow. "Could this here be her bucket?"

Brendan took a closer look and then said, "It might be. Yeah, I think it is."

Cimarron dropped the bucket and got back into the saddle. "She probably hit a rock and jolted it off her wagon. Let's move out."

They had not gone far when Cimarron reached up and untied the bandanna from around his neck. He handed it to Brendan. "Tie it around your nose and mouth. It'll make breathing a bit easier."

Brendan reached out for the bandanna and then hesitated. "What will you use?"

"Me? Don't you worry none about me. I don't mind one bit if a snowflake or two finds its way down my nose or throat. They might help to douse the fires of hell a saucy lady I once met in Tennessee told me were burning hot and bright in the depths of my soul."

Brendan laughed and took the bandanna, which he tied over the lower half of his face as he had been instructed to do.

"Hey, now, take yourself a look at that!" Cimarron pointed to the ground a little to the right.

"I don't see anything," Dean said.

"Tracks. Wagon tracks. Traces of them, anyways. Look there. Look close. See how there's those little narrow dips in the snow? They're lower than the rest of the snow cover."

"Ma's wagon, you think?" Brendan asked.

"Likely it's the very thing that made those tracks. I can't conjure up the thought that anybody else'd be moseying about out here. Not in this storm. Not the way the wind's rising. We three are about to find ourselves in the belly of one helluva big blizzard, or I miss my guess."

"Goddammit!" Brendan exclaimed.

"God's got nothing to do with it," Cimarron said, grinning. "He's far too busy to sit around up there stirring up storms, since he's got sinners like me to keep an eye on. Now, what the three of us've got to keep our eyes on at the moment is those tracks and where they'll take us. Let's move out and be thankful the wind's at our backs."

The three men rode on in silence across the plain while the freezing wind seemed bent on whipping them on.

Cimarron, his jacket collar turned up, shivered from time to time as snow was whirled between his collar and neck. He kept his eyes on the faint wagon tracks that were becoming fainter as the wind howled on and sent the snow on the ground swirling into drifts which grew tall and then shifted shape as the wind changed direction.

Before long, all trace of the tracks had vanished in the shifting snow.

"Spread out!" Cimarron yelled, trying to make himself heard above the whine of the wind. "Dean—that way!" He pointed to his left. "Brendan—over there!" He pointed to his right. "Both of you keep your eyes open in case she's lost her bearings and started to circle."

As the distance between Cimarron and his two companions widened, he yelled to them, "Not too far. Stay close enough so we don't lose sight of each other!" He thought it unnecessary to add a warning about the danger any one of them would face should he become separated from the others.

He rode on, keeping his head down, only occasionally raising it to make sure he could still see Dean and Brendan. He flexed his fingers in an effort to get the blood moving in them. When that didn't work he slapped his hands against his thighs, which helped.

The mane of his sorrel was caked with snow and the steam from the animal's nostrils flew up around its head, momentarily melting the snow before it quickly froze again.

Brendan's startled yell caused Cimarron's head to snap to the right. But Brendan was nowhere in sight. Cimarron swore. And then he spotted Brendan's horse. The animal seemed to materialize from the snow-covered ground, and almost immediately he guessed what had happened. "Dean!" he yelled and waved an arm in the direction of Brendan's horse, which was plowing through drifts as it made its way north.

Dean rode toward the animal in an effort to head it off, but the horse veered and, swiftly circling Dean, galloped north to disappear in the thickening snow.

Cimarron yelled to Dean to join him and then rode to

148

the spot where he had seen the horse rise like an apparition out of the ground.

He found Brendan buried in the snow and struggling desperately to climb out of it. He leaped from the saddle and cautiously felt his way down the side of the dry wash that the wind had filled with snow.

"I fell!" Brendan cried out, reaching for the hand Cimarron was holding out to him. "My horse did."

Cimarron, as Dean appeared above him, seized Brendan's hand and pulled. At the same time, he yelled up to Dean, "Keep back from the edge of the wash or you'll land down here too."

Brendan let out a cry of pain.

Cimarron continued to pull on his hand, scrabbling backward up the sloping bank of the wash.

"My leg!" Brendan yelled. "It's broken!"

When Cimarron had him up on level ground again, he asked, "Which leg?"

"My left."

Cimarron ran his hands over the leg and then grunted. "Broken, all right. Just above the ankle." He looked up at Dean. "Those cedars we passed a ways back. Think you can find them again?"

"I can find them."

"Good. Now, here's what you do." Cimarron gave brief instructions, and a moment later, Dean rode north and vanished in the falling snow.

"Brendan, you just sit still for a minute." Cimarron hurriedly scooped up snow and packed it into place until he had built a windbreak. He put his hands under Brendan's armpits and hauled him to its leeward side. "Dean'll be back soon. Then we'll fix you up."

It was some time before Dean returned. When he did, Cimarron immediately set to work freeing the cedar saplings Dean had felled from the rope by which they had been dragged.

He told Dean what he intended to do, and both men set to work as the snow, which now had some sleet in it, stung their faces and bare hands.

Fifteen minutes later, they had fashioned a rough travois consisting of two poles of cedar saplings over which they had placed Dean's saddle blanket, which was held in place by lashings of piggin strings Cimarron had cut from his saddle. They fastened the ends of the poles to Dean's saddle with lengths of his rope.

"You'll have to take it slower than you might want to move in this weather," Cimarron cautioned. "But the snow'll help you some. The travois'll slide fairly easy, I figure. Once you get him back to your ranch, see if you can splint his leg."

"Hell, Cimarron, I'm no doctor!"

"Listen up, Dean." Cimarron told him what to look for and what to do about it when he found it. "Now you're a doctor, or the closest thing to it around here."

They lifted Brendan into the travois, and then Dean stepped into the saddle.

"Cimarron," Brendan said, "I'm sorry."

"Nothing to be sorry about. You did your damnedest, and that's all anybody can ask of any man."

"Do you think you'll be able to find Ma?"

"Sure I will. These old eyes of mine have found honeycombs a bear couldn't't've found, not to mention feminine pulchritude where other men saw only crossed eyes, a hooked nose, and no trace of a chin." He stood and watched Dean move out. When Dean looked back over his shoulder and waved, Cimarron returned the wave and then got back into the saddle and started south, the wind roaring in his ears.

He was almost upon the wagon before he actually saw it. It lay on its side, snow banked up against it. The horses that had been pulling it were gone.

He spurred the sorrel, and it struggled through the deepening snow cover. He got out of the saddle and crunched through the snow, circling the wagon and calling Tess's name several times. He got no response. He hunkered down and peered through the wagon's cover, which was as white as the snow heaped upon it. Inside he saw only overturned household goods and boxes. Crackers which had fallen from a shattered barrel lay everywhere.

There was no sign of Tess.

He stood up and surveyed the scene around him. No Tess. And no tracks.

The sorrel eased up to him. Absently, he put out a hand and stroked the animal's neck. "Now, why wouldn't she have sheltered inside this broken-down wagon?" he asked the horse.

It nuzzled him and moved closer, seeking the warmth of his body.

The wind? He stiffened, listening. Was it the wind that had keened? Was he hearing things? Imagining them?

No!

The sound reached his ears again, and this time he knew it for what it was. A woman's scream. He leaped into the saddle and galloped in the direction from which it had come.

He found Tess only minutes later. She wore a shawl around her shoulders and was gripping it tightly in both hands. The wind whipped her skirt about her legs. Her red hair, a beacon in the snow, flew free.

She screamed again as the pack of wolves formed a circle around her. She spun around, her eyes darting from one to the next and then on to the next.

Cimarron counted seven timber wolves, and he suspected there might be more lobos lurking just out of sight, waiting for the seven to bring Tess down so the feast could begin.

She'd be better off with seven bears, he thought, as he charged toward the nearest wolf. Bears usually eat only what's already dead. He jerked the reins hard, and the sorrel, snorting its fear, reared, its front legs lifting off the ground.

Cimarron brought the animal down. Its hooves missed the wolf he'd hoped to put out of action, and the animal snarled as it slunk backward, its wet teeth bared.

The sorrel tried to make a run for it, but Cimarron held it in check as he drew his Colt. He fired, but the sorrel suddenly pranced to the side to escape one of the wolves, and the shot went wild.

"Cimarron!" Tess screamed as the wolf directly behind her sprang forward and nipped at her ankles.

"Kick it!" he shouted at her.

She did, and the wolf sprang backward and then almost immediately began to approach her again from behind.

They'll try to hamstring her, he thought. Bring her down that way and then jump her. He fired again, and this time he wounded one of the lobos and it went loping off into the storm.

The others stood, most of them rigidly, their eyes darting from Tess to Cimarron and back again.

He got off another shot, but it too went wild because the sorrel wouldn't stand still. Then, before he could fire again one of the wolves sprang forward and leaped into the air.

As the lobo came down, its claws raked the sorrel.

The horse screamed and reared, throwing Cimarron from the saddle.

The snow cushioned his fall, and he was about to get his legs under him when another wolf went for him. He rolled over, his arms flying up to shield his face. His revolver fell from his hand as the body of the wolf collided with his own.

He thrust the wolf away as the others came racing toward him and pulled his knife from his boot. He plunged the blade of his knife into the wolf, and its snapping and snarling ceased. It whimpered and went limp.

He reached out and quickly retrieved his revolver. He holstered it and then, holding the knife on which the body of the lobo was impaled with both hands, he sprang to his feet and ran toward his sorrel as blood dripped from the body of the wolf to redden the snow beneath it.

The sorrel was rearing and sunfishing, also bleeding, as it tried to avoid the wolves. He grabbed the horse's bridle with one hand.

"Get into the saddle!" he yelled to Tess.

She remained motionless where she stood, her eyes wide with terror, her hands still clasping her shawl in front of her as if it would protect her from the fanged danger that surrounded them.

"Tess! Get into the saddle!"

The sorrel tried to break free, frightened by the scent of its own and the wolf's blood, but Cimarron kept his hold on its bridle, his chest heaving, his breath steaming in the cold air.

Tess moved. She took a single step in the direction of the horse. She stopped suddenly as a wolf snarled menacingly not far from where she stood.

Cimarron kicked a wolf that lunged at him and sent it flying backward. He began to lead the sorrel toward Tess.

It fought him. He fought it back, and when he reached Tess, she managed to climb into the saddle. He thrust out his arm and let the body of the wolf fall free of the knife in his hand. Before it hit the ground, he was up behind Tess in the saddle and shoving the bloody knife back into his boot.

Seizing the reins, he turned the horse, and as he did so he saw the five remaining wolves lunge toward the carcass of the dead member of their pack.

Their teeth ripped into it. Gore smeared their gray muzzles and teeth.

Cimarron gave the sorrel its head, and the animal galloped away from the carnage behind it. With Tess sobbing in the saddle he shared with her, he drove the horse on, aware that the animal might give out on him at any moment, but determined to put as much distance between them and the lobos as he could before the wolves finished devouring the dead member of their pack and decided to come after them.

The sorrel faltered.

Cimarron slowed it. I've got to, he told himself. If I don't, this animal's going to die under me with the double load it's carrying and the way it's stood up to all I've put it through already.

As the sorrel walked slowly through the snow, he reached out and stroked its neck. Your heart's bigger than a barn, he thought, and continued stroking the animal.

Tess's sobs finally subsided.

Cimarron slipped out of his buckskin jacket and gave it to her. "Put it on over your shawl."

"But you need it," she protested.

"Put it on and don't argue with me. If there's anything I can't abide, it's an obstinate woman."

The cold pierced his body, and he held himself rigid in the saddle as he tried not to shiver so that Tess would not begin arguing again about the jacket.

"Why didn't you stay in your wagon?" he asked her.

"I did. I unhitched the horses so they'd have a chance to find some kind of shelter, and then I crawled into it, but—" She sobbed once. "The wolves came. I could hear them howling in the distance, and then they were close to the wagon. I guess I lost my head. I was so afraid—terrified, in fact. I climbed out of the wagon and ran. They came after me. It was horrible. I was so frightened and I didn't know what to do or where to turn, and then you

153

came riding out of the snow and I couldn't believe what I was seeing. Oh, Cimarron, I was never so glad to see anyone in my entire life! Did you trail me through the snow?"

"There weren't any tracks. The wind must have blown snow over them before I got to your wagon."

"Then how did you find me?"

"You got yourself a good set of lungs, Tess."

"I don't understand." And then she did. "My screams."

"You got it."

"What luck for me that you were in the neighborhood when I needed help."

"It had nothing to do with luck. I came hunting you."

"You did? But how did you know that I had crossed the border and come down here in my wagon?"

Cimarron explained how he knew, and when he had finished, Tess said, "You told me that Brendan and Dean Carlisle came with you. Where are they now? Are we on the way to them?"

"Nope. They're both back at the Carlisle ranch by now. Or close to it. I sent them back because—because the storm was getting real bad."

He wondered if Tess had believed his lie. When she didn't question him any further, he decided that she had.

They rode on in silence for a time, and he began to worry, because there was no way for him to determine where they were heading. No pole star in the sky. No landmark of any kind. He searched for the stand of cedars he had spotted on the ride south. He needed to build some kind of shelter, and the need was almost as painful as the cold that held him in its icy embrace.

He looked back over his shoulder. No sign of the lobos. He turned back and saw the shape, almost as insubstantial as a shadow in the falling snow, off to his right. He squinted at it and then turned the horse and headed for it.

The shadow solidified as he came closer to it.

"A cabin!" Tess cried.

"Line shack, looks like. We must be on Carlisle range." He got out of the saddle and then helped Tess dismount. He led her into the shack, found a lamp, lit it, and then went and got the sorrel and brought it inside the shack. Hastily, he stripped his gear from it and then looped his

154

rope around its neck and tethered it to the iron leg of the single cot in the one-room building.

He searched the shack until he found what he was looking for.

"What are you doing?"

"We could do with a fire, Tess," he said as he poured grain from the sack he had found into a tin cup and then sloshed whiskey from the bottle he had found on a shelf into it. He mixed the two with his fingers and then fed the sorrel by hand.

"You think more of that horse than you do of yourself," Tess commented as she knelt and started a fire in the fireplace, her tone faintly accusatory.

"Tess, this horse means more to me right now than all the money in any bank you might want to name. He's our way out of here. He might mean the difference between life and death for us."

Tess turned to him, a puzzled look on her face.

Cimarron didn't answer the question he saw in her eyes, because the howl of a wolf outside the shack answered it for him.

He went to the door and bolted it. Then he shuttered the shack's single window.

11

Cimarron and Tess ate a meal of baked beans and hardtack as the lobos prowled and howled outside the line shack, both of them silent, lost in their own thoughts.

Cimarron picked up his tin cup that was filled with coffee, looked at it a moment, and then set it down without touching it. He got up, took another cup from the wall shelf, and sloshed whiskey into it. He emptied the cup faster than he had filled it as the sorrel to his left pawed the dirt floor.

As Tess watched him, he poured more whiskey into the cup and downed that too.

"My mother used to say," she began tentatively, "that at first whiskey unlocked the door to dreams but later the door to nightmares."

"Every man lives with a nightmare or two in the back of his mind, Tess. Lucky's the man who gets through life without at least one to give him some sleepless nights and maybe the shakes too from time to time."

Tess cleared her throat. "Maybe it would help if you'd talk about it."

"About what?"

"What's troubling you. I can see that something is." In a less somber voice, she added, "Maybe there's something I can do to help."

Cimarron shook his head and reached for the whiskey bottle. He practically filled the cup. "Nobody can help."

"A woman?"

He looked up at her and then raised the cup to his lips. He drank, put down the cup, and said, "A dead woman." He wiped his lips with the back of his hand. "I haven't had much time to think about her lately. But now—here—it's pretty quiet, except for those damned lobos

156

outside, and it's almost as if she were here with me, as if I could see her as plain as I can see you."

"You loved her?"

Cimarron pinched his closed eyes between the thumb and index finger of his right hand. "I don't know. Maybe I did. I do know I liked her a lot." He paused. "She said she loved me. My son——"

"I didn't know you were married."

"I'm not."

"What was her name?"

"Lila." Cimarron opened his eyes and reached for the bottle, but then withdrew his hand before touching it. Words began to flood from him as he told Tess what had happened at Lila's cabin. When he had finished his account of the tragedy, he propped his elbows on the table and dropped his head in his hands.

"I'm so very sorry," Tess said softly and reached out to place a hand over one of his.

"Me too."

She sat at the table without moving, her hand still on Cimarron's, as he squeezed his eyes shut again and then, knocking her hand aside, wiped the tears from his eyes with both fists.

"I'm sorry," he said a moment later, his face grave. "I didn't mean to slap your hand away like I did. It was just that——" He made a vague gesture.

"We are such frail creatures, and——" Tess began, but Cimarron angrily interrupted her.

"There's nothing frail about me!"

She ignored his outburst and continued, "Our bodies are so vulnerable to so many diseases and injuries. But our hearts—ah, there lies a story to be told. Our hearts sing one moment and lie shattered within us the next. We love and sometimes we lose that love. It's a miracle that we pick up the pieces of our lives and go on."

"You're talking about your husband?"

Tess nodded, lowering her head.

Cimarron reached out and took her hand. "Your son loved him too. Him and me, we had a talk."

Tess looked up. "Brendan idolized his father. But I've told you all about that. Your Lila, what was she like?"

"Well, first off, I've got to say she wasn't my Lila. I mean, she couldn't belong to anybody, not that woman.

Most independent woman I've ever known. She was—I don't know how to tell you how nice she was."

"Someday there'll be another woman, Cimarron. You'll marry. Have children."

"I don't know." He ran his fingers through his hair. "It does get lonely living the kind of life I do. When I'm having a woman"—he glanced almost apologetically at Tess as if he expected to see disapproval on her face—"part of me holds back. It's almost as if I'm not sure she'd really want to be with me if she knew me for what I really am."

"I know you for what you really are."

He shook his head as he heard the ghost of the father he had murdered howl outside the shack with the wolves.

Undaunted, Tess continued, "You're a man I would trust with my purse or my life. You're both enterprising and courageous, and, at times, a gentleman."

"Gentleman?" Cimarron echoed, not looking at Tess. "I didn't tell you what I did to that Creek who killed Lila and my son."

"Even a gentleman must seek vengeance when he has been greatly wronged. Perhaps it is not vengeance at all that he is really seeking at such times. Perhaps it is justice."

Cimarron stared at her, hearing the echo of her words.

"I'm not young anymore," she said, dropping her eyes. "I'm not pretty—certainly not at the moment, I'm not. But in the dark—with the lamp out—you could be with me and pretend I'm Lila. It might help to ease the hurt you're suffering."

"I couldn't do that. You shouldn't even think it."

"I was wrong. I shouldn't have said anything about Lila. But the rest of what I said—what I'm offering you—I mean it only as a kindness." She pointed to the bottle. "This won't help. I might be able to. At least for the time we are together here."

Cimarron glanced to his left at the cot to which his sorrel was tethered.

When he looked back at Tess, she was reaching for the lamp. She raised its globe and blew it out.

He watched her rise from the table and move through the room that was suddenly filled with shadows cast by the flickering light of the fire in the fireplace.

The sorrel nickered softly as she sat down on the cot, and its springs squeaked.

"You don't have to do this, Tess."

"I know I don't. I want to do it. For you. For both of us."

He watched her drape her dress and her underclothing over a chair and then slip beneath the blanket covering the cot.

He got up from the table and moved through the shadows to the bed, where he quickly stripped and got under the blanket with her.

Neither of them moved for a moment, and then Tess turned on her side and put an arm around him.

He moved closer to her, turning his head in order to see her face. As the warmth of her body seeped into his own, he embraced her.

They lay there locked together without speaking for some time as the night outside the shack was pierced by the mournful howls of the still-prowling wolves.

He kissed her lightly on the mouth and then rested his head in the crook of her arm. He was not sure just how it happened, whether she had made the first move or he had, but he was hard and she was soft and she was whispering to him and he was whispering to her and their bodies, seeming to act of their own volition, joined together into a single world of pleasure that soon soared into ecstasy.

Their world exploded and drifted down around them as they lay quietly on the cot, Cimarron still covering Tess, their arms around one another, their breathing the only sound in the firelit shack. It began again with a slow ascent they shared just as they shared kisses, touches, and still more kisses. Higher they went, and Tess cried out as Cimarron lunged into her as far as he could go, her nails bitting into the flesh of his back as he moaned, his body trembling and aflame.

Her breath on his neck was hot and her body beneath him was hotter. He raised his head and kissed her, and she eagerly returned his kiss, his hands rising and clasping her head between them, her legs wrapped tightly around his thighs.

Their kiss ended. Cimarron withdrew from her. They adjusted their bodies and, once as comfortable and as

159

close together as they could get, they let sleep settle on them and blot out the world and the wolves that filled it.

Cimarron stood fully dressed the next morning at the window he had unshuttered and stared out at the white and now wolfless world upon which the sun streamed silently down.

It was still cold, but no wind blew now and already patches of ice were falling from tree branches as the snow began to surrender to the onslaught of the sun that was already high in the sky.

Near to noon, he thought. I keep this up and I'll sleep my life away. He turned from the window when he heard Tess stir.

She looked up at him sleepily and then smiled. "Good morning, Cimarron."

"It is that—a real good morning—and it was a good night—the best—and I thank you for making it so for me."

"You look rested. Relaxed."

"Tess, a real woman like you—a good and kind and considerate woman like the kind you are—she can rest and relax a man like me."

"You're all right then?" she asked tentatively, her voice low.

"I'm all right. You did your best to soothe me, and you helped some. But if the truth's to be told, it'll be a while—maybe a long while—before my hurt's altogether healed." He went over to the cot, leaned down, and kissed her lightly. "But your brand of doctoring eased both my body and my mind." He straightened up and smiled down at her. "I've made coffee. I'll get you a cup. No, don't get up. Stay put right where you are. I'll be but a minute."

He crossed the room, took the pot from the fire, filled a tin cup with coffee, and carried it to the cot. He sat down beside Tess and handed the cup to her. "It's hot as the hinges of hell," he warned her, "so watch out."

She thanked him and then, when she shivered, he got up and shuttered the window.

He resumed his seat on the cot beside her and kissed her again, this time on the cheek.

The blanket she had wrapped around herself slipped, baring her left breast.

160

He lowered his head and kissed its nipple and then wrapped the blanket around her again. "I thought we'd skip breakfast, if that's all right with you. We've got some riding to do, and the sooner we do it, the better."

She nodded and drank some more coffee.

He got up from the cot and stretched. "It's a pretty day waiting for us out there. You'll see. I'm going out to have a look around and try to figure out exactly where we are. Be right back."

Once outside, he looked up at the sun and then off to the horizon. He walked around the shack and saw, in the distance south of the Cimarron River, the peaks of the Glass Mountains, which were white with snow and would have been white without snow, he knew, because of the millions of selenite crystals that covered their gypsum surfaces.

He returned to the shack and told Tess, "I've got my bearings now, thanks to the sun and the glimpse I got of the Glass Mountains south of us."

She was dressed, and she waited while he fed some more grain to the sorrel before saddling and bridling it. She followed him as he led the horse from the shack and shielded her eyes from the glare of the sun on the snow as she came outside.

He helped her into the saddle and then mounted the sorrel himself.

They rode in a northeasterly direction.

"Where are we going?" Tess asked.

"I'm taking you to the Carlisle ranch—to Brendan. Then I'll be riding on alone."

"Where are you going?"

"Up to the border to try to put a stop to any shooting that anybody might be planning on starting. All I hope is I'm not too late. I'm hoping that blizzard kept the soldiers and the settlers from reaching for one another's throats."

"Snow in April," Tess mused.

"It's March."

"You've lost track of the days, Cimarron. Today is April first."

"Guess I have at that. Been paying attention to more important things than what day it is."

"In New York City snow in April would be a rarity."

"Well, out here spring comes late sometimes. But even

when it does come early, you can still get your share of snow. It's good for the crops to come. I've heard folks say, 'Year of snow, crops will grow.' We've had a lot of snow in the Territory this past winter. Maybe that means a bumper crop come harvest time."

"The snow is melting fast," Tess observed.

"Glad it is. Makes traveling easier."

They were silent then as they rode on.

It was Tess who finally broke the silence. "I owe you an apology, Cimarron. I encouraged Brendan to join that gang Mr. Lomax organized to get you. I'm so glad they didn't find you."

"Oh, they found me all right."

"What happened?"

"Well, it wasn't what you could call an amicable meeting, no, sir, and no, ma'am, it sure wasn't."

"They didn't hurt you, did they?"

"Nope." Another lie, Cimarron thought. How come a man has to lie so much to keep from hurting other people?

"I'm relieved to hear that. It was just that—I don't know if you can understand why I wanted Brendan to go with those other men when they went after you. You see, I was so angry with you for trying to keep us from settling down here in the Strip. To me, you were the one person who was trying to destroy the dream I'd cherished for so long and fought for so hard."

"There's all kinds of ways to make dreams come true, Tess. If one way won't work, a person ought to try another."

"I'm afraid I don't follow you."

"I'm not surprised you don't. You weren't meant to understand, not yet anyways."

"Cimarron, you are a puzzle sometimes!"

"I am? Why, all along I thought I was about as easy to read as any primer Mr. McGuffey ever wrote."

Tess laughed.

"There it is," Cimarron said, pointing. "The Carlisle ranch."

"Oh, I'm so eager to see Brendan!"

"I reckon I ought to prepare you for what you might see." Cimarron told her about Brendan's accident.

"Do you think he'll be all right?" Tess asked anxiously.

162

"He's young and he's strong. I see no reason why he shouldn't mend in next to no time."

They had ridden for only a short distance when Brendan hobbled out of the front door of the ranch house on a cane that had been made from the limb of a shin oak, its end under his armpit bulbous as a result of having been wound with multicolored pieces of cloth.

"Brendan!" Tess cried and waved, although they were too far away for him to hear her.

As they rode up in front of the house, Cimarron dropped down from the saddle and then helped Tess dismount. He tethered the sorrel to the hitch rail as Tess ran to Brendan and embraced him.

"Hey!" he shouted. "You'll break my neck holding on so tight, and I already have a broken leg." He freed himself from her embrace and made his way to where Cimarron stood. He held out his hand and said, "I know you'd find her." He shook hands with Cimarron. "I told everybody you would."

"Well, I tried, and I guess I got lucky."

Brendan shook his head. "It wasn't luck. It was you."

"Brendan," Tess exclaimed, "there were wolves—ever so many of them, and Cimarron killed one of them with his knife and then the others—" Her gaze, frankly admiring, fell on Cimarron.

"I used to be a pretty good pig-sticker," he commented, "when the smokehouse back home was all fired up, so that old wolf gave me no trouble at all."

"Cimarron!" Dean rushed out onto the porch. "Pa's a whole lot better. He still wants to talk to you. Come on inside."

Cimarron let himself be led into the house with Tess and Brendan following him. "Dean," he said, "this is Mrs. O'Malley, Brendan's mother."

"Pleased to meet you, ma'am."

Victoria appeared in the doorway leading to the west wing and halted, her eyes on Tess.

Cimarron caught the coldness in her gaze, and he quickly said, "Victoria, Mrs. O'Malley here told me she wanted to apologize to you just as soon as she got here. Tess?"

Tess turned swiftly toward him.

"Tess, are you about to make me out a liar? Is a good

Christian woman like yourself going to drag my good name through the mud?"

Tess softened. She smiled sweetly. "What I was about to say was that I did not tell you I intended to apologize to Miss Littleton *as soon as we got here*. I told you I intended to see my son first."

"I guess I misunderstood you."

Tess went over to Victoria, and Cimarron heard a few murmured words pass between them. He watched as the two women shook hands—a little stiffly, he thought.

"Cimarron, there's somebody else here who wants to talk to you like Pa does," Dean told him.

"Somebody else?"

"Mrs. Lomax."

"Orajean? She's here?" Cimarron pushed his hat back on his head and stared in disbelief at Dean, who merely nodded and then said, "She's in the privy out back—or was. She's—"

"Here I am, Dean. Oh, Cimarron, you're here at last!" Orajean ran from the doorway and threw her arms around Cimarron, who stared over her shoulder at Tess and Victoria, who were both regarding him with amused expressions on their faces.

"What in the world are you doing here, Orajean?" he asked her as she released him and stepped back.

"I'm going with you."

"You're going with me?" Cimarron scratched his head. "Where are you going with me?"

"East!"

"You're going east with me?"

"I've made up my mind," Orajean announced loud enough, Cimarron thought, for the wole world to hear her. "That man I saw you with in the lobby of the hotel in Kiowa—Mr. Doby. He told me you were coming here. Well, I got my horse from the livery and I came here after you. But once we get to Fort Smith I'm afraid we'll have to part."

"Part," Cimarron echoed numbly.

"Yes. You see, I'm going downriver from there." She leaned over and whispered the rest of what she had to say in his ear. "To New Orleans. I've heard wicked stories about that city, so that's where I'm going. I told you when we were in bed back in Kiowa that I intended to be will-

164

ful from now on. Well, I do. What I didn't tell you is that I'm through for now and forever with being a prim and proper wife and lady. I found out something about myself that has absolutely changed my life in an astonishing fashion!"

"What'd you find out, honey?" Cimarron managed to get out.

Orajean's words, though whispered, were a shout of triumph, a declaration of more than mere independence. "I found out— Are you listening to me?" When Cimarron nodded, she continued, "I found out that I'm really a whore at heart, and I never knew it until I left Bill Lee and bedded those two men and then you!"

Stunned, Cimarron could only nod.

Suddenly, the sound of a cow bell pealed through the house.

"What the hell—" Cimarron turned toward the sound, which was coming from the west wing.

"That's Pa's bell," Dean said. "He wants something or somebody. He's still bedridden."

"Well, I'll go see what he wants," Cimarron volunteered, "seeing as how he wants to have a talk with me anyways. You all will excuse me, I hope." He crossed the room and made his way into Carlisle's bedroom.

"You!" Carlisle bellowed at him from the bed. "I figured you'd turn up sooner or later. Probably later. I told Dean to tell you that I wanted to have a talk with you, Cimarron. That was *yesterday!*"

"I've been busy. I see you're still giving orders to everybody you set eyes on."

"Sit down and don't talk back to your elders."

Cimarron went over to the bed and sat down in a chair next to it.

Carlisle grunted.

"I've decided to pay those damned savages a grazing fee!" he announced without preamble, looking as if he had just been bitten by a wasp.

"Well, now, isn't that good news?"

"Not for me, it isn't good news. It means I'll probably be bankrupt before the year is out." He glared at Cimarron. "That will square me with the law, won't it? With you?"

"It will, Carlisle. But as to working out the details, you'd best deal direct with Mr. Marcus Doby."

"Me do business with that damned Indian?"

"That Cherokee Indian, who happens to be a member of the tribal council and the legislature, has had to deal with conniving sonsabitches from the Bureau of Indian Affairs, so I'm next to sure he won't mind too much doing a bit of business with a stump-jumping, shit-kicking, conniving, *and* cantankerous cattleman like yourself."

Carlisle sat up in bed, his glare deepening, his mouth opening and closing, his fists clenching on the blanket covering him.

Cimarron calmly met his gaze. He raised an eyebrow questioningly.

Carlisle collapsed on the bed in a fit of laughter. "Did you hear the whippersnapper?" he boomed to no one, his body bouncing in the bed as he continued laughing, unable to control himself. "Calling me a stump-jumping—what else did you call me, Cimarron?"

"A stump-jumping, shit-kicking, conniving, *and* cantankerous cattleman."

Carlisle jabbed a finger in Cimarron's direction. He tried to speak but could only continue laughing until tears ran down both of his cheeks.

Recovering finally, he said, "I'll talk to Doby and make the arrangements."

"By the way, Carlisle, did Dean tell you how he helped me hunt for Mrs. O'Malley? How he brought her broken-legged boy back here all by himself in a blizzard that was blowing Sunday right out of the week?"

"He did that? He didn't tell me. Not a word, he didn't."

"I'm telling you that you've got a son any man would be proud to flaunt before the world."

Carlisle looked away. Then he looked back at Cimarron. "Do you think I can make it up to the boy?"

"The *boy?*"

"To my son?"

"You didn't build up this fine ranch without a heap of trying, I reckon, and you don't look to me like a man about to quit trying to do whatever needs doing."

"It's good to see you again, Cimarron," Carlisle said softly. "I swear I never did meet a man like you before."

"I'll take that as a compliment, Carlisle."

"To tell you the truth, I'm not sure whether I meant it as one."

Cimarron smiled and, a moment later, so did Carlisle.

"Pa."

Cimarron turned to find Dean standing in the doorway of the bedroom.

"Pa, Johnny Warren just drove the supply wagon in. I was talking to him out front. He says he heard shooting as he drove out of Kiowa. He's pretty sure it was either the soldiers shooting at the settlers or the other way around. Maybe both."

Cimarron was on his feet at once and striding across the room. "Will you ride into town for me, Dean?"

"Sure I will."

"Find Marcus Doby and bring him back here."

"Where are you going now, Cimarron?" Carlisle yelled from the bed. "You just got here!"

"Be seeing you, Carlisle," Cimarron called over his shoulder and then moved swiftly through the house with Dean trailing him.

Once outside, the men mounted their horses and rode north at a gallop. As they neared the border, Cimarron veered northwest and Dean continued heading due north toward Kiowa.

Cimarron heard the sound of the shooting before he saw the men who were doing it, and he reined in his sorrel a moment after spotting the troops spread out in a skirmish line just ahead of him. He gazed north and was surprised to see that there were no wagons in sight. But there were men south of the border, and they were firing on the troops.

He turned his horse and rode west and then north again. Now he was able to make out the figure of Lomax crouching behind the men, none of whom he recognized, and shouting orders from his relatively safe vantage point.

Where the hell, he asked himself, were the settlers? Who was doing Lomax's work for him?

He decided to get the answer to his first question. He circled around to the west and, when he arrived at the settlers' camp, found the wagons he had expected to see on the border.

People looked up at him as he rode into camp, his eyes

roaming from face to face. When he spotted the brawny man he had seen trying to comfort Tess during the earlier attempt at a border crossing, he rode up to him and asked, "What's going on down there south of the border?"

"Lomax hired some guns in town," the man answered.

"You boys don't do your own fighting, is that it?"

The man looked down at the ground. "Most of us are family men. We want land and we want to homestead, but we aren't willing to kill to get what we want."

"Sounds to me like you got a camp full of sensible fellows and Kiowa's got more'n its share of gunfighters."

"Those men who are doing all that shooting aren't really gunfighters. They're merchants, most of them, and they want to see Kiowa turn into a boom town and themselves get rich once the Cherokee strip starts getting settled." The man paused a moment and then said, "My name's Michael Maguire. You wouldn't happen to have seen Mrs. O'Malley, would you? She left the camp and I've—we've been worried about her."

"Don't doubt for a minute that you're worried about her, Maguire. I noticed how you showed some concern for her when all those wheels were falling off your wagons a while back. I take it you'd like to meet up with her again."

"I would indeed, Mr.—"

"Cimarron."

"Tess—Mrs. O'Malley's a fine woman, she is that."

"Maguire, she's at a ranch owned by a man named Carlisle. Now I want you to herd these people down south to that ranch."

"Why?"

"I'll tell you why."

After Cimarron had done so, Maguire let out a whoop of delight and threw his hat into the air.

"Go east," Cimarron ordered him, "and then, once you've cleared Kiowa, head due south."

"Thanks, Cimarron! We owe you a lot, we most surely do."

"You've still got a ways to go before you get what you've all got your hearts set on, so you'd best be moving out."

"Listen to me!" Maguire yelled to the settlers. "We're heading south!"

Cimarron didn't hear the rest of Maguire's shouted words because he was galloping back the way he had come.

When he spotted Lomax, he drew rein and leaped from the saddle. He made his way stealthily on foot toward the man, his six-gun in his hand.

Lomax never heard him until Cimarron was standing directly behind his quarry and the barrel of his Colt was pressed against the small of Lomax's back.

"Lomax."

"Who—"

"Walk backwards and don't attract anybody's attention. Let's go!"

"Cimarron!"

"The same. Now move, Lomax!" When they reached the sorrel, Cimarron said, "Get aboard."

When Lomax was seated in the saddle, Cimarron climbed into it also and galloped toward the eastern end of the townsmen's skirmish line, where he halted his horse and let out a loud yell which attracted the attention of Lomax's hired guns.

"I'm taking your boss to Fort Smith to stand trial for trespassing on Indian lands!" he yelled. "Has he paid you yet for the work you're doing for him?"

"No!" someone yelled back.

"Well then, I have to say that it sure don't make any kind of sense to me to see you boys chancing getting yourselves killed for free!"

One of the men broke from the skirmish line and came running toward the sorrel. "Lomax, you owe us and I aim to collect!"

Cimarron put a bullet into the ground directly in front of the man's boots, halting him. He gestured with his gun, and the man hurriedly backed away.

As the townmen's skirmish line began to crumble, he turned the sorrel, spurred it, and rode south at a gallop until he reached the troops. "Captain Soames!" he yelled, his hands cupped around his mouth.

When Soames came running up to him, he said, "Told you I'd be back. I think maybe now you can march your boys back to Fort Supply."

"In the midst of this battle?" Soames spluttered.

"What battle?"

Soames pointed north.

"I don't hear any shooting, Captain. The other side seems to have had enough."

Soames watched incredulously as the gunmen withdrew and headed back toward Kiowa.

"Why, they're retreating!" he declared. "We've won the day!"

"It's clear your men were the superior force, Captain. Have yourselves a good trip back to Fort Supply."

Soames shook his head. "We'll remain here. There might be further trouble."

"There won't be, Captain. I can guarantee it."

"Look there!" Soames shouted. "Wagons—crossing the border."

Before Soames could shout an order to his troops, Cimarron told him where the wagons were going and why there was no need to stop them.

Captain Soames nodded and then held up his hand to Cimarron, who shook it, turned his horse, and continued riding south, Lomax cursing in the saddle behind him.

When Cimarron had finished tying Lomax's ankles and wrists, he left his prisoner lying on the floor of the tack shed, went outside, and padlocked the shed's door.

As he came around to the front of the Carlisle ranch, he found that the first of the settlers had arrived, Maguire's wagon leading them.

He went up to Maguire and said, "I'll get Doby if he's here and be right back."

He found Doby inside the house talking to Victoria Littleton.

"Cimarron!" Doby exclaimed when he saw him. "Dean Carlisle came to get me in Kiowa and— Is there going to be trouble?"

"Not now, there isn't. The troops are probably on their way back to Fort Supply by now and the settlers are gathering outside waiting for you to tell them about the arrangements you've made for them."

"I still think you've made a bad decision, Marcus," Victoria said sharply.

"Perhaps," Doby admitted.

"Victoria," Cimarron said, "the world out west here's changing, and it's changing fast. Towns are springing up all over. Railroads are poking down into the Territory, and all the way across it too. What Marcus is doing is the sensible thing, though I'll admit it may not be the happiest thing from the Cherokee point of view."

"Call it bowing to the inevitable, Cimarron," Doby said without bitterness.

Orajean suddenly appeared in the doorway leading to the east wing. "Victoria, where's the salt?"

As Victoria answered her question, Orajean yelped at the sight of Cimarron.

"You're back! Now don't you go away. I'm busy in the kitchen but I won't be forever!"

She disappeared.

"Let's go outside," Cimarron suggested.

As they left the house, Cimarron pointed to the seat of Maguire's wagon. "Climb up there, Marcus, so they can all see and hear you."

Doby did, and Cimarron leaned back against the wall, his arms folded and his ankles crossed, listening as Doby told the gathered crowd about the arrangements he had made for them to settle in Cherokee Nation.

". . . and in addition to my land you may also settle on the lands owned by two of my friends," Doby was saying. "You will be granted resident permits by Cherokee Nation and you will be asked, in turn, to accept tenant-farmer status under the terms of which you will give your landlords part of your annual crops in exchange for a right to live on and use the land granted to each of you."

Victoria came out of the house. "Well, you've settled it, I guess."

"In a way that's better than bloodshedding," Cimarron remarked. He glanced at her. "You'll be going back to New York now?"

She shook her head. "Cimarron, I didn't mean to lead you on. I hope you won't be angry when I tell you the news."

"What news?"

"About Dean. I think I'm in love with him."

"Why, that's *good* news!"

"I thought you might be angry. I thought you might have imagined that I—that you and I—"

"Hell, honey, I haven't got that wild of an imagination. A good-looking and educated eastern woman like yourself and a lout like me? It wouldn't've worked out."

"You're wrong," she said, smiling, "and you are not a lout. I think it would have worked out fine, but then Dean came along and——well, I'm just glad you understand. These things happen."

"Oh, I understand all right. You've got eyes as bright as a prairie fire lately and they get even brighter, I've noticed, when Dean's around."

A cheer went up from the settlers.

"I'll get pencil and paper," Doby told them. "You can all sign your names and I'll arrange for the allocation of acreage to each of you."

Another cheer went up from the crowd as Doby climbed down from the wagon and came up to Cimarron. "By the way, Cimarron, did you see Lomax up north?"

"Got him hog-tied out back in the tack shed."

"What will happen to him?" Victoria asked.

"Probably Judge Parker will slap him with a fine. Maybe he'll sit in jail for a spell. Whatever happens, he'll have learned his lesson, I'll wager."

"I've talked to Mr. Carlisle, Cimarron," Doby said. "He's prepared to sign a lease for the land he's using here in the Outlet."

"I hope you got a good price out of the old curmudgeon."

"Forty cents a head for full-grown cattle and twenty-five for stock under two years of age. Did you know Carlisle's got two thousand head, give or take a few, and most of them full-grown?"

"Bet he had apoplexy by the time you two'd concluded your deal."

"He did raise an objection or two at first, but I managed to make him see things my way."

"Oh, no, you damn well didn't!" Carlisle thundered as he came out of the house to glare at Doby. "It was duress, pure and simple." He turned to Cimarron. "I only went along because you threatened to throw my ass——beg pardon, Miss Littleton——in that Fort Smith jail of yours if I didn't."

"I never——" Cimarron began, but Carlisle's grin silenced him.

172

"Cimarron, you're back!" Tess cried as she came out of the house. She yawned. "What's going on out here? I was taking a nap and all the commotion woke me."

"Maguire!" Cimarron yelled, and when Maguire came running up to them, he said, "You'll want to be telling Mrs. O'Malley that she's to start living on land in Cherokee Nation."

"Cherokee Nation?" Tess asked, looking from Cimarron to Maguire and then back again.

"It's not going to be too much of a change for you, I reckon," Cimarron said to her.

"What are you talking about?" she asked him, frowning.

"Maguire's not a name that's all that different from O'Malley."

"Cimarron!" Tess exclaimed, her face reddening as she avoided looking at Maguire.

"Tess," Maguire said, "Cimarron's right. You must have known I wanted to ask you to marry me."

Tess gave him a shy glance.

Cimarron said, "Have at it, Maguire. Now's as good a time as any."

"Tess, will you marry me and help me raise my boy?"

"Mr. Maguire," Tess said primly, "is a widower. He has a nine-year-old son and he—"

"And he asked you an important question, Tess," Cimarron prompted.

"Michael—yes, Michael, I will marry you if you'll have me."

"Have you?" Maguire shouted. "Have you indeed!" He threw his arms around Tess's waist and lifted her off her feet. "You think Brendan will like it where we're going?" he asked as he put her down.

"He won't be coming with us, Michael."

"He's staying here," Carlisle interjected. "I've made Dean foreman of the ranch so that I could get the rest I've so richly deserved but have been deprived of for more years than I care to count. The first thing Dean went and did is hire Brendan as a hand. According to Dean, he'll make a top hand out of Brendan in less time than it takes a preacher to pass the collection plate. The pair of them went out in the spring wagon to tally the stock for Doby."

"Carlisle," Cimarron said, "there's something you can do for me if you've a mind to."

"Name it and it's done."

"That book I saw in your library. The one by that fellow Marcus Aurelius. I'd be obliged to you if you'd let me borrow it. I'll get back this way someday and I'll return it to you then."

Carlisle disappeared inside the house, and when he reappeared he had the copy of Marcus Aurelius in his hand. He gave it to Cimarron. "No need to return it. It's yours."

"Thanks, Carlisle. Appreciate it. Well, I'd best be starting back to Fort Smith now."

"Not without me, you won't," Orajean declared as she appeared in the doorway, flour smudging her face and covering both of her hands.

"You'll leave tomorrow, Cimarron," Carlisle decided peremptorily. "But tonight we'll all have ourselves a party to celebrate the way things have turned out."

"I've been baking a cake for when you returned, Cimarron," Orajean declared.

"That sure is awful nice of you, honey."

"Oh, I just can't wait to get to New Orleans!" she cried, clapping her hands and sending small puffs of flour into the air. She threw her arms around Cimarron's neck and gave him a floury hug.

As the others made their way into the house, Carlisle, his wistful eyes on Orajean's jauntily swiveling hips, said, "I envy you the company you'll have on your ride back to Fort Smith."

"I don't look forward to riding back with Bill Lee Lomax, who is, by the way, trussed up out back in your tack shed."

Carlisle turned and glared at Cimarron. "That's not what I meant, and you damn well know it isn't!"

Cimarron, grinning, put an arm around Carlisle's shoulders, and together they entered the house.

1

The trail he was following suddenly veered to the left, so Cimarron turned the blood bay beneath him and rode south toward the ambling north fork of the Canadian River.

When he reached it, he rode out into the shallow water, and upon emerging on the opposite bank he searched along it in both directions until he found the spot where Jake Farley had ridden out of the river.

The hooves of Farley's horse had made three sharp impressions in the ground and one that was blunted, the latter the result of the shoe the animal had thrown which Cimarron had found many miles back along the trail, one bent nail still clinging to it.

Farley was heading west now, and Cimarron, judging by the spacing of Farley's mount's hoofprints, knew he was galloping. If he keeps up this pace, he thought, he's liable to find himself a man on foot before too long. He smiled.

He had not ridden far when he came to an expanse of dunes. The sand of which they were composed had once been part of the river bottom but now lay unevenly humped under the bright July sun.

He kept as close to the riverbank as he could without losing sight of Farley's trail in order to avoid the dunes, which would slow his pursuit by providing uncertain footing for his bay. But as the westerly wind began to rise, it sent particles of sand swirling up into the air, which stung his face and hands.

He pulled his blue bandanna up until it covered his nose and the lower part of his face and rode on, squinting down at Farley's trail, which was gradually being erased by the wind as it whipped across the surface of the dunes. But the trail was still visible when Cimarron left the dunes behind him and continued riding west into a heavily timbered area which was dominated by black-barked oaks.

He pulled down his bandanna as the bay moved through the thick shadows of the densely packed trees, its hooves shattering some of the many brittle branches which littered the forest floor. Soon it emerged into an area of ragged sunlight which fell through the leafless branches of many dead trees.

Cimarron noted the holes and glyphs in the trees' trunks which had been made by boring beetles. The beetles had also begun to bore, he noticed, into other oaks nearby, which, he knew, would ultimately succumb to the devastation wrought by the beetles as they bored between the bark and the wood of the still-living trees.

The bay moved out of the sun and into the cool shade of the forest again, and as it did so, Cimarron used his bandanna to wipe the sweat from his face. He bent down low over his horse's neck to avoid low-hanging branches, and later, as the bay came out of the forest into the sun flooding the Osage Plains, he pulled his black slouch hat down low on his forehead and squinted into the distance.

The plain was covered with plants and grasses, all of them lusty with life beneath the sun which indiscriminately nourished them. Bunch grass predominated, but in places there were clusters of crested wheat grass, and Cimarron didn't miss the several broken stalks directly ahead of him. He began to move forward again, scanning the vast plain which stretched out around him and noting the crushed plants in his path, fleabane and dock among them.

He continued riding at a fast trot until he saw the low-growing branches of a wild rose bush ahead of him move and then become still. He halted the bay, his eyes on the bush.

Snake? He sat his saddle, watching, and when a jackrabbit bounded up from beneath the rose bush where it had been lying, his eyes followed its erratic flight.

Something's wrong with that critter, he thought. Then he saw the dried blood on the animal's rear legs. Something almost got it, he thought. It's near to dead.

His stomach rumbled with hunger, and he swallowed the saliva that suddenly filled his mouth. As the rabbit went to ground again, unable to continue its flight, he got out of the saddle and walked over to it.

When he reached the animal, it tried to rise, its eyes wide with fright, but it could only stir slightly while its nose twitched and its front paws made feeble movements.

Cimarron stared down at it in disgust and disappointment. There were other wounds on the animal's body, he now saw. Maggots squirmed in most of them. The critter's not fit to look at, let alone eat, he thought. He went back to the bay, swung into the saddle, and continued following Farley, occasionally dismounting to examine the ground for sign.

When he spotted horse droppings, he knew he was not far behind Farley, because they were still moist despite the blazing heat of the merciless sun which was wringing sweat from his face and body.

When the sun above him momentarily darkened, he looked up, expecting to see a cloud. There was none. But there was a golden eagle soaring in the sky, and the bird, as it flew between Cimarron and the sun, had blocked the light. It flew high, its wings spread wide as it rode the updrafts, banking off them as elegantly and as effortlessly as if it were a part of the wind itself.

Cimarron reached behind him, and his right hand closed on the stock of his booted '73 model center-fire Winchester.

But he let go of the rifle, his eyes following the flight of the eagle. You shoot, he warned himself silently, and

177

the noise you make'll likely as not bring Jake Farley gunning for you if he's anywhere in the neighborhood.

But, he thought, I just might be able to turn that eagle into my dinner without firing a single shot. I've seen how the Indians do it. Maybe I can do it too.

He turned the bay and galloped back to where he had last seen the jackrabbit.

It was still there and still alive but barely so. He slid out of the saddle, scooped it up, got back in the saddle, and rode for the hummocks which rose out of the plain a little to the south. When he reached them, he selected a shady spot between two of them that would give him cover and then led the bay around behind the highest hummock and left it, its reins trailing, beneath a ragged outcropping. He rounded the hummock then and quickly tore up the grass and plants growing near it in order to expose the ground. He tossed them aside, and then, after tying a piggin string he took from his saddle around the rabbit's front legs, he dropped the animal on the ground and, playing out the piggin string, took shelter in the shade between the hummocks. He lay belly down on the ground without moving except for his right hand, which did move as, hidden under his chest, it jerked the piggin string and the jackrabbit scampered along the ground as it tried to escape.

He turned his head slightly so that he could see the sky. He waited a moment and then jerked the piggin string again, watching as the eagle dipped sharply, then circled, its head angling sharply to one side.

He pulled the piggin string once more and then let go of it as the eagle came plummeting down toward the rabbit that was still struggling to free itself. As the great golden bird spread its wings wide to brake its descent and its talons opened to seize its prey, Cimarron's right arm shot out and seized one of the eagle's legs. The bird screeched and began to struggle, its curved yellow beak descending again and again to tear the flesh on the back of Cimarron's hand. He sprang to his feet, and as the eagle's wings flapped furiously and its feathers flew into the air, he deftly wrung its neck.

He dropped the bird then and watched its body flop about on the ground for several minutes, its wings shuddering and its talons convulsing, before it finally lay lifeless at his feet.

He picked up his kill by the legs, boarded the bay, and rode for the river. When he reached it, he got out of the saddle and dropped the eagle into the cool water to rid it of its body heat, since he intended to skin and cook it immediately and he knew that body heat tended to give game a nauseating flavor.

He found a flat stone, pulled his knife from his right boot, and yanked the eagle out of the water. He girdled the skin of both legs with his knife, peeled the skin back, girdled the tail and anus, cut an abdominal incision from tail to rib cage, and then ripped the bird's internal organs free. He severed the bird's legs, wings, and head and then washed it in the river before gripping the bay's reins and walking to a stand of cedars, where, using broken branches he found on the ground, he made a spit and then a fire with his flint and steel.

He hunkered down before the fire he had made, slowly turning the spitted eagle and blowing on the smoke rising from the fire to disperse it so that it would not betray his presence in the cedar grove. He looked up and was pleased to see that the tendrils of smoke that had escaped him were being dissipated among the leaves of the overhanging branches.

When the bird was golden brown, he lifted the spit's crossbar with both hands and began to eat, tearing hungrily at the roasted flesh with his teeth and hardly taking time to chew as he sought to appease the hunger that was so strong within him.

When he had finished eating, no shred of meat remained on the bony carcass, which he tossed into the flames, causing them to spit and crackle as they consumed the grease on the bones they quickly began to char.

He rose and kicked out his fire, drank from his canteen, and then climbed aboard the bay and rode out of the cedar grove.

As he did so, two things immediately claimed his attention. East of him smoke was rising. Campfire, he thought. In the northwest, clouds of dust billowed in the air. Riders, he thought.

Both the smoke and the dust made him uneasy. Both

raised questions in his mind. Whose campfire had he spotted? Who were the invisible riders hidden in the swirling dust?

The answers to his questions were important at any time for a man riding alone almost anywhere, but here, in Indian Territory, he knew the answers were of major importance.

He rode back the way he had come and in among the cedars again. He watched the rising dust almost without blinking until he was able to make out the half-hidden figure of a man in the midst of it. Then, another. Both men, he saw a moment later, were wearing cavalry uniforms, and out of the dust behind them appeared other figures. Indians. The men mounted, the women on foot. All of them flanked by troopers, twelve in all.

He glanced south. No sign of smoke now. He left the protection of the trees and rode toward the cavalry's long line that was moving slowly in the dust hovering above the guards and the guarded alike.

When he reached the haggard officer with the rugged face who was leading the long column, he nodded a greeting. "Bound for the Darlington Indian Agency, are you, Lieutenant?"

"We are, sir."

"Cheyennes?" Cimarron asked, pointing to the Indians.

"Northern Cheyennes, yes. Major Linnett, the Fourth Cavalry's commanding officer at Fort Reno, sent us out to gather them up. It's been a long journey and they're tired. It's time we stopped to rest." The lieutenant turned in his saddle and spoke to the man riding behind him. "Sergeant, we'll halt here for a brief respite. See that our men and the Indians have enough water."

"Lieutenant, my name's Cimarron. I'm a deputy marshal out of Fort Smith and I'm hunting a horse thief by the name of Jake Farley. Did you happen to spot a lone rider heading west?"

"I did not," the lieutenant replied as he and Cimarron dismounted. "I'm Lieutenant Henry Kendrick." He held out his hand, and Cimarron shook it. "You're something of a rarity, I must say, Cimarron."

"Me?"

"I've never seen a marshal out here before."

"Deputy marshal."

"From what I've beeen told, deputy marshals are seldom seen west of the Katy railroad."

"Some of us do get farther west than that from time to time. Me for one." Cimarron watched the Indians as they stood or sat in silence. "They're a woebegone bunch if I ever saw one."

"It's been a long march for them. They were settled on the Red Cloud Agency up in Nebraska until someone in Washington, apparently in conjunction with the Central Superintendency in Lawrence, Kansas, decided they should be moved down here to the Cheyenne-Arapaho reservation."

"Those politicians, whether they happen to be back in Washington or up in Kansas, got themselves more ideas of what to do with these Indians than a dog has fleas."

"More is the pity," Kendrick commented.

"I take it you don't exactly relish marching them all over hell's half-acre."

"It is my duty. I do it." Kendrick glanced at the Cheyennes, all of them still silent and expressionless, and grimaced. "Most of them didn't want to come south. But they finally agreed to do so. They really had precious little choice in the matter, and they knew it. If you ask me, it's an injudicious decision, whoever made it. These northerners never did get along all that well with the southern Cheyennes, and now, with so many southerners already on the reservation down here, well, there's bound to be friction if not outright trouble of one sort or another."

"You called me a rarity before, Kendrick. Seems to me you're one yourself."

Kendrick's eyebrows arched questioningly.

"You're a pony soldier who's clearly got some sympathy for the Indians. Most troopers I've known in my time were either scared shitless of Indians or they wanted to kill as many of them as quick as they could."

"I've killed Indians," Kendrick said slowly. "I am not boasting. I am merely stating a fact. I've fought the plains tribes more times than I like to remember. But that was war. This . . ." Kendrick waved a hand toward the Cheyennes. "this is—well, it is not the kind of duty I prefer."

"Some of those writers in the eastern papers, they'd most likely call it shameful."

When Kendrick said nothing, Cimarron studied the Indians gathered in the distance. The men avoided his eyes; the women busied themselves with their babies and the packs strapped to the countless dogs among the group. He began to feel uncomfortable, as he always did in the presence of men who would not meet his eyes. Such men, he had long ago learned, were either dangerous or, as in the case of these Cheyenne braves, beaten.

"So you didn't see the man I'm trailing," he said finally, looking away from the Indians and back at Kendrick.

"I'm afraid not. He must be a very dangerous man for you to have come this far west looking for him."

"Jake Farley's not all that dangerous. Shifty, yes. Sly, yes. But no more dangerous than a sidewinder when you've got a big stick and some clout. I almost had him west of Wewoka but he gave me the slip. Well, Kendrick, I'd best be moseying along after him. It was a pleasure meeting up with you. Haven't had anybody to talk to in so long my tongue's turned rusty."

"Good luck, Cimarron. I hope you apprehend your man."

"I'll get him," Cimarron said as he stepped into the saddle and then, with a wave to Kendrick, rode west.

How long had it been? he asked himself. Days. He really wasn't sure exactly how many. But he was sure that he had used his tongue for more than talking when he had last met someone on the plains.

She had told him her name was Carrie. She was, she said, driving her team and wagon north to Tulsey Town in Creek Nation for supplies.

He had told her that was a coincidence, since he happened to be heading in the same direction, which was a lie, because he was heading southwest. But she had been pretty. Young and pretty, and she never seemed to stop smiling at him, and he felt warmed and encouraged by her smiles, and he almost whooped with delight when it began to rain and there was no shelter in sight on the plain.

They took cover under a tarpaulin in the bed of her spring wagon, and as the rain spattered it, they talked a little at first and then they touched a lot and before long he was on top of her and she was moaning with pleasure.

Cimarron, remembering Carrie now as he rode along, smiled to himself. He never did learn her last name, not that it mattered. But he had learned other things about her. He had learned that she was both passionate and, once she had gotten used to being where she was with him, uninhibited.

It's a wonder, he thought, that it ever got soft again on me considering the way she carried on with her teeth and her hot hands and her hotter tongue that she knew more ways to use on me than any other woman I ever had.

He glanced to the right. Kendrick had said he hadn't seen any lone rider. So it was likely that Farley was still heading west, although there was no way to be certain of that. He looked to the south and saw only the empty plain in that direction. Remembering the campfire smoke he had seen earlier when the cavalry came into sight, he looked back over his shoulder.

A rider. In the distance and coming toward him.

He drew rein and sat his saddle, watching the rider approach, his right hand resting on the butt of his Colt. He was surprised when the rider suddenly turned north. He continued watching until both horse and rider disappeared among the trees that were growing along the river.

Something's not right, he thought. Something's wrong. A rider doesn't ride in one direction and then up and change direction for no good reason I can spot.

Am I being trailed? he wondered. Or am I just getting spooked out here with a horse thief somewhere up ahead of me and somebody I don't know riding behind me?

He turned the bay and continued riding west, looking back over his shoulder from time to time but seeing no one behind him. Could the rider have been Jake Farley? Had the man doubled back and then come up behind me? This job I've got is getting to me, he thought. It's turning me as skittish as a bronc that's wearing a saddle for the first time. The rider was probably heading for the reservation, he decided. An Indian maybe. Probably. An Indian that got a sudden notion to turn north away

183

from the reservation? His explanation made little sense, and he knew it.

When he came to a dry wash, he rode down into it after a speculative glance in the direction of the timbered region to the north. He halted his horse and got out of the saddle. He waited a moment and then climbed up the low bank on his right. Taking off his hat, he peered over the edge of the bank. He saw only the trees near the river. He looked back over his shoulder and saw only the plain, littered in places with boulders. He clapped his hat back on his head and then slid down the bank. Taking the reins in one hand, he led his horse to the western end of the wash. He walked up its slight incline and then, when he saw nothing ahead of him—

But there was something ahead of him. In a grassless stretch of ground in the distance he saw the hoofprints. Three sharp. One blurred.

Farley.

He swung into the saddle and spurred the bay. As it came racing out of the wash, a shot rang out.

He turned the bay with one sharp tug on the reins, and as the horse galloped back down into the wash, he leaped from the saddle, drawing his Winchester from the boot. The bay ran on and then stopped, swinging its head around to look back at him.

He flattened his body against the sloping side of the wash and then scrambled up it to peer at the trees in the north. That rider I spotted, he told himself, must be holed up in those woods. He braced the barrel of his rifle on the level ground and sighted along it, waiting for the next shot from whoever it was who was trying to take him.

When the shot he had been expecting did come, it took him by surprise, because it came not from the trees but from behind him. Instantly, he slid down into the wash and then quickly scrambled up the other side to peer south, the direction from which the second shot had come.

You're a damn fool, he told himself angrily. You spot a rider heading north. You see trees in the north. You get yourself shot at. You figure the rider did the shooting from the trees. Damn fool, you jump to conclusions quicker'n some men jump another's claim.

The boulders.

His gaze darted from one to the next and on to the next. Any one of them was large enough for a bush-whacker to hide behind. One pile was almost as big as a battlement.

Minutes passed.

He decided to try to provoke some action. He squeezed off a shot, and chips of stone were torn from the nearest boulder.

A man's head and arms suddenly appeared above a more distant boulder. He raised a rifle and fired.

Cimarron fired simultaneously, and the man ducked down out of sight—the man he had recognized as Jake Farley.

Farley must have decided to wait for me, he thought. He must have decided to put an end to me and my trailing. Now how the hell am I going to take him alive? If I go and kill him, I won't get paid my two dollars for bringing him in. What's worse, I'll have to bury the bastard.

His thoughts were dispersed as Farley, crouching, ran forward and then dropped down behind a boulder closer to the wash.

Cimarron got off another shot at his quarry, which went wild as the dry ground beneath his boots crumbled and he slid partway down the bank.

He was up again and aiming almost at once, bracing his boots in holes he had toed into the bank.

No sign of Farley.

Got to do something, he thought. Got to flush Farley out without getting a hole in my hide in the process. He scrambled down the side of the wash and went running back through it. He hesitated a moment at its mouth and then came up shooting and running for the boulder closest to him.

Farley got off a shot as Cimarron dived behind the boulder, but the shot missed him.

Close, though, he thought. The jasper's almost as good with a rifle as he is at stealing horses. He got to his knees and peered around the side of the boulder he was crouching behind. Still no good. Farley had circled his boulder and remained out of sight.

Cimarron swore.

There was another broken mass of boulders to his left. Not a very high mound, he realized, but high enough for a man bellying down on the ground to hide behind. He'd be taking a risk if he came out into the open again. But it might be worth it.

Farley rose and fired again. His shot struck the boulder behind which Cimarron crouched. As the sound of the shot died away, Cimarron heard another sound, a distant one. He pressed his ear to the ground and covered his other ear with his free left hand. A horse. Coming this way. He straightened and looked around but saw no horse.

Farley rose from behind his boulder, and Cimarron fired at him before he could squeeze the trigger. Farley dropped down without firing.

Hoofbeats sounded. Closer now.

Cimarron eased around the boulder. There it was! The horse he had heard galloping. Horse and rider were coming from the northeast. He recognized the horse as the one he had seen earlier coming up behind him.

His gaze darted from the horse and rider to the boulder behind which Farley remained invisible. Now what exactly is going on here? he asked himself. Who's that rider after? Farley? Or me?

He saw the rifle in the rider's hand rise, and he ducked down as a shot blazed from it.

Somebody let out a yell.

The rider? Farley?

Cimarron heard another shot. He peered around the boulder and saw that Farley was up and running.

Well now, he thought as he stood up, took aim, and fired at Farley, who kept on running.

A moment later, Farley darted behind the low battlement, and then he reappeared aboard a horse and went galloping north.

Cimarron raced back to the wash. He jumped down into it and climbed quickly into the saddle. He spurred the bay, and a moment later, as he came out of the wash, he went riding north after Farley.

"Cimarron!"

He turned in the saddle and looked back in surprise at the mounted rider he now realized was a woman.

"Cimarron!" she shouted again and gestured wildly. *"Stop!"*

He drew rein, turned the bay, and headed back toward the woman he was sure he had never seen before in his life but who seemed, in some strange way, familiar to him. As he drew abreast of her, he came to a halt. "You know me?"

"Now what kind of question is that?"

"Sensible kind, seems to me."

"After what I just did for you don't tell me that you have the unmitigated gall not to thank me for it?"

"Just what is it you figure you just did for me?"

"Why—why—" she spluttered and pointed.

Cimarron stared at the retreating figure of Farley and watched as the man disappeared in the trees.

"I drove him off, that's what I did for you!" the woman cried. "I may have saved your life!"

He studied her. Slim figure but noticeable hips and even more noticeable breasts. Deep cleavage visible because the top buttons of the man's shirt she was wearing were unbuttoned. Her jeans were dusty and her boots scuffed. She's done some traveling, he thought.

"I'm almost sorry I did!" she cried in exasperation.

"Did what?"

"Save your life!"

"What you did is you went and run off the man I was after."

She had smooth skin which was naturally dark and darkened still further by the sun. Indian, Cimarron thought. Full-blood. Her nose was straight, and so was the line of her lips. Her eyes were inky and her hair, unbound and hanging well below her shoulders, was as black.

She pushed her Stetson back on her head and booted her Spencer carbine.

"How come you know my name?" Cimarron asked her.

"Oh, I know quite a good deal about you, not just your name. I know, for example, that you're a deputy United States marshal and I know how you got that scar on the left side of your face. You were helping your father brand cattle when you were a boy and accidentally let a calf get away from you. Your father became angry and swung the red-hot branding iron he had in his hand. It raked your face."

"How do you know how I got my scar?"

"Do you remember a woman named Alma Ralston?"

"Alma Ralston," Cimarron repeated thoughtfully, and a moment later his eyes lit up. "Why, sure I do. I met her down in Tishomingo in Chickasaw Nation."

"Well, I can tell you, she hasn't forgotten you or your ways."

"Is that a fact? Alma and me, we had us some good times together." Cimarron paused, remembering. "But how'd you recognize me? By my scar? Or did Alma describe me to you?"

"The picnic."

"What picnic?"

"Alma would be very sorry to hear that you've forgotten the picnic you and she attended at which a photographer took a picture of the two of you together. She showed me the picture, which she sets great store by."

Cimarron recalled the picnic on the bank of the Washita River as the woman's eyes left his face and roamed down his body. "Who are you?" he asked her.

"My name is Beatrice, and I'm still waiting."

"What're you waiting for, Beatrice?"

"For a word of thanks for what I just did for you."

"I thought I made it clear to you. You didn't do me any favor. More like a disservice, to tell the truth. Now I'll have to ride out and try my best to find Farley again, and who knows where he might be by now?"

"I'm sure you'll find him, if that is what you are still intent on doing."

"Well, what else would I be intent on doing? Finding Jake Farley's my job. You said you knew I was a deputy marshal, so—"

"You make me feel as if I owe you an apology for what I did—for trying to help you."

"I spotted the smoke of your campfire. Then I spotted you. Tell me something. How come you headed north once you knew I'd seen you?"

Beatrice lowered her head a moment and then looked up, avoiding Cimarron's eyes. "I had to answer a call of nature and I wanted to do it privately, not with you watching me, so I rode for the trees growing along the river." She reached up and buttoned her shirt to the neck.

Cimarron immediately decided he was going about

matters the wrong way. It was time to change course. "How is Alma Ralston? I mean, the last time you saw her, how was she?"

"Oh, she's fine. She confessed to me that she still pines for you, and now that I've met you, I can, I think, understand why."

"She sure was a good—" Cimarron managed to suppress the bawdy word he had been about to utter and concluded, "—friend."

"A man like you must have, I suppose, a goodly number of women friends."

"I have a few." An image of Carrie flitted through his mind, although he wasn't at all sure that she could qualify as a friend. He was sure, though, that she could qualify as an interesting acquaintance. He decided to give Beatrice what she wanted. "Thanks for keeping Farley from drilling me."

"You're welcome."

"It's good you showed up when you did. You were about as welcome as ice in hell," he lied.

"I was on my way to visit my father when I heard that man you called Farley fire on you. I felt I had to help, and then later, when you came close to me, I recognized you. Isn't it a small world?"

"You're traveling all alone?"

"Yes. As I said, I'm on my way to my father. He's a cattle rancher north of here in the Unassigned Lands." Beatrice patted the stock of her Spencer. "I can take quite good care of myself."

"I believe you can. Well, I'd best be riding out after Farley. Since you're heading north and so is Farley, you and me we could ride along together if you've no objection."

"I'd like that."

"Me too. I might just have need of you in case I find Farley and he starts shooting at me again."

Beatrice laughed. "I'm really not as brave as I pretended to be a moment ago," she confided. "So I might have need of you. As Alma told me she did," she added.

Cimarron, as he and Beatrice rode north, wondered what she had meant by her last remark. Had she been referring to the fact that he had run off the man who had been harassing Alma when they met? Or was she referring to the other needs of Alma's which he had met later?

He noticed that Beatrice was opening the top buttons of her shirt.

"It's hot, isn't it?" she asked without looking at him.

"I am," he answered, and, when she glanced at him, an unreadable expression on her face, he gave her a big grin.

ABOUT THE AUTHOR

LEO P. KELLEY was born and raised in Pennsylvania's Wyoming Valley and spent a good part of his boyhood exploring the surrounding mountains, hunting and fishing. He served in the Army Security Agency as a cryptographer, and then went "on the road," working as dishwasher, laborer, etc. He later joined the Merchant Marine and sailed on tankers calling at Texan, South American, and Italian ports. In New York City he attended the New School for Social Research, receiving a BA in Literature. He worked in advertising, promotion, and marketing before leaving the business world to write full time.

Mr. Kelley has published a dozen novels and has several others now in the works. He has also published many short stories in leading magazines.

JOIN THE CIMARRON READER'S PANEL

If you're a reader of <u>CIMARRON</u>, New American Library wants to bring you more of the type of books you enjoy. For this reason we're asking you to join the <u>CIMARRON</u> Reader's Panel, so we can learn more about your reading tastes.

Please fill out and mail this questionnaire today. Your comments are appreciated.

1. The title of the last paperback book I bought was:
   TITLE:_____PUBLISHER:_____

2. How many paperback books have you bought for yourself in the last six months?
   □ 1 to 3   □ 4 to 6   □ 7 to 9   □ 10 to 20   □ 21 or more

3. What other paperback fiction have you read in the past six months?
   Please list titles: _____
   _____
   _____
   _____

4. My favorite is (one of the above or other): _____

5. My favorite author is: _____

6. I watch television, on average (check one):
   □ Over 4 hours a day □ 2 to 4 hours a day
   □ 0 to 2 hours a day
   I usually watch television (check one or more):
   □ 8 a.m. to 5 p.m.   □ 5 p.m. to 11 p.m.   □ 11 p.m. to 2 a.m.

7. I read the following numbers of different magazines regularly (check one):
   □ More than 6   □ 3 to 6 magazines   □ 0 to 2 magazines
   My favorite magazines are: _____
   _____

For our records, we need this information from all our Reader's Panel Members.

NAME:_____

ADDRESS:_____

CITY:_____STATE:_____ZIP CODE:_____

8. (Check one) □ Male   □ Female

9. Age (Check one): □ 17 and under   □ 18 to 34   □ 35 to 49
   □ 50 to 64   □ 65 and over

10. Education (check one):
    □ Now in high school   □ Graduated high school
    □ Now in college   □ Completed some college
    □ Graduated college

11. What is your occupation? (check one):
    □ Employed full-time □ Employed part-time □ Not employed
    Give your full job title:_____

Thank you. Please mail this today to:
   CIMARRON, New American Library
   1633 Broadway, New York, New York 10019